I0625706

A TIDE OF ICE

Also by Erin L. Snyder

Novels
A COUNT OF FIVE
FOR LOVE OF CHILDREN
FACSIMILE

Short Fiction Collections
TENDING THE FIRE
25 CHRISTMAS EVES

A TIDE OF ICE

THE CITADEL OF THE LAST GATHERING
BOOK II

BY ERIN L SNYDER

A TIDE OF ICE

This is a work of fiction. All characters, events, and ideas are the product of the author's imagination and any similarity to real events or people is completely coincidental.

Copyright © 2015 by Erin L. Snyder
www.erinlsnyder.com

Cover art by Erin Snyder and Lindsay Stares

All rights reserved. No portion of this book may be reproduced in any form without written permission of the author, excluding brief passages embedded in reviews or other scholarly works.

ISBN 978-0692578568
Idyll Themes Press

I'd like to thank Bryan Yarrow for his invaluable help with both this book and its predecessor, and Ainsley Yeager for her fantastic feedback and suggestions on the cover image.

I'd also like to thank my wife and editor, Lindsay Stares, to whom this novel is dedicated. There's no way I could have gotten this done without you.

PART 1: EPILOGUE

1

From the top of the ridge, Alaji could see Boars Lake to the southeast and the fields to her north. She continued on until she reached the cliff's edge, which provided an unobstructed view across the plains. It was a clear day, so after a few minutes searching, she was able to make out a small slope in the distance, marking the spot where she'd long ago tracked down the warlord she'd held responsible for her brother's death.

It all seemed trivial now. Her failure to avenge her blood had been rendered moot by the flow of time. The warlord was as dead now as he'd have been if she'd succeeded, and his name was a topic for only the most obsessive of historians. Whatever legacy or empire he'd left behind had faded beneath the footprints of grander enterprises, which in turn had been wiped away.

As for Alaji's family and their people: she alone remembered them as they were. The world which had grown over theirs had dismissed them as simple. And perhaps they were. They'd allowed themselves to be enslaved by superstition long before raiders from the north and kingdoms from across the sea claimed their land.

The fields themselves had been tamed. Farms stretched out along the plains, and she could make out the tiny forms of people tending them. It occurred to her that there were more of them by far than had come with the army of the north.

Here on the ridge, at least, things were as she remembered them. The hill was covered with brambles and shrubs. She even found a bush holding brier berries, though they were smaller and less flavorful than the ones she'd grown up eating. Even so, she'd picked a handful for later, wrapping them in a brown cloth and tying it around her shoulder.

Alaji knelt on grass just beginning to sprout and shut her eyes. Wind tossed her hair, and she focused inward. She aligned her breathing to her beating heart almost instantly. It was so easy now, like blinking. She touched one of the pendants around her neck to reassure herself it was there. Of course it was, just as the other ten shards of the talisman were tucked securely in her pack. They echoed her heart and breath, as if alive.

She exhaled and began the count of five. One for her people's gods, which she now knew never existed. Two for the plants her nonexistent gods had never seeded into the earth and three for the animals they couldn't possibly have given gifts of magic. Four for men who once served the false gods and five for spirit.

She stepped back to one. Overhead, the sun had slid back and the wind and clouds repeated the last steps of whatever dance they'd performed. Birds and bugs reset to where they'd been, pollen shifted in the breeze, and leaves which had already fallen did so again. And no doubt a mouse or a shrew or perhaps even a fox shat out the same shit it had shat before, all the while unaware the whole of time had been jarred from its course by a girl in a field practicing a spell which should be commonplace in this time, but, through some bizarre accident or conspiracy, was known by her alone.

Backward. Easy. Time for something harder. She opened her eyes and tore a handful of grass out of the ground. Then she rose to her feet and began the count. She cycled through it several times to gain a feel for the pace then held her fist in front of her face as she cycled back to one. Then she opened her fingers slowly and allowed the wind to catch the strands of grass.

And she stepped forward to five.

It's not so much that this was harder than stepping back, as it was more unnerving. It was like leaping into a dark room with no guarantee there'd be ground underfoot.

The grass in the air was gone, or at least she didn't see it immediately. If she took the time to examine the ground, she knew she'd find the pieces, but she'd experimented enough to trust the spell was functioning.

It had taken a great deal of work to reach this point. She'd spent the winter in Elsimi experimenting with her magic, then a part of each night since. Rather than explain what she was doing, she'd simply waited until Imn Orith fell asleep, then she snuck off to do her research. Her traveling companion wouldn't have been bothered by her study, but he'd almost certainly want to observe and ask questions. She'd long since lost patience with his fascination with her powers.

She felt she was finally getting the hang of this variation. Whether she'd be able to rely on it under less ideal conditions remained unclear, but at the very least this was a strong start. More than that, it was something she'd developed on her own, from theory to practice. She hadn't stumbled upon it by accident (or, if Yemerik was right, by design). She wondered what else she could do with the magic of the gods, now that it was truly hers.

Her people would have been horrified at the notion. That she'd stolen the spell from the gods was bad enough to warrant a punishment of death: how much worse that she relished it, claimed it, and twisted it? But their opinions were less than trivial: for the time being, they were centuries gone, buried and forgotten. If and when she managed to return to them, she'd already settled on a plan to survive: she simply wouldn't tell or show them what she could do. This assumed she managed to return to a time of her choosing, of course, which was far from certain. If she wound up on the battlefield she'd left, things would be more complicated.

But those were details for another day. It was getting late, and she was growing hungry. The inn she was staying at offered middling food, at best, but it pleased her to eat fish harvested from these waters once more, even if they were smaller than what she'd grown up eating.

She began making her way back, following trails she remembered, even though they'd long since grown over and been lost. Before she was halfway down the hill, she came across a goose drinking from a small pool. She froze as soon as she saw it and began the count. Then she charged forward, moving without concern for the noise she was making. The goose leapt into the air to fly away.

Alaji stepped back in time, and the goose was once more on the ground. She kept running, and stepped back a second time after it took off again. By then she was on top of it, and she grabbed its neck.

The bird thrashed at her, beating its wings and kicking, but she held it firmly and met its gaze. Beneath her breath she whispered the chant the women of her village had used for centuries to charm chickens and pigs, and before that to control horses on the plains. She'd seen it used in this time as well, by wizards in Elsimi to train their dogs and by street performers in Hathari to master the movement of snakes. But it seemed that it had been taken from her sex a long time before: she'd yet to see another woman cast that or any spell since arriving in this era. She took some pride in the fact she was better with the spell than most of the wizards she'd encountered.

The bird went limp, lost in Alaji's enchantment. She held it loosely with one hand and drew her knife with the other. She brought the bronze blade to the goose's throat and rested it there.

"You're lucky you're not worth hauling back," she muttered, returning her knife to her belt. Then she half dropped, half threw the goose away from her. It remained limp for a second, still lost in the spell, but it snapped to attention in time to flap its wings and slow its descent. It landed on its back in the shallow pond, flipped itself upright, then turned and started away. As soon as it recovered its balance and built up the speed, it leapt into the air. Droplets of water shook from its wings as it took off. Alaji watched it fly away and turned towards the town, content that being waited on all winter hadn't cost her the skills she'd developed on the plains.

With mixed emotions, she realized she was a better hunter than her brother had ever been. "I'll save you," she whispered. But her promise rang hollow, even to her. Theojin had died like the rest of her people. Saving him would mean going back, and she had little idea how to return. Even if she managed to reach her time, a sure method for changing the past, as well as what the costs might be, was still unclear to her. Yemerik had grown elusive when she'd brought up the possibility. Then again, she had little faith in Yemerik's knowledge or judgement in these matters. He was the best chance she had of finding her way home; that didn't mean she fully trusted or believed in him.

The walk back to town took less time than the trip up into the hills. When she neared the inn, she saw Imn Orith standing outside. He raised his hand to greet her, then withdrew it quickly when it passed before his face, reminding him he'd only three fingers remaining on that hand. He glanced around to make sure no one was staring at him.

"Alaji," he said, before briefly having to turn aside to cough, yet another cruel reminder he'd picked up during their arrival to this time. "I'm sorry – the season has never agreed with me. I was wondering if you've given any thought to when we should continue onward."

"Tomorrow morning," Alaji said, somewhat downcast. Part of her would have liked to stay longer, but she was risking much as it was. She had to find Yemerik and leave this era before something horrible happened. Besides, she was growing tired of the bards' tales about these lands and their histories. In the past three days, she'd heard it said the earlier inhabitants lived underground like worms, hunted dragons for their meat, and drowned deformed infants in the lakes as a sacrifice: she wasn't sure how much more she could take.

2

"I told you not to come here!" The woman shouted, hurling an apple core at the man crouched in the street. He cringed as it struck him in the center of his back and broke in half. Then he turned to look at her.

"I'm sorry," he said, in a warped accent. "Has anyone—"

"No one's asked for you!" the woman spat. "No one has ever come asking for you, except looking for money. Now get away from my inn."

Yemerik stood slowly. Then he turned, concentrated, and said as clearly as he could manage, "Someone will come… for… to find me. Please, tell… to stay, and—"

The woman kicked a cloud of dirt in his direction. "No one's coming," she replied. "And if they ever did, I'd tell them I'd never heard of you. Now get on your way!"

Yemerik nodded and began to slouch away. He gripped his side as he went, and occasionally made eye contact and extended a hand towards some well-dressed couple. Most ignored or insulted him, but a few fished a coin from their pockets and handed it over. He'd smile and mutter something about one twice-ascended god or another protecting them, then hurry towards the next place he wasn't welcome.

It was mid-summer and extremely hot in Hathari's stone streets. He rested briefly in the shade of the newly-finished inner wall, meant to protect the palace of Tikt-Minot, regent of the New Hatharian Empire. What, exactly, they thought it would protect them from was less clear. There were no cities in the west still capable of raising a force a tenth the size needed to attack Hathari. There were a few in the east, of course, but the largest had little interest in attacking their own vassal. And if the smaller nations wanted to strike out against Hathari, they'd be better served burning crops and leaving the capital to fall to infighting. The wall was a waste of resources that could have been better spent elsewhere in the empire before it crumbled to the point the term "empire" would no longer apply.

Once he felt rested, Yemerik began to shuffle away from the shaded wall. He moved towards the Hur-Thun district, one of several nicer areas housing some of the city's shopkeepers, successful entrepreneurs, and a handful of wizards of mediocre repute. A number of people he'd never met sneered at him, while those who recognized him from his time in the neighborhood simply avoided his gaze. He passed the building he'd lived in for several years and sighed. But it really made little difference: the bed he missed was only modestly less bug-infested than the streets, and the comforts this city offered were almost a step backwards from the era a thousand years earlier.

This wasn't how things were supposed to be, of course. The Hatharian Empire was supposed to be the crown jewel of the ancient world, a power stretching around the globe and through time. It was supposed to have access to magic and knowledge beyond these petty peoples' dreams. But then Yemerik himself was supposed to be a scholar of the Last Gathering, not a beggar in a broken line of history.

For what it was worth, he was happier now than he'd been six months before, when he'd made his living entertaining merchants and travelers with stories his customers found strange and marvelous. He'd been welcomed with open arms and free drinks into taverns that now ran him off. That was before he'd been, in their words, stricken dumb. He'd gone from an articulate scholar to a babbling fool. And, in that instant, his livelihood was gone. He had almost nothing saved, and within a week was on the street.

Things were finally looking up.

What Yemerik knew and they did not was that he hadn't lost his ability to speak eloquently: in fact, he'd never had it, at least not in their language. A magic pendant far beyond their comprehension had changed his words into theirs. Then one day in the middle of winter it had simply vanished, along with a pouch full of pieces of a talisman.

Losing these objects wasn't in itself a positive development – far from it, in fact. Each piece was more powerful and valuable than every enchanted trinket this backwards era had crafted, put together. But their absence meant something vastly more fortunate: someone was coming to find him.

Actually, it didn't necessarily mean that. There were several other plausible interpretations that were growing slightly more likely as the days and months drew out. Still, it represented a very real chance, which was far better than he'd had since he'd pulled a girl out of a skirmish in the late pre-Hatharian period to determine how she'd learned to control time hundreds of years before such magic should have developed.

He'd yet to actually pin down an answer to that question, though he had several promising hypotheses.

Regardless, someone had presumably acquired his possessions in the future and traced them back to this time. It was almost certainly someone from the Citadel, which – he had to admit – wasn't entirely without a downside. He'd have to provide several hard explanations when he returned home, and even once everything was fixed, it was very possible he'd never be cleared to leave the Citadel again. But that was the worst-case scenario. It was just as likely the knowledge he'd acquired would be used to uncover a complex plot to undermine the progress of history and his discoveries would more or less make up for his transgressions. Well, it was almost as likely.

It hardly mattered. He'd had enough with adventuring in the distant past. If things went well and he came out looking like a hero, perhaps he'd take a few vacations into some of the later golden ages of the world at some point. If not, the Citadel was far preferable to this place and time.

"Wait. Is that Yemerik?" He'd been lost in thought, so his name caught his attention. His head perked up, and he turned, half expecting to see the High Lord Archivist of the Citadel in person.

What he saw instead was a handful of teenage boys holding stones.

"Thought you weren't coming back," one said.

Yemerik sighed and tried to recall the boy's name, not that he really thought it would help. "I'm... passing through," he muttered, looking around in hopes that someone might step in. Even in Hur-Thun, there were laws against assaulting a man on the street. Not that he really expected a city guard to intervene on his behalf, but he hoped one of these boys' parents might use this as a sort of teaching moment.

But either none of their parents were around or the ethics of this era were as backward as everything else here. The first of the boys threw a stone, which Yemerik ducked. Then the others followed, charging and hurling projectiles.

Yemerik turned and ran blindly while the pack raced behind, throwing rocks and laughing. A few hit, leaving painful welts, but either the boys were too weak to do much real damage or they were more interested in tormenting than seriously wounding him. He decided that stopping to find out probably wasn't in his best interest.

He headed out of Hur-Thun, hoping the gang wouldn't come after him, but they kept up the attack. A few stones struck bystanders or merchant carts, eliciting threats and curses. Whether these were directed at the small mob responsible or at him seemed mostly academic.

He was growing tired, and he headed into the alleys, again hoping the boys wouldn't follow. Once more, he was disappointed: they stayed on his heels and the rain of projectiles continued. The only reason they hadn't caught him was that they had to constantly stop and collect ammunition.

Yemerik rounded a sharp corner, and a stone – one of the largest – slammed into the building behind him, just missing his arm by a few inches. But, despite the danger behind him, he froze in place.

He was staring into the yellow eyes of a goblin chewing on the carcass of a rat. Yemerik felt something against his foot and looked down. He'd knocked over what seemed to be a rotting piece of fruit on a pile of clay shards and discarded hay.

The goblin looked down at the defiled offering and growled. It bared its teeth and tossed its half-eaten rat behind it. Then it leapt, clawing at Yemerik.

The creature struck him and knocked him over. It raked him with its claws, tearing his ragged clothes and leaving deep, bleeding scrapes.

Somewhere around the corner, Yemerik heard the boys laughing. The sound infuriated him more than the goblin's attack: after all, it was only protecting its territory. But it was also the more immediate threat, as well as the one in the immediate vicinity, so it received the brunt of his anger.

Yemerik kicked the creature's legs out from under it, and it toppled over towards him. Its claws and teeth bit into his leg, so he punched it simultaneously in the ears. The creature howled in pain and reared back, giving Yemerik a chance to kick it squarely in the jaw, which sent it reeling.

This gave Yemerik a moment to roll over, crawl backwards, and reach for the large rock that had landed in the corner. He grasped it and turned just as the goblin jumped at him once more. It went for his neck but was still disoriented. Yemerik struck it in the forehead with the rock. It fell to one side and caught itself against a building with a free hand.

Yemerik didn't give it an opportunity to regain its balance. He gripped the stone with his right hand and swung. The creature managed to block with an arm, but the force knocked it to the ground. It showed its teeth and hissed, and Yemerik hit it again. Again. Again.

Yemerik was dizzy when he rose. The stone, covered in blood, slipped from his hand and fell to the dirt street. Then he turned and saw the eyes of a half-dozen boys, standing completely still, mouths agape and eyes wide.

One of them shouted, "Let's get out of here!" and they all tried to flee at once, which resulted in a number of them tripping over the others. They scrambled to regain their feet and fled out of the alley.

All but one, who Yemerik caught by the back of his tunic. "Let go of me!" the boy shouted. Yemerik hurled him at the goblin, and their bodies collided. The boy screeched in terror and disgust and pushed it away, which gave Yemerik a chance to grab him again and hold him near the dead creature.

"Your name!" Yemerik demanded.

"Let go!" the boy yelled again.

Yemerik pushed him closer and closer to the body of the goblin, until he was almost touching it. "Tell me name," Yemerik said.

"Si-Terrigue," the boy said.

"Verril-Si-Terrigue?" Yemerik said, and the boy nodded. "Father is Verril-Si?"

"My father has friends in the—"

Yemerik shook him to shut him up. "Listen!" he snapped, when the boy's attention seemed drawn back to the goblin. "Someone... come looking for me in Hur-Thun. Tell them—"

"I won't say anything," the boy said, shaking. "I promise."

"No!" Yemerik shook him. "Tell them Jels. You know?"

"I... I... I...." Yemerik shook him again, and the boy said, "I know where it is."

"Good. Swear."

"I swear! You're at Jels!"

"Only if looking for me," Yemerik said. "If you go to guards...." Yemerik kept one hand on the boy's tunic while he reached down with the other and recovered the rock on the ground, still wet with goblin blood. Then he rose it above his shoulder and glared into the boy's eyes. "Understand?"

"Yes. Yes!" the boy said. Yemerik flung him towards the

entrance to the alley, and the boy ran out. When the child was gone, Yemerik released the rock again. Then he collapsed onto the ground in pain and exhaustion. He looked at the dead goblin for a few seconds. Then he looked at the overturned stack of broken jars and hay. He pushed it together and returned the piece of fruit on top. Then, cringing, he regained his footing and began tightening his rags to conceal the scratches and bites, along with the bloody abrasions left by the stones. Once he'd done what little he could, he hobbled towards the other end of the alley.

After all, he still had three more stops before nightfall.

3

Yemerik tried to peel away the makeshift bandage, but the pain was too intense. He cringed and grasped his side. He was breathing quickly and was damp with sweat. He lowered his head and tried to sleep. But, once again, the pain prevented that, so he began to cycle through the locations. His old home in Hur-Thun, the bar north of the pond, the library at the mouth of the wall, the market....

There had to be something he'd missed. They should have found him by now. Since the shards of the talisman had vanished, he'd focused on returning to the locations he'd be most likely to have been. The places he'd have included if he'd prepared a list of spots to look for him during this year. He'd made several such lists already, carefully dated and compiled, so that another traveler could find him. It should have worked. It made no sense.

On the contrary, it made perfect sense. The agents of the Citadel had his belongings but not his notes. They knew he existed here, in this time, but not where he was. Or worse: the ones who'd brought the artifacts back might not be from the Citadel at all. They could be the ones who'd orchestrated all of this. Either possibility meant he'd died in vain.

"Getting ahead of myself," he muttered. "Not dead yet." It was only a technicality, of course. A bitter, itching, tortuous technicality. His wounds were almost certainly infected. What should he have expected from a goblin bite?

He tried to recall his survival training. They'd barely covered infections – there were simple protections, after all, that anyone from the Citadel would have. There were more intensive trainings, of course, but those were reserved for agents working in dangerous eras or times when carrying a talisman might draw too much attention. They'd never offered him such information, and he'd certainly never asked. What need would a constructive historian have with advanced survival training?

He trembled and felt his side erupt in pain. "Alright, academic," he whispered to himself, "what are the odds of surviving a serious infection?" He had no idea, but he bet it depended on the kind of infection and the degree of magical or medical attention. An image of the goblin tearing into the flesh of a rat with its teeth leapt into his mind. What else had the creature chewed on that day before biting him? He cringed, swallowed, and tried to imagine something else to counter the nausea accompanying the thought.

Prospects for medical attention were even less promising. There were wizards in the city who had the power to help, but they wouldn't lift a finger without payment. He could try to keep the wound clean, but that seemed like an overly ambitious exercise given the fact he was currently curled up in a gutter beneath a bridge.

Besides. It was unlikely to accomplish anything more than prolonging his death. His best course of action was to wait to die.

He clenched his eyes shut and ground his teeth to distract from the pain and depression. He didn't want to die here. No one wanted to die, but it meant more for him than most. This was the great sacrifice the Citadel elders always went on about: the willingness of an agent of the Citadel to offer up their soul to repeat the torments of the ages. To go from one end of time to the other twice, maybe more if you believed Jiover's hypothesis. They called it the most awe-inspiring tribute to the mission of the Citadel imaginable. And Yemerik had absolutely no desire to make it.

But that possibility was looking increasingly likely. Even if he survived the infection, the likelihood he'd be found was low. In the scheme of hundreds of millions of years, what did it really matter if he died tonight, tomorrow, or a decade from now?

Not for the first time, he contemplated taking his own life. But the act was easier imagined than done. What was he to do? Climb to the top of the regent's palace and jump? He'd be arrested before he reached the base of the stairs. He didn't have a knife or poison or anything of the sort. And trying to find a cliff to throw himself off of was out of the question: he was too exhausted to crawl out of the city, let alone go on an extended trip.

That left lying here. Beneath a bridge far too low to the ground to kill him, with only a few inches of foul smelling water flowing beside him – nowhere near sufficient to drown in. All he could do was wait to see if he lived or died. His head dipped to rest on his chest again, and he shut his eyes. Once more, the pain shook him awake. But he was stubborn. He adjusted his position despite the damage it did to his wounds and rested his head as best he could. He was asleep.

Then he was awake again. How much time had passed? Had any? He coughed and tried to concentrate. Had he heard his name? He reached to his eyes to try and clear his vision, but moving his arm stretched the skin near one of his deeper cuts and he spasmed in pain.

"Yemerik." It was a woman's voice. Then a pause. "It's him, I think." Another pause. "Yemerik," the voice said louder.

He forced himself into a sitting position, then rubbed his eyes. It was still dark out, but someone was here. He looked up. There were two people standing over him: an old man and a young woman.

He didn't know the man, but the girl…. He began to laugh then to cry. He was in so much pain. Was he hallucinating?

"Yemerik, are you alright?" She sounded worried. Then again, she should be worried, assuming she was actually here.

"Alaji?" he managed, before falling unconscious again. It was a blur after that. A sensation of pain and darkness. Propped up and walking like a marionette. He would remember the feeling of cold rain against his skin, even after being told days later the night was clear. He'd remember the sneering innkeeper, though he wouldn't remember entering the inn. Everything was too dark and too bright at once, a nightmare of contrasts. He stumbled and fell, retched and coughed. His memory was a patchwork of sounds and images against a black backdrop; more was missing than present, and when he finally tumbled into the rented bed, he wasn't sure any of it had actually occurred.

But he forced his eyes open, and Alaji was there. Or, at the very least, she seemed to be. She was different than he remembered her. She was better nourished and wore clothes from this time. "It's all wrong," he began, drearily. "Hathari… I'm so sorry. It's not—"

"I know," she cut him off. "This era in history isn't right. They can't move in time and haven't spoken to the Citadel's delegation."

"How… how are you here?" He asked. "Are you really here?"

"I came back through the gate," she said.

He shook his head. "Different me," he said. "You must have known a different me. The Alaji I knew drowned. I'm sorry. It's—"

"I understand," Alaji replied. "But I didn't drown. I was trapped on the other side of the gate. I opened it again and met… an older you. He sent me back with the shards and your pendant."

"What did I do…." Yemerik was interrupted by a cough. "What did I do to piss myself off so much?" He laughed, then cringed at a sharp pain in his head. "I need one of the—"

"The shards," Alaji filled in. "You're sick. It will help."

"Yes. How in the world do you know that? Oh. The older me."

Alaji dug out one the shards of the talisman and placed it in Yemerik's palm. He squeezed it tightly.

"I'd have died," he said. "Thank you. For coming for me. You saved my...."

Alaji nodded and bit her lower lip. "I didn't expect to find you like this. In the future, you seemed healthy."

"I was. Either the other me didn't realize what taking the pendant would do to me, or he didn't care. I've been living in the streets since winter. How did you find me out there?"

"You gave me instructions. I asked around. A fat man with a scar said you slept beneath the bridge."

"I never expected Din Corbil to be useful." He smiled for an instant. "Would you get me some water?"

"There's some by your bed," Alaji said, moving a clay cup close to him. He grabbed it and drained it quickly.

"I don't suppose there's some food here, as well?"

"I can get some," Alaji said, starting towards the door.

"Please. I don't need much, but I haven't eaten all day." Of course, he was asleep the moment she left the room.

4

Alaji stood in a daze outside the door. Yemerik's state was jarring; his gratitude, even more so. The older version of him had seemed sincere, but she hadn't expected this reaction from the younger. True, this Yemerik was older than the one she'd originally known, but it was more than that: he'd been humbled, something even the older version hadn't really experienced.

Had the other Yemerik known? He must have realized giving her the translation pendant would have ramifications. Surely he'd known his grasp of the local language wouldn't be good enough. Then why do it?

"Alaji?" Imn Orith's voice shook her back to the present. He was standing halfway down the hall by one of the rooms they'd rented. "I've sent for physicians, but they won't be here until morning. I have… some experience with these things. He looked unwell. We should at least clean the wounds. Perhaps your wizard spells could help."

She shook her head. "The wounds are infected. I have a different way to counter that, but I'm not sure whether my… wizard spells… would make him better or worse." Even after months of use, the phrase still felt strange in her mouth. These were the spells of women, the magic given to them by the gods to heal their husbands and children. Given by gods who didn't exist, perhaps, but that didn't make it any easier. Even without her gods, the power was hers: the way this era's wizards claimed it disturbed her.

"You're sure the infection will be halted? I realize this sounds naive after all we've been through, but that's not power I've seen any wizard or physician master."

"I'm sure," Alaji said. "He'll be stronger in the morning. You saw the extent of my spells when you fell off your horse. I can make do, but it sounds like your people are better at this one than I ever was."

Imn Orith rubbed his shoulder where he'd landed weeks before. "Not that I'm complaining," he said with a wry smile. "Yes, our physicians are adept with arts of healing. They study differently than the conventional wizards. They're far more focused."

"Good. My mother always told me there'd be better healers. I don't think she ever imagined they'd be men."

"Your world sounds fantastic," Imn Orith said. "Forgive me. I meant no disrespect, it's simply that everything you've told me… the concepts are staggering."

Alaji shrugged. "The changes were a lot to get used to. The

buildings here, the technology, and the food: they're unlike anything I dreamed. And Yemerik says the world keeps changing. The shape and feel and even the creatures. It's difficult to fathom."

"I've read more philosophy than most men have heard of, and I've never come across these ideas. It is amazing." He yawned. "I'm sorry. It's been a long day, and a long time since I've had an actual bed to sleep in. Oh, the innkeeper will be up with breakfast in the morning. He believes Yemerik is your father and my son. It seemed easier that way. I hope that's acceptable."

"Yes. Yes, thank you. I'm going to stay a few minutes in case Yemerik needs anything."

Imn Orith cast a glance at Yemerik's door. "He's so different. I wouldn't have recognized him."

"He's different than when I knew him, too," Alaji replied. "Time does that."

Imn Orith chuckled, running a hand across his own wrinkled face. "I suppose it does. It's funny, though. I can't help but think how young he looks. His beard's barely started turning grey."

"The Yemerik I first met didn't even have a beard," Alaji replied. "And the only lines he had were around the eyes. Now, his whole face has aged."

Imn Orith yawned. "I am sorry. All of this is catching up with me. You'll wake me if I'm needed?"

"Yes. Thank you."

He smiled, nodded, then hurried down the hall to his room, leaving Alaji to reflect on Yemerik's transformation. She sat down outside his door and leaned her head back against the wall.

—

She was woken by the innkeeper the next morning. It took her a moment to determine where she was. When she realized she'd fallen asleep in the hall, she apologized and followed the innkeeper into Yemerik's room.

"He looks better," the innkeeper said sternly, glancing at the side of the bed in case there was a need to charge them extra. The room looked clean, so he set a plate of food and a mug of beer beside the dish from the prior night, muttered something about being back with more, then hurried out.

Alaji sat and began to nibble at the food before switching to beer. The idea of going back to the muddy, clouded version she'd grown up with depressed her. At least it would likely be a while before that occurred. She scolded herself for the thought: her brother was dead and would remain so until she found her way back. While she was enjoying the comforts of the distant future, his bones were rotting in the ground.

She sneered. It was her mother's voice, coming from her head. She'd return and do right by Theojin when and if she could, but she saw no reason to miss out on the pleasures afforded to her in the meantime. She swallowed another gulp defiantly.

"Careful." She jumped a bit and spilt a few drops on her shirt. "That's more alcoholic than you're used to." Yemerik's eyes were open, though he hadn't moved.

"I don't know what that is," she replied.

"Alcohol… it's what makes you… no, the stuff you used to drink probably wasn't strong enough to get you drunk. Drunk… it's… difficult to explain."

"The sense of dizziness, like you're neither awake nor asleep? I've been here for months already. Even longer twenty years from now. I'm used to the drink." She swallowed another gulp.

"Yes. Of course. I'm sorry – I'd forgotten. I suppose you've already learned restraint." She grinned, then quickly finished the mug. She laughed. Yemerik did as well, though he immediately stopped to rub his forehead. He raised a hand to tell her he was alright.

"The innkeeper's coming with more food. You're welcome to what's left here in the meantime."

"Please," he said, and she brought the plate over. He lifted a piece of bread and used it to gather some eggs. He took a small bite and chewed it slowly, savoring the taste and warmth.

"I didn't think they were that good," Alaji remarked.

"You haven't been picking at discarded food in the street," he replied. "It's not exactly the best thing I've ever eaten, but it's good in comparison." He took a larger bite. "There was someone else with you. Last night, I think… I can't really recall much clearly, but I remember a man."

"Imn Orith. I brought him back with me from the future. He's sort of been my guide here."

"I convinced the people in the village in Ilpinthi to bring me here," Yemerik said.

"Elsimi," Alaji corrected him.

"Pardon?"

"The village. It's called Elsimi."

"Yes, of course. It should be called… never mind. I convinced them to set me up with guides, guards, and a small sum of money. If I'd known what I was going to find, I'd have pushed for more. At the very least, I wouldn't have dismissed my servants when I reached Hathari."

Alaji cleared her throat. "They sent someone with me in the future and sheltered us through winter. I didn't want to trouble them further. They did give us horses and supplies, though."

Yemerik chuckled to himself. "I don't suppose they gave you any money."

She removed a folded cloth bound with twine from the bag that held the shards of the talisman and a few other items she was never without. "Imn Orith said I should keep it hidden when I'm around people." She untied and drew back the sides. "He has more. I also have the coins you traveled with, though the other you said I should avoid using them."

Yemerik looked at the handful of coins Alaji was holding and smiled. "It should be more than enough to keep us alive."

"Will it be enough to get us back to Elsimi?" Alaji asked.

"Why would we want to go back there?"

"For the gate. We can't stay here. You told me you'd be able to help me reach the Citadel."

"I know," he said. "But that was before I arrived here."

"No. I don't mean when we were on the plains. The older you sent me back, because waiting for the Citadel didn't work. He said we should try for it on our own."

The color drained from Yemerik's face. He laughed awkwardly, and his eyes darted around. "That's... that's difficult to fathom. It would be extremely dangerous."

Alaji shrugged one shoulder. "It's that or die here," she said.

"It might be better to die here," he replied. It was clearly a joke, but he didn't seem any more amused than Alaji was. "I'm sorry. I didn't mean that to sound so grim. It's just... there could be a lot of time between now and when magic becomes advanced enough to reach the Citadel. And the gates aren't always reliable. They can't be easily destroyed, but they're only as useful – or as safe – as they're accessible. Rockslides, changing water levels, volcanoes... we can't just go back to Ilpinthi and take that fifty or a hundred million years into the future. We'll have to go from gate to gate, moving in smaller jumps at a time... I'm not even certain it's possible."

"You said there was a chance we'd be able to find someone from the Citadel near one of the gates. Or that there might be a way to contact them."

"I must have been extremely optimistic. It's not impossible, but it's a toss in the dark. The alignment of iteration and timing makes it statistically unlikely."

"There's nothing else we can do, is there?"

"I'm not sure," Yemerik said. "Give me some time to think."

"The last time I saw you, you'd had twenty years longer to think, and this is the only plan you came up with."

"It's a damn stupid plan," he said.

"I know," Alaji replied, laughing.

He laughed, too. Slowly, at first, but within a few seconds, he couldn't speak. Once he regained his composure, he said. "It's good to see you again. It's been awful."

"It's good to see you, too," she replied, only realizing it was true after she'd said it. For all his faults, she'd grown to like Yemerik, even if this version was more timid than the ones she was used to. "But we have to go on. I think I understand why we're doing this now, at least in part. Your people aren't here, and they're not coming for us. We need to find them."

Yemerik shut his eyes and nodded. "I know. It's just... I thought I was going to die in the streets. I thought... never mind. It doesn't change what we need to do. It's just hard to imagine right now."

"We'll wait until you're healthy before booking passage to Elsimi," Alaji promised.

Yemerik cracked a smile. "No. Not Elsimi. The gate at Ilpinthi will be dangerous soon. We'll go east, to Urolmore. Then, we'll leave this broken age behind us."

"Iron's next, right?" Alaji asked

"Pardon?"

"In the future I left, you called this an age of bronze, and that the next was iron."

"Well, yes. Chronologically. This was actually supposed to be a great deal more. They were supposed to have learned to travel ahead and acquired the skills and magic needed to smelt iron, create steel alloys, and even to transform metals into entirely new materials. But that hasn't come to pass."

"Then that's our next step, isn't it? The age of iron?"

"No, no. They should have iron worked out in a few thousand years. After that, innovations should speed up in frequency. Assuming nothing goes horribly wrong, they'll have cities inhabited by tens of millions in five or ten millennia. We can safely push fifty thousand years using the gate at Urolmore. Even that's barely a step forward, but we'll want to know more before we go any further."

"Where is Urolmore?" Alaji asked.

"In Rathara, across the ocean. It'll be easier to book passage to the east than back to Ilpinthi, anyway. Far more trade."

Alaji nodded. "Across the ocean," she whispered back. It was an amazing thought, as foreign and enticing as anything she'd experienced so far in her strange journey. She'd grown up being told the water beyond the land was infinite. She'd seen enough of Yemerik's maps to figure out that wasn't the case, but it was one thing to see masses of land drawn on parchment and another entirely to realize she'd step foot there herself.

"You should know, things may be different," Yemerik said, softly. "Not so much in this time: Eastern Hathari is more or less the same as the West. But the era we'll be traveling to won't be like the ones I know. It's easy to talk about the early ages: stone, bronze, iron, early magic, and all that. But the advancement of magic is only predictable for so long, and its long term effects aren't predictable at all. Where we'll be going… it's more or less assured five or six civilizations unlike anything you've seen will have risen, supported millions, then fallen to war or plague or worse. We could just as easily arrive in the middle of an era of learning and peace as we could find… I don't know… a time where fire is flowing through the sky like rivers and rats the size of this building are roaming around. If we keep going long enough, we'll see things better than the first and worse than the second. If we live long enough, I mean. But other than that, history is in disarray. I have no idea what we'll find."

"I understand," Alaji said. "But this is important. Besides, it's the only way I'll ever be able to return home."

Yemerik nodded. "If we can reach them, the Assembly at the Citadel will make it like…" he stopped abruptly, hesitated, then said, "They'll send you home."

"There's something else," Alaji said. "I need to save my brother."

"That may prove difficult," Yemerik said.

"I know. We've had this conversation. I had it, anyway, with the other you. But you promised you'd do what you could. You told me to tell you that."

"Fine," Yemerik replied. "I'm not sure what I can do, but I'll do whatever that is."

"You'd better," Alaji said, wryly. "I went through a lot to get back here. They wanted to cut me open and drain out my blood." She cracked a smile.

"They what?" Yemerik asked. "Who the hell wanted to do that?"

"Imn Orith, for one." She motioned towards the hallway with a nod of her head. "Mostly his lord, Minot-Rin."

"Wait. Rin? They gave the city to the runt? Was he still just a regent, or did they reinstate the imperial titles?"

"Everyone called him 'regent.' You can ask Imn Orith about the rest."

"Why'd you bring him, if he wanted to kill you?"

"He didn't, exactly. And I didn't mean to bring him through the gate. There were others, too, but... it doesn't matter. He's the only one who made it to Elsimi, and he wanted to come back to Hathari."

"I'd imagine. He'll be able to make a fortune betting on Rin's ascension. Minot-Sil is favored to inherit the kingdom."

"Imn Orith will want to come with us," Alaji added. "But he'd slow us down. We should leave him here."

"I agree," Yemerik replied. Alaji couldn't tell if he was relieved or disturbed by her conviction; perhaps a bit of both.

After a few seconds of silence, she added, "When he asks, I'll explain it to him. He'll want to talk with you first, though. He has questions about the future I couldn't answer."

Yemerik sighed. "It's not something we should really be spreading."

"Then lie to him. The older you always did. I once overheard you tell him that lions walk around on their hind legs when there's no one watching."

"Really? He believed that?"

"He seemed to believe a lot of what you said. But that was when he thought you knew the secret of immortality. I'm not really sure what he'll think now."

"Ah, that makes sense."

"It does?"

"Immortality. Someone must have recognized your language, pieced together that you were older than you possibly should have been. That's why they'd want your blood."

"Someone recognized me, actually, from decades before. I still haven't figured that out. You – the older you – said something about reflections of me visiting times I've never seen. He said there would have been other me's created in the past."

Yemerik lowered his head to the pillow. "I'm not nearly awake enough to be thinking about any of this," he said. "Go away and tell the innkeeper to hurry up with something to drink. Don't you know better than to trouble a man with paradoxes when he's half dead from starvation and goblin attacks and wild dogs?"

Alaji smiled and turned towards the door. "I'll make sure they don't forget you." She began to leave.

"Wait. Thank you again. For coming back for me. I'd have died out there."

"You'd have died back on the plain, too," she reminded him, smiled, then hurried out before he could respond.

5

The fire slowly ground its way through the log, and the man who had once been Imn Orith wondered if it was worth replacing. It was growing late, and he was tired. But there was little time these days when the sun was up, and there was a great deal he hoped to accomplish. He didn't need its light – he had a bright-stone hanging from the ceiling for that – but it was difficult to work the ink in the cold and harder to work his joints. So he crossed the room and tossed another log onto the first, which split in two beneath the weight. Embers scattered around the room, small but comfortable, and the flame began to push back the cold once more.

He reached for his reed brush with his right hand before the reality set in. Even after all these years, the instinct always won out. He balled his right hand, covering his remaining fingers with his thumb, and lifted the brush in his left. Then he dipped the tip into the ink he'd mixed before starting, straightened his blank scroll with his closed fist, and touched the brush gently to the papyrus. A single black dot formed beneath it, and the author inhaled. He shut his eyes and considered yet again what to write.

"This is the secret history of Imn, the Left-Handed," he began. He'd considered other options: the 'Man Not Born' or perhaps the 'Twice Lived,' but these didn't have the right ring to them. Even 'the Left-Handed' seemed forced, but it was the best he could come up with. He couldn't very well go by his actual name, since – contrary to Alaji's supposition – it was still in use by a young man. He'd actually crossed his other self's path once near the west wall, where the younger Imn Orith was purchasing rare metals. The older knew perfectly well what they'd be used for, since he recalled the time all too clearly. He was trying to distill the essence of the metals in order to use them to prolong the life of men. It was still years before word of his studies would reach the newly ascended regent, Minot-Rin, who would become a patron of his work and provide him with money, supplies, and servants. And, of course, subjects, in the form of convicted prisoners who'd be made to test the elixirs.

He shivered a bit. How many men had he watched die after drinking his creations? The number escaped him. Regardless, he would leave those tales out of his history. Perhaps the other Imn Orith would recount them, when he reached this age.

His younger self had seen him and stared at him for a moment. The elder had thought perhaps he'd recognized himself, but the young man looked away and returned to his bartering. Whether he'd thought he'd seen a distant relative or just someone who bore an uncommon resemblance, it obviously hadn't troubled him too much. The old Imn Orith left quickly after.

"I have seen the fabric of time split asunder," he wrote, and almost immediately regretted it. He liked the turn of phrase, but it was too direct, too blatant, to entice a reader's interest. It read like the ramblings of a braggart, not a wise man unveiling the world's unknown mysteries. He'd almost wished he could throw it to the fire and start again. But papyrus was expensive, and his income had dried up. For several years, he'd made a tidy profit on Yemerik's advice: wagering on the outcome of events and investing in merchants he'd remembered were successful. But this no longer worked as well as it once had: things had begun to diverge from the history he knew. It began small, with a few trivial details shifting, but had reached a point where he could no longer trust his knowledge of events or individuals. The weather patterns remained unchanged, but he wondered if even that would last. Still, he had enough money to survive under his assumed name, and more coming in thanks to several partnerships with sailors and importers.

Again, none of this would be in his treatise. He wanted his writings anonymous, in case someone actually believed him and came looking for their money back. Besides, he had more than enough to fill the page.

"I say to you that the world is not as it seems. That which has passed is not truly gone, and that which is yet to be may change. In the west, there lies a gate, built by the god self-sacrificed who alone has ascended to the highest throne in the highest heaven." If there's one thing Imn Orith had learned reading every ancient (and not-so-ancient) scroll he could get his hands on, it was to attribute all mysteries to the god who sacrificed himself to himself to gain his own favor and ascend. He'd asked Yemerik about the stories, only to hear him laugh out loud. But this would better the chances the scroll would survive and be copied.

"And here lies the mystery of this gate: a man may pass through it as he walks beneath a tree and nothing may change. But if the man carries a key, then this same gate will open to a time of his choosing, to eras of the past or future, wherein dwell strange beasts and people, where wild creatures reign as kings, or the heavens and the sea have changed places." Poetic license, of course, but necessary additions if he wanted this to last.

"Keys lie in the hands of few, chosen by the ascended to walk the earth. They possess powerful magics, and those who meet them would be wise not to incur their wrath. I have met such travelers and gone through the gate. I have seen their power over time and men's lives, seen bodies of six fall before the might of one—"

He paused to consider how scholars would react. They might accept it, for who's to say what power the gods could grant, even to a lowly girl? But there was no sense taking chances: "one warrior holding nothing but a plank of wood."

He read over what he had so far and smiled, satisfied. There were no guarantees, but this could well convince the sages. He'd have to tear the page to make it look like there was more that had been lost. Then he'd need to scorch a few edges, spill a few drops of wine on the corner, and perhaps coat it in ash or soil for a day, to make it appear older than it was. Then there was the matter of getting it into the hands of a scribe working in the regent's library, but he had some thoughts on that.

With luck, they'd accept it as an authentic work of an ancient philosopher, copy it, study it and work with the ideas. And then, perhaps someday, Alaji and Yemerik might come across the writings in their travels. And was it too much to hope they'd come back for him? They said they might return, but Yemerik had said many things to him in two times, and Imn had grown skeptical of his words. Besides, each year that passed made the prospect of discovery seem less enticing and more exhausting. But even so, he was unwilling to give up the hope. What they'd shown him was but a fragment of the whole. Perhaps only a fragment of a fragment.

—

The old man calling himself Imn Kirpalith died twelve years after arriving in Hathari, shortly after Imn Orith became an associate of the young regent, Minot-Rin, who was widely rumored to be obsessed with eternal life. Imn Orith died several years younger than Imn Kirpalith: he was executed by order of Minot-Rin during an illness contracted by the regent. Minot-Rin was said to regret his decision after recovering from his sickness and discovering no other scholar in Hathari seemed as knowledgeable on the theories of eternal life than his former friend. At age forty-six, upon his birthday, Minot-Rin drank an elixir made of viper's blood, deer's milk, and something described as a metal that flowed like wine. His last words offered detailed instructions for carrying out the execution of the philosopher who'd mixed the potion.

The Secret History of Imn, the Left-Handed was not widely distributed, but neither was it lost or destroyed. It came into the possession of a merchant, who took it across the sea and sold it to an advisor of King Elid the Just, who made the merchant his advisor. The text was shared between them alone, as it was deemed too powerful a secret to be shown to others. In fact, the secret became known to one alone when the advisor was poisoned. To his credit, King Elid granted titles and gifts to the advisor's family far beyond what would be expected.

It would be centuries before the Secret History would be read once more.

PART 2: A TIDE OF ICE

1

"It's as large as the world," Alaji said, gasping for breath at the top of a hill. The land sloped away into a valley containing a small village nestled beside a brook. In the distance, a lake stretched to the east, and it reflected the clouds overhead. Beyond that, the tips of mountains larger than any she'd seen were slightly obscured by a thin haze.

Yemerik laughed. "It's all part of the same world."

"You know what I mean. The world to the west. My world." She motioned back towards the distant hills. Somewhere, beyond those, lay the ocean, and beyond that the shore they'd departed.

"Your 'world' is a continent," Yemerik replied, "It's generally referred to as Hathari, but that name didn't stick in this timeline. This is a different continent, and it's called—"

"Rathara. I know."

"Actually, it's different in this era. But it will be called Rathara. I mean, probably not in this timeline, but once everything's corrected—"

"Shut up," Alaji said good-naturedly. "I want to enjoy the view." They'd been hiking for weeks after arriving in Linport. The city hadn't been a third the size of Hathari, but it was still dizzying, especially after spending four phases of the moon in a cramped merchant vessel. By the end of that voyage, even Alaji decided she'd had enough of the sea, though she was already beginning to grow nostalgic for the open water again.

Alaji gazed at the scenery while Yemerik tended to their donkey. They'd purchased the animal after being told by several sources the terrain they were moving towards wouldn't support horses. It was either lead a donkey by foot or travel by roads in the south, charter a ship to move them past Ghathari Bay, then meet up with the eastern roads into the mountains. This was faster.

Once the animal was settled, Yemerik came over to stand by Alaji. He took in the view for a moment and grinned. "I've seen better," he said, needling her.

"How many more are there," she asked. "How many continents?"

"Five in all. At least, there are in this time."

Alaji looked at him, alarmed. "They… appear?"

"No. Nothing like that. But they drift. If you go back far enough, they were all connected. Not that there's any reason to go that far back. We'll likely cross a few eras when a couple of the continents reconnect, though. And there's always a chance some sorcerer will do something rash. It's not easy to sink a continent, but timelines have certainly existed where it's occurred. It's more likely for someone to split one in two."

Alaji swallowed and cleared her throat. "That's the kind of thing your Citadel stops, isn't it?"

"Sometimes. We try to improve the lives of everyone throughout time, and drowning tens of millions of people is an awfully large impediment to a better world. But eternity is a long time. Sometimes, horrible things have a positive impact."

"You told me once that the Citadel would create floods."

"Just the coasts!" Yemerik replied. "We've done things to wipe away cities, but we've never intentionally destroyed a continent."

"Elsimi was on the coast," Alaji replied coldly.

"The sort of interference you're describing, we don't do that until long after the Hatharian period."

"It's still horrible."

"I know," Yemerik agreed. "It's unimaginably horrible. But... there was an iteration in the Citadel's history when the Gathered Assembly thought it might be possible to eliminate pain and suffering. They worked towards that end, but achieved negligible results. They tried working through time from the past to the future removing events like floods and wars. But they only succeeded in changing the form of the atrocities into something more subtle or pushing them forward into eras when magical power was more potent. There was one egregious attempt that led to the death of every man, woman, and child on the planet less than halfway through history. After that, the hypothesis fell out of favor, and we've worked to understand the patterns. Events don't occur in isolation: there are repercussions, which result in further repercussions throughout time. The better we can understand these causes and effects, the better we're able to achieve the best results possible. The best world possible, given the limitations of magical development, natural disasters, and human nature. It's a more compromised mission, but we've been far more successful: a fourteen percent decrease in suffering is already achievable with a series of just over two hundred targeted interventions, and there are strong indications we'll be able to improve things further. Don't feel bad if you don't understand – the models are over my head, too. But the methodology works. There are patterns in history that can be manipulated to prolong periods of peace and minimize... unpleasantries."

"I still don't like it," Alaji said.

Yemerik took a deep breath and sat on the ground near Alaji. "No. Of course not. I don't like it, either. But... when I decided to become a constructive historian, they brought me to a time where the Citadel had... interfered. It wasn't a flood that time. We'd magically altered a kind of locust to... the details don't really matter. We did something to disrupt a kingdom's food supply. They brought me, along with a dozen or so other students, to one of the cities to show us the devastation. It was awful. People were starving. They were eating anything – absolutely anything they could get their hands on. And it was all for nothing, because it was just a matter of time before they'd be invaded. They knew it, too. That any day a neighboring kingdom was going to ride in and slaughter every man, woman, and child after… I'm sorry. You don't need the details. It was going to be horrible."

Yemerik paused to take a drink from his waterskin. He was squinting, and every muscle on his face was tense. "They didn't bring us there to teach us how to impact a civilization or for research or anything like that. They'd already taught us the theory and methods. They took us there so we'd have to face the consequences of what we'd be doing. Because if we couldn't handle it – and a few of the students couldn't – there was other work they could do.

"You see, we already understood the other side. We knew that if the Citadel hadn't hurt that kingdom, they'd have grown stronger and stronger, then eventually swept across the continent, burning and pillaging dozens of larger nations and creating a legacy of violence that would last for centuries and inspire others to act mercilessly. The loss of life would have been fifty times worse and the suffering almost incalculable: we knew that. The thing we had to understand was that the only way to stop it was to let it happen to that kingdom instead. It's an awful choice to have to make. And I hate it. But the alternative… you're going to see it. If we last any amount of time on this journey, you're going to see things that are unimaginably horrible."

Alaji looked at the ground. "I understand. I didn't mean to judge you."

"No. It's okay. I should be judged. The Citadel's work needs to be judged and examined and considered from every possible angle. Altering time is an awesome responsibility, and we have to make sure we don't become complacent. That's why it was so important we confronted the consequences of our actions."

Alaji thought for a moment. "I don't know what will happen

when I return to my time. I need to save my brother if I can, but after that… there's a chance they'll want to kill me. A good chance. Even if I manage to hide my magic, I'd just be back where I started. I'm not sure I want that anymore, after everything I've seen and done. As long as I can save Theojin, I'd be willing to go to the Citadel and help. If that's an option."

Yemerik sat completely still. "Alaji, it doesn't really…." He scratched his arm and adjusted how he was sitting. "I can't promise anything except… if nothing else, I know I can get you home. And your brother, I can at least get him another chance. I'm not sure what the result will be, but I can definitely do that. He'll have another chance, and you'll never…." He paused and drew in a deep breath and bit his lower lip. After thinking for a moment, he added, "You'll at least have a chance, too. Your people won't remember the things that happened at that battle. Those things won't have happened when we're done."

"The more I see, the harder it is to imagine spending my life by the lakes."

"I understand that," Yemerik said. "And I'll do what I can. When we reach help, I'll explain what you can do, and I'll make your case. You're a good person, deep down. I'll make sure they understand that. And, who knows, maybe they'll want you at the Citadel, at least for a time. It's just… we're not supposed to do things before the rise of the Hatharian empire. I wasn't even supposed to be there."

"Then… they shouldn't want to send me back, right? After everything I know? That would damage the future. Or past or whatever it is to you."

"I'm not sure," Yemerik replied quickly. He stood up and dusted himself off. "We should get moving. I want to reach that town before nightfall. I don't know about you, but I'm tired of sleeping on the ground." He hurried towards the donkey.

Alaji watched him carefully then rose herself. She looked back in the direction they'd come and thought of the sea and all the marvels before and since. Then she looked back at Yemerik and tried to piece together what he might be thinking.

2

It took them two more weeks of traveling before they saw their destination and several more days to reach it. Because they weren't on the water, Alaji had imagined this gate would be smaller than the one beside Elsimi. She'd expected something subtler, something less conspicuous. She couldn't have been more wrong.

Stretching between two mountains, the gate spanned a massive valley. Beneath its shadow, a forest surrounded a thin river. A modest sized village even lay before the mountain. The distance across was more than ten times that of the other gate, and the height seemed incredible. When they were first close enough to see it, Alaji froze and stared in disbelief. She was somewhat relieved when she saw Yemerik's eyes open and mouth ajar. Even he wasn't entirely prepared for the sight.

"The river," Alaji said, after she had a chance to catch her breath. "You could move the entire river."

Yemerik turned to face her and shook his head. "It's so much more," he said. "The gate, it's not even for water. Well, I suppose it sort of is, but not like you're thinking. Not like that. It's... I can't. I can't even begin to explain. You'll see, once we're through. You'll see."

She let it drop, in part because she was used to him avoiding her questions, and in part because this was different. It didn't seem like he was trying to be evasive, at all. He simply looked tired and perhaps a little dizzy. This journey wasn't like the last one they'd taken, when they traveled through the ancient world to open a portal to Hathari. In part, Yemerik was different: eleven years in a timeline different from what he'd known and months in poverty had humbled him. But it was more than that – he had fewer expectations about what they'd find. He was moving through unknown lands, and the things he did know left him diminished.

As they approached, they met up with one of the roads connecting the area with the eastern provinces. Groups of pilgrims were camped at the edge.

"Of course," Yemerik whispered. "The ascension point. They think this is where it happened. Of course they do."

"What is it?" Alaji asked, growing annoyed at his habitual vagueness.

"I heard them talking about it all the time in Hathari, I just never realized it was the gate. Their sacrificed god, the one who—"

"I remember," Alaji cut him off. "What about it?"

"This is where they think it happened. They believe this is where he supposedly sacrificed himself to his own glory and ascended to the highest heaven." He looked up at the far-off arch. "I should have expected," he added. "If you were superstitious, where else would you attribute that kind of significance?"

Alaji didn't speak. She simply glanced at the people lining the road.

"This will complicate things," Yemerik added. "There's no telling how many of them will be crawling over the gate. If we're not careful, we could wind up pulling dozens, even hundreds, through with us. We'll need to be quick and wait until most of them are gone."

"We could go when it's dark," Alaji suggested.

"That's assuming they don't flock there at night. They're always blathering on about light cutting through darkness. I'm not sure whether it's relevant here, but it's certainly a possibility." He cursed quietly under his breath.

His opinion of the pilgrims didn't improve as they traveled on. There was no shortage of wandering groups gawking at the strange sight or pausing to greet anyone coming the other direction. They kept passing or being passed by families moving towards the mountains at a similar pace when one group would stop to rest and the other would catch up. The pilgrims seemed overjoyed to see them each time and kept attempting to start up conversations. Their words were gibberish to Alaji, but Yemerik grew more and more irate as time went on. Alaji suggested that she take the pendant to translate their words, but Yemerik shook his head and replied that it might seem odd if she suddenly gained the power of speech after he'd told them she was mute. "It's unfortunate we didn't think of it sooner," he added sardonically.

The town on the outskirts of the mountain pass seemed to live off the pilgrims' money. And, by the look of their homes, they appeared to live quite well. Every house they passed had a sign offering a room for the night or food for sale. Even without the ability to read them, Alaji could infer their meaning from the brightly painted illustrations. Not for the first time, she wondered how they mixed paints so luminous.

There was a field set up for open trade. Yemerik sold their donkey and the supplies they couldn't carry, then used the money to replace their boots and buy some new clothes. They purchased some fresh food, as well, though most of what was being sold was rotten or stale. Then they began the hike up the western peak. The path twisted, bringing them directly beneath the long, slender arch on multiple occasions. They were still a long way from the top, and the wind was strong. The stone bridge itself looked thin from below, like a rope stretching between the mountains.

"Are we going to need to go up there?" Alaji asked, swallowing.

"There'll be an altar near the gate itself," Yemerik replied. "The one at Ilpinthi should have had one, as well, but it would have been under water. This one should be accessible."

"Good," Alaji replied.

"Keep in mind I said it should be accessible. There's a chance it could be buried beneath a rockslide or something. If so—"

"If so, you can climb up on your own," Alaji replied, looking at the impossibly long drop between the center of the arch and the valley far below.

Yemerik laughed out loud, which startled her. "I was thinking I'd send you up," he said. "Maybe we can draw lots or something."

"Suits me. I can always step back a few seconds and change the outcome."

He smiled and shook his head, then paused to drink from a waterskin the village had charged them to fill. He wiped a line of sweat off his forehead and pushed on.

It was late afternoon when they reached the arch. It wasn't at the peak of the mountain, but rather about three quarters of the way up. The gate met the mountain near a cliff, though there was some room before the drop.

The scene was worse than they'd expected: hundreds of pilgrims – men, women, and children – were there. Many were camping on the mountain. A crowd was gathered by the arch itself. The nearest were holding their palms against the rock; others were trying to get close enough to do the same. Alaji followed the line of the arch across the chasm. She squinted, and saw a similar mob at the distant mountain forming the other side of the gate.

Yemerik swallowed and took a deep breath. "I'm thinking," he said before Alaji could speak. "Just give me a moment."

That moment would have to wait. "Welcome!" A rotund man hurried up carrying a bowl full of water. "You must be thirsty." He offered them the water, and Yemerik nodded and took a sip. "Is this your first visit to the western point?"

"It's our first time here," Yemerik replied.

"My name is Rishic. I live in Fothelle below," the man said, motioning to the town lying beneath the mountain.

"I see," Yemerik said. "Then how much do we owe you for the water?"

Rishic laughed. "I am no man of business," he said. "I have devoted my life to the service of He Who Ascended." As Rishic spoke, he moved his arm in an arch, mimicking the shape of the gate.

"There is fresh water nearby. Come, I'll show you around."

It took almost a quarter of an hour before Rishic left them, and not before clasping them both on the shoulder and whispering a prayer to the self-sacrificed god. Then he went off to greet more new arrivals.

"He seemed nice," Alaji said when they were relatively alone. "What did he say?"

Yemerik ran through where they could find water and who would give them food. Apparently, it was expected that anyone would share what they had, so they'd want to keep their supplies hidden. Then he inched towards a drop-off nearby and looked down.

"Just like he said," Yemerik said beneath his breath.

Alaji walked over and peered off the edge. Below them, on an outcropping of rock, lay a pile of skeletons and a few decomposing corpses. She could see what looked like a knife sticking out of one. "What happened here?"

"Is happening," Yemerik replied. "These are the 'self-sacrificed.' A few every year. Devout worshippers trying to follow the example of their god thinking their spirits will be carried to him in the heaven that lies past the night sky of the second heaven."

"It's disgusting."

"Well, yes."

"It's all because of the gate again, isn't it? They saw it open once, and they built stories around stories."

"It's possible, but hard to say. There's no reason to think the gate has ever been open in this timeline, at least not while humans lived here. Besides, their description of what happened is very different. They think their god's spirit split in two, walked across from each side, then met as one not in the middle but in a heaven above all heavens."

"That makes no sense."

"The religions that make sense don't tend to survive. No mystery. Regardless, it's just as likely their beliefs came first and they wrote the gate in when they came across it. If it wasn't here, they'd just have found the tallest mountain or a rock that looks like a face or something else."

Alaji glanced down at the bodies below once more. "There are so many," she said.

Yemerik shrugged. "History gets unpleasant. It'll be easier if you get used to it now, before we come across truly horrific things."

"It doesn't bother me," Alaji said, defensively. "I've seen dead bodies before. It just seems so… meaningless."

"It had meaning to them," Yemerik said. "That's more than most people get in exchange for their lives." He stepped back and looked around. A pair of children were playing with sticks nearby. He shook his head and added, "We should push on. If I understood Rishic, the altar will be nearby."

"How are we going to get the pilgrims away from the gate?" Alaji asked.

"We'll wait until night. You were right before. There won't be as many around."

"But there'll be some?"

"Yes. Still quite a few in fact. That's why… I have an idea, but… you're not going to like it. It involves…."

"You're going to sacrifice them, aren't you?" Alaji asked.

Yemerik cringed when she said the word. "No. I'm not going to kill anyone. At least, that's not what I'm trying to do. But we'll have to open and close the gate a few times before we go through. That should scare some of them off."

"And lure others through," Alaji added.

"Yes. Into a different time than the one we'll be going to. It will be disrupting to their lives, but there's no reason to think they'll die."

"But they might. If they wind up in the middle of winter or surrounded by a storm. Or if it's a bad era. They won't be able to leave like we can."

"I understand your concerns. But I don't have a better solution. If we go through with them, they'll be in the same situation. Only then they'll be a danger to us, as well."

Alaji nodded. "It makes sense," she said. "It's better than having to kill them."

Yemerik started to say something, but stopped. "Yes," he said, after a moment. "Exactly. And it's unlikely anything will happen to them. They'll probably be hailed as prophets, like we were in Elsimi."

Alaji nodded. "We should find water and repack our supplies, in case the weather worsens. We'll also want to have weapons available."

"Of... of course," Yemerik agreed.

Alaji looked overhead. "The day's in its last fifth," she said. "Good. I'm ready to be done with this time."

"Me, too," Yemerik said. Though his heart didn't seem in it.

3

The altar was unassuming, but obvious: a small stone table rising out of the rock. They'd missed it the first few times they'd searched, because an old woman had been using it as a seat. Once she left, Yemerik spotted it and ran over to inspect it. The same indentation was present in the center, just like the one they'd seen on the other gate. They waited until nightfall, and then Yemerik readied the gate, using a shard of the talisman to connect to a different time. He then stayed behind while Alaji moved into position: the gate could only be opened by passing beneath it, and her spell of time would allow her to disrupt the connection and close it at will. She'd be able to prevent it from staying open longer than they planned and shut it immediately if the gate opened to a truly inhospitable setting. They'd agreed on a section of the trail about an eighth of a mile away that passed under the arch. She was out of view, and he was alone again.

He went through the plan again and again, all the while keeping an eye on the pilgrims who were preparing to sleep near the arch. Many went to lay a hand on the stone structure once more. Parents were gathering their children in an attempt to keep them away from the cliffs before it grew dark.

He'd have to watch them carefully, he thought. He could deal with the idea of a few pilgrims wandering through the gate and ending up ten or twenty thousand years in the future – in fact, he found the notion rather humorous – but the thought they might close the gate with a young child thousands of years away from their family horrified him. If he was vigilant, maybe he could warn some of them, convince them to move away from the gate instead of perceiving it as an opening to the world of the gods.

His gaze followed the archway until it vanished into the darkening sky. Beyond it lay the shadow of the eastern peak. Beneath that, lay the other side. There'd be people gathered around it, just as here. He had no way of knowing whether they were closer or further away than those he could see. He'd have no way of shouting to try and get them to flee. Whatever happened there was out of his control. And entirely his responsibility.

He knew Alaji would almost have reached the gate. There were still a handful of faithful waiting beside the stone constructs. Would it matter if they had waited all night instead? If they stayed a week and waited for rain? Or perhaps they should have remained until the winter to see if the snow dissuaded the followers of this god. He doubted it would have made much difference. There'd always be someone here to worship. Perhaps there'd be fewer, but… no, it did not matter. He was an agent of the Citadel of the Last Gathering Before the Falling Stars. He was a member of the Assembly. There was a mission far larger than the lives of a few or a few dozen or even a few million. Besides, all of this would be undone. Why was he having such a hard time focusing?

He considered this as night turned to day in a flash. Confused, birds began hovering at the portal in a panic. A blast of wind poured out of another time, carrying different pollens. The air was damper and warmer, with a different smell and weight. Sunlight spilled out across the mountaintop and down on the valley. He could see the tops of houses in the village below illuminated.

And he saw the pilgrims approaching enraptured. At first, they were silent, taken in by the miraculous sight. And it was certainly that: another world juxtaposed against their own. It shone through a door thousands of feet high. And the edge of that door ran along their encampment. Was there really a question whether these people would touch it? Was it really in doubt whether they'd wander through and lay on the warm rocks beneath the midday sun?

When their silence broke, there were no sounds of fear or panic. There were only prayers and exaltations. There were cheers and praises and hymns. And why not? This place was overseen by a god. What else could any of this mean?

It was as though he blinked. The light was simply gone. The wind lingered for a moment, and a small cloud of confused birds spiraled into the brush around them. Somewhere down the path, out of sight, Alaji must have flickered, breaking the connection between the gate and the shard of talisman that had opened it.

And then there were other sounds. Mothers calling for their children. Men calling for their lovers. Confusion and fear. Some clawed at the ground by the gate, hoping to get through.

They needn't have worried, of course: the plan called for them to open the gate again. Reluctantly, Yemerik gazed down at the tablet. He placed the shard of the talisman in the indent. Its presence meant every time Alaji closed the gate, a duplicate of himself was left in an alternate timeline. In the scheme of things, that now seemed as trivial as everything else.

He began turning the shard. It occurred to him that if he could somehow match the number of turns precisely, he'd be able to reopen the portal at the same moment as before. But it was an absurd and naive ambition. A one-percent shift in angle could alter the result by centuries; a quarter turn, millennia. When the portal opened a second time, it was night, albeit a different night than this. It was cooler, harsher, and dark. Grey clouds rolled out into the valley below. Where the clouds broke, the stars were different through the opening than above the gate.

The pilgrims seemed far less enthusiastic than before. They did not panic, but many backed away. A few shouted that they were seeing their god's displeasure towards the unfaithful, and they ran through lest they anger him further. A few more entered hoping to locate lost family members. Why shouldn't they assume the opening led to the same destination?

But most were wary and held their ground. When the gate shut this time, there was far less surprise. A number of the pilgrims gathered to pray.

From his spot, Yemerik began preparing the portal for a third and final time. He turned the shard for twice as long as before, then returned it to his pouch. Then he ran as fast as he safely could.

"Are you alright?" Alaji asked, when Yemerik rounded the bend in the trail, panting.

"I'm fine," Yemerik replied. "We need to go now. We need to be quick."

Alaji nodded. "It's right here." She motioned to a line in the sand she'd drawn with her foot. "All we have to do is step over it to open the gate. You should give me the—"

Yemerik didn't wait to let her finish. He handed over the shard of the talisman, they hurried across the line together, and all around them the world changed. It was cold. Not freezing, but certainly the coldest time they'd opened to. In the back of his mind, it occurred to him that he should consider going back through and starting again: he may have gone too far. But the idea of risking yet another portal sickened him. Besides, with a glance off the cliff he could see the ground was still below them: that was all that really mattered. He turned back to Alaji. "Hurry," he said. "Close the gate. Quickly."

From Yemerik's perspective, she simply vanished and reappeared. But everything behind her vanished, as well.

There was a blast of wind, and the seasons changed around

them. Alaji shivered and began removing her pack. "We can try again," she suggested, digging for a cloak. "Now that the others are gone, we can try for summer."

Yemerik motioned up the trail. "They're not all gone." A man was moving back and forth, dazed. He hadn't seen them yet, but he would in a moment. "Besides," Yemerik added, starting towards the pilgrim, "I think this is summer."

4

There was a thin coat of snow beneath Alaji's boots. It looked and felt like winter or late fall at the earliest. She followed Yemerik as he hurried up the path towards the man they'd spotted. They were calling out to each other, but their speech was unintelligible to her. Rather than listen to their sounds, she wandered up the path further. Once she crested that section of the path, she came to the opening where the camp had been. Everything up here was bright, despite the overcast sky. It was almost blinding, so she squinted to try and take in the sight.

The land around them was different, but she'd expected this. Many of the stone formations had fallen, and the small trees and shrubs looked nothing like she remembered. None of this surprised her, nor did the presence of a few more pilgrims. One, an elderly man, was kneeling on the ground in prayer. Another, a woman only a few years older than Alaji, was staring out at the northern horizon. Alaji moved closer and looked, as well.

"Yemerik!" she screamed, running down the path. "Yemerik!"

He was where she'd left him, and he was handing over one of his blankets to the man he'd been speaking to. He looked over to her, but he didn't seem worried.

"Across the plain! There's… something. I don't understand. I thought they were…." She shook her head, and Yemerik simply raised a hand to settle her. Then he said something to the man, patted his shoulder, and started towards her. "It's okay," he said softly in her language.

"It's impossible," Alaji replied, moving back towards the outlook. She motioned out to the northwest and then swept her arm to the east. "What is it?"

"Remember what I said, about the gate being intended for water?"

"That's not water," Alaji whispered.

"No," Yemerik admitted. "It's ice."

As soon as he said it, she realized he was right. It was ice, as far away as the horizon, as tall as the mountain she stood on, and – as far as she knew – as long as the world was wide.

"It's called a glacier," Yemerik added. "It's a moving plateau of ice. No, more like an ocean of the stuff, slowly flowing over the continent. It's good we didn't come too much further: it would have been on top of us."

"If we're staying in this time, we should get as far away from it as possible."

"It's fine. Glaciers move slowly. It will take thousands of years for it to reach us here." Yemerik looked around. "It looks like there's a settlement to the south. That seems as good a destination as any."

"Wherever we're going, we should leave soon," Alaji said.

Yemerik nodded. "We should round up the pilgrims first. Make sure they don't stay up here and freeze to death."

It grew warmer as they moved down the mountain, but the cold was only one of many concerns. The path they'd followed up was long gone. Sections were overgrown with briars, blocked by fallen rocks, or had dropped away completely. Other areas, shaded from above, were slick and frozen over. An elderly pilgrim woman lost her footing at the edge of a cliff and was only saved by the man walking beside her.

The trip was even more precarious due to the strange wall of ice on the northern horizon. Alaji found it difficult to take her eyes off it whenever they came to an open section. She wasn't alone in her fascination, either: the pilgrims looked on and muttered to themselves. Alaji wondered what they were saying. Sometimes, they attempted to communicate with her, but she simply shook her head. Then they'd laugh or clasp her shoulder or try again more slowly before giving up and turning their attention to one another or the archway far overhead.

They found the ruins halfway down, a little while after reaching the tree line. There were stone walls three times as tall as Alaji, built from blocks too large for a man to carry. Moss coated the walls, while ivy had torn holes straight through. An oak stood nearly in the center of what once must have been an incredible structure. Rubble covered the floor, hinting at a roof long since fallen. It was another impossibility in a world crowded with impossibilities. The pilgrims were even more excited than Alaji. They laid their palms against the northern wall and cried with joy. Alaji glanced back towards Yemerik for some explanation, but he simply shrugged.

It was growing dark when they reached the bottom of the mountain. Alaji located some fallen branches from trees that were shorter and thinner than those they'd passed on their way up. She looked at the pilgrims around her. They wouldn't be familiar with a woman who could use magic. She lit the branch and chuckled to herself. What did she care, anyway? Yemerik was the one who'd have to explain.

None of the fifteen pilgrims who'd followed them down the mountain were watching when Alaji cast her spell of the hearth, anyway, but there was a flurry of activity and confused expressions when they noticed she was carrying a burning stick. A few began questioning Yemerik, who responded in their language while several of the more pragmatic pilgrims started collecting firewood.

They ranged in age from children to the elderly. Some seemed elated; others looked as though their gods had abandoned them and they'd lost everything they'd ever loved. Alaji wondered how long it would take the joyous ones to realize the others were right.

It grew colder as the night set in. Yemerik was seated around the fire which had been made from the remnants of Alaji's spell. He kept an eye on the youngest two of the group, a pair who were being looked after by a few of the women. Even without the use of their language, Alaji could tell their caretakers weren't related to the children.

"What now?" she asked, somewhat bluntly.

"Get some rest. We could use some food, as well, if you think you can find anything in these woods."

"I haven't seen much yet. Just songbirds and squirrels, but there must be larger game."

"I wouldn't be so sure." Yemerik kicked at a patch of greyish snow.

"I can try. You should send a few of them after water, if they'll go." She paused for a moment, then asked quietly, "Do they know what's happening?"

"No, but they suspect we know more than they do. It actually helps us, at least for now. Lends us credibility. Let's just hope they keep thinking it's got something to do with their god. With luck, we'll be free of them in a few days, anyway. As soon as we find that town, we'll hand them over, go back to the portal, and go back another thirty or forty years."

"Why?"

"We're going to try and send a message to the Citadel," Yemerik replied.

"You can do that?"

"Not directly," he said. "But there is something we can try."

——

They reached the town at dusk the next day. The houses were different in ways Alaji couldn't understand. The wooden exteriors were smooth to the touch: no evidence they'd ever been covered in bark remained. One building, built beside the river, had a strange wheel attached. The water turned it slowly, and it in turn rotated a rod, which extended into the structure. Whatever else this accomplished, Alaji couldn't imagine. She found these marvels fascinating, but she was used to the sense of newness by now. The pilgrims, on the other hand, gawked in awe at each new thing: at the statue on the outskirts of the town painted gold, at pigs twice as large as any they'd seen, at ornate fabrics strewn about.

There was a crowd to greet them. Men, women, and children, dressed in clothes that bore small imprints, were staring at them, just as they were staring at everything. Almost everyone was holding a bowl or plate or pitcher full of food or drink.

Yemerik, of course, seemed unaffected. He motioned for the others to stop, and he remained still, studying the townspeople until their murmurs turned to words. Then he strode up and demanded, "Do you remember?"

The town grew silent, and the crowd parted for a single old man to approach. Alaji didn't know what was being said, but she thought of the town with the dragon's head warning. She even thought of her own town: it was always an old man. Across tens of thousands of years, this was constant.

Yemerik stared at the old man silently, as if judging him. Then he nodded, and the speaker said, "We remember the name and oath."

"Speak, then, the name," Yemerik said, forcefully.

"Yemerik,'" the old man proclaimed.

"And the oath."

"When the stars touch the mountains, the blessed people are coming. And on that day, they will join us, as brothers and sisters, and we will welcome them. And they shall bring us joy and prosperity."

"This gift is not just for you, but for your children and their children. For a hundred generations, this town is blessed."

"It is written for all to see." The old man pointed towards the statue.

"You must tell your children what happened. You must tell visitors. All must know that heaven rewards the faithful."

The old man turned, and with nothing more than a nod, elicited a cheer from the crowd, who began at once to descend on the pilgrims with their offerings.

Alaji and the pilgrims looked to Yemerik. "Eat!" he said, in Hatharian, then in the tongue of Alaji's people. He was already reaching for a leg of lamb.

It would be several hours before Alaji was able to pull him aside. "I heard them say your name," she said.

"Yes." Yemerik began running through the conversation.

"Then... the Citadel has been here. They knew we were coming?"

"No, but I'm trying to tell them."

"But you knew the villagers."

"No. I just realized they knew me."

Alaji sighed. She was exhausted and confused. But she was also well fed for the first time in weeks, so it was difficult to muster anger.

Yemerik smiled. "They knew we'd be coming, because we're going to tell them in the past. You and I, once we're done here, we'll go back up the mountain, travel back in time, then tell the village to wait for the sky to appear between the mountains once more, and that will mean we've returned with a bunch of holy people."

"This is like Elsimi. They think we're messengers from the gods."

"Exactly. Which means they'll listen to us, give us whatever we need, and – more importantly – tell stories of our appearance. Their stories will become legends that will last, I don't know, a few hundred years. Maybe a thousand, if we're lucky."

"That's not long enough, though."

Yemerik shrugged. "If we're extremely lucky, a member of the Assembly might overhear something while exploring the era and investigate. I doubt it, though, especially with something as unimportant as a crowd of confused followers of a forgotten god. We'll need something more noteworthy if we really want to make an impression and open a significant window of opportunity. We need a prophecy that will last ten thousand years, even if it becomes warped and confused."

"How do we create something like that?"

"Trial and error," he said, looking back up the mountain. "Trial and error."

5

"My name is Yemerik." The proclamation was punctuated with the butt of a walking stick striking the dirt road. Alaji, of course, only recognized the name, though she was able to infer a great deal more from the body language of the villagers. Or, more accurately, the lack of body language from the lack of villagers.

As planned, they'd opened the portal into the past, about forty years earlier. Then, once again, they'd made their way down the mountainside, through the forest, and back to the small village. Only this time, their arrival was unmarked. A handful of children stared at Yemerik as if he were a madman while an older woman blocked the space between them, perhaps worried he might be dangerous.

"Did you not see my sign?" Yemerik screamed. He pointed towards the mountain pass. "Did you not see the sky rendered like a butchered pig?" He shouted this at the woman, who made a point of avoiding eye contact while she began herding the children away. A few men holding farming instruments began approaching. Yemerik ignored the threatening look in their eyes and approached. Alaji stayed close behind with the count of five turning in her mind.

"You there!" one of the men said. "What's your business here?"

"Did you see it?" Yemerik demanded. "They sent a sign of my coming!"

"You're scaring the kids," the largest of the men said, holding a shovel. "If you have business here—"

"Oh, I have business," Yemerik said through gritted teeth. "But not with witless heretics who have forgotten the gods!"

They began to chuckle. Another of the men whispered something to the large one, who burst out laughing. At least they seemed less likely to attack than a moment earlier.

"Hear me!" Yemerik shouted again. "Hear me, and watch for the second sign. Watch for the third! The sky shall rip open and merge darkness and light. And then I shall come again. And if I am not shown proper respect, the gods will swallow up this land! Do you understand?"

It was difficult to determine whether or not they understood. Their laughter now drowned out his words. One of the children broke away from the group, picked up a clod of soil, and hurled it at Yemerik. It broke apart against his cloak.

He turned to Alaji and said, "We're leaving," in her tongue. His voice remained grim, and his expression remained stern.

She started to ask a question, but he shook his head and began walking away. A second dirt clod sailed through the air and missed him. Behind them the laughter echoed.

"That went better than it could have," were Yemerik's first words upon leaving the village. He caught a glimpse of Alaji's expression and added, "We still have some work here, of course. But overall, that was a decent start."

"I liked it better when they were feeding us."

"Wait until next time," Yemerik said, grinning.

—

It was frigid on top of the mountain at night. With one hand, Alaji clenched her cape closed while she tried to hold a shard of the talisman still with the other.

"Nine or ten hours would be best," Yemerik said through chattering teeth. "That would give us the effect we want. Plus we could step through and be done with this damn cold."

"I'm not that precise," Alaji replied. But she was being modest.

She'd done this several times and was gaining a better feel for the rippling waves of time that spilled over the indentation in the rock and emanated through the portal. She couldn't explain how it worked, how the tilt and number of rotations controlled the amount and magnitude of the rift, nor could she have planned in advance how to move the stone fragment to get the desired distance. But operating by touch, she could shape the pulses of magic into the form she was after.

She stopped and returned the piece of the talisman to the pouch holding the others. "That should be close. At least, I think so."

"As long as it opens into the sunlight, it'll be better than this," Yemerik replied. He turned and began moving towards the gate. "As long as you don't send us into the ice wall or lead us back to the beginning of time or something."

"The gates can take us to—"

"No," Yemerik cut her off, more coarsely than he intended. "But they go back a long ways. Further than you'd ever want to go, unless…. no. There'd be no reason for that."

"For what?" Alaji demanded.

"Well, the oldest gates go back to before the continents split apart. It'd be one way to get between the Urgryn and Thistrive gates, assuming you could figure where you were going and were willing to walk a few hundred miles. I suppose that might be easier than sailing several thousand. Once the plates shift, the gates wind up on opposite ends of the world." In the dark, Yemerik didn't realize he was nearing the gate until Alaji motioned for him to stop. It wouldn't have mattered if he'd crossed; he wasn't holding any pieces of the talisman, so he wouldn't be able to activate it. But it was easier for them to cross over facing the same direction. The alternative would have been a bit confusing. "You understand the plan?" Yemerik asked.

"I open the gate, we go through, then I close it after a minute."

"As long as there's daylight. If it's dark, we'll just close it and try again."

"And if it's dawn or dusk?"

"I don't know. I guess it depends on the amount of light. I'll know when I see it open. Let's just get this over with."

Alaji stepped beneath the gate, and the boundary opened. Once more, light pooled into the valley below. The air brightened, illuminating the land in both directions.

"Perfect!" Yemerik said, following through himself. "They'd better notice this. Give it a moment, just to be safe."

Alaji waited by the portal while wind swept from day to night and back again. When she decided she'd had enough of the breeze, she found her count and stepped through time. The gate, cut off from the shards of the talisman, snapped shut.

—

They found themselves back at the town a little before dusk. Skipping the prior night meant they were exhausted, but Yemerik concealed it well. He marched into the town and stood ready, waiting for someone to take note of his presence.

This time, he didn't have to wait long. And their reception was far more dramatic than before. Dozens of people moved towards them, gawking in awe. Children were held back by the men, who stared in silence.

The large man from their previous visit was among them, but this time he'd left the shovel behind. His expression showed equal parts terror and humility, though it was difficult to make out either due to the dark bruise over his left eye. He opened his mouth to speak, but nothing more than a gasp escaped.

Yemerik addressed him directly. "Did you see the sign of my return?" he demanded.

"I saw," the man said, almost too soft to hear. "I... I'm sorry for the way I was. If I'd known—"

Yemerik silenced him with a motion of his hand. The large man froze, and Yemerik glared at him. Some in the crowd shifted away, others moved in closer towards the large man. These looked on him with wide eyes and flaring nostrils. Their hands were rolled into fists, and their muscles were tense. "Do you fear the gods?" Yemerik asked.

"I do." He was whimpering now, and he seemed to shrink.

"Do you trust in them?"

He nodded, notably less enthusiastically. "I… I trust in the gods."

"Good," Yemerik said. He walked towards the man and stopped a few feet before him. "Then you will hear their message." The leaned over and whispered something to the man. When he finished, he moved back. When he spoke again, he did so loud enough for the crowd to hear. "I have trusted you with a message from the gods themselves. On the next midwinter, you must share this news with your neighbors, but until then, it is for you alone. Do you understand?"

He nodded frantically.

"Good. Tonight, my companion and I require beds to sleep in and food to eat. Tomorrow, we begin a long journey. We'll need food and water for our trip. There will be another sign in the coming days to mark our passing. Past that, you know what to do."

Hasty arrangements were made for their lodging while Yemerik and Alaji waited. "What was that about?" Alaji asked, motioning to the large man.

"I made him our prophet," Yemerik replied. "It had to be someone, and if I'd chosen anyone else, our friend would be dead in a few days. Now they'll probably make him their mayor or priest or something."

"Well. We've… closed the circle. That's what this is, right?"

"That's simplistic phrasing, but yes. We've aligned a future and past event. It's almost certain the Citadel's magic will connect them. Almost."

"It was your phrasing," Alaji muttered so quietly she wasn't sure if Yemerik even heard her. "What do we do now?"

"Eat something hot, get a night's rest, then take everything of value we can carry."

"Shouldn't we wait? To see if the Gathering Before the Falling... if your people hear about this?"

"If they get our message, they'll likely be here before we were."

"You mean... they might be here now?"

"No. They'd have met us already. We'd have closed the circle, stabilized the timeline, then the Citadel's agents would have retroactively intercepted us before we got this far. That's another way of saying they didn't get our message."

"Then we try again," Alaji said.

"As many times as it takes. Or until we die. Whichever comes first. It's just a question of when we want to go. This time feels relatively stable but too backwards for our purposes. We can't go too far into the future without risking the glacier catching up with us, and I don't want to risk jumping over it yet. Five or six hundred years should be a good bet, though. That should give their magic and technology enough time to develop but hopefully not enough time to turn on them."

"Turn on them? What does that mean?"

Yemerik shook his head. "I wouldn't worry about it. We should be safe with a mere five hundred years."

PART 3: THE HUNT

1

They arrived in daylight, as close to five hundred years later as Alaji could manage. At first glance, it seemed promising. It was warmer than the era they'd left, despite the approaching glacier. From the mountainside, they took a moment to gather in their surroundings. There were signs of what Yemerik called development: large swaths cut from the forests and distant settlements. They selected the nearest, a collection of buildings nestled on the shore where a northern lake fed a river flowing south. They'd be able to cover most of the distance by following what looked to be a large road cutting between the mountains and running parallel to the river. It was only a matter of reaching it.

They took the same path down the same mountain they'd been on in the past. But it had changed, of course. "It's longer," Alaji mused. "I'm sure it's a little larger. I thought it was changing last time, too, but I figured I was just imagining it."

"It might be, at least a little," Yemerik replied. "The land changes even without the glaciers shaping it. There's geothermal activity, earthquakes, and…. I'm sorry. I'm sure you have no idea—"

"I know earthquakes," Alaji said. She wasn't annoyed this time. It was too nice a day and too interesting an experience to be bothered by his assumptions. Besides, she was actually interested. "I didn't know they could build land up, though. Just shake rocks loose."

"Well, they do more of that. But the world is always moving. The continents are floating and shifting. Earthquakes are mostly just symptoms of that. Imagine you're holding a leaf from two sides and you push the edges in towards each other. The middle will fold and rise up. That's what mountains are. Sort of. It happens slowly."

Alaji nodded. The scale was incredible, but the idea was simple enough. She looked out over the valleys and hills, trying to recall how they'd changed. The world below was being carved and recarved through time, shaped like wet clay over the ages. She smiled. It was astonishing.

They reached the bottom and began moving southeast towards the road they'd seen from above. The forests were thick. The trees were taller and thinner than they'd been in the past, and there was far more brush along the ground. After several hours, they reached their road.

Only it wasn't a road. Tree trunks lay scattered in a mesh of branches, where they'd been left to rot. Some had been upended along with massive patches of earth; others were snapped off at the stumps. There were slashes in the wood, long and deep, like cuts left by a dog's claws in an unprotected arm. To one side, flies swarmed around a giant mound of brown excrement.

Alaji froze instinctively. Yemerik did the same while they surveyed the scene. "What did this?" she asked, glancing towards him.

Yemerik shook his head and whispered, "We need to leave. We need to get back to the gate." Alaji didn't argue. In moments, they were racing through the woods. Thorns and bristles caught in their clothes and hair. Occasionally, something scraped a hand or ankle and left a bloody welt. They didn't slow down.

Something wasn't right. There were too many birds overhead and too few rodents in the underbrush. The forest knew something they did not, and a sudden crash behind them drove home the point. Something was tracking them. Something was coming.

Alaji gasped as she caught sight of bare rock through the trees. In their haste, they'd veered north and lost the path back to the gate. They'd reached the base of the mountain, but from the wrong angle. Instead of a soft incline, Alaji gazed up at the face of the cliff.

"There's no time to circle back," she said as the sounds grew closer. "Whatever it is, we need to face it." She motioned towards an opening to their right, and Yemerik nodded, handing over his shards. Alaji drank a few gulps of water and a few more of beer before picking up a broken tree branch and readying a short spear they'd brought from the village in the past. The shaft was smoother than any she'd ever seen, and its metal head was sharpened to a point. She paused to reflect on what her brother would have been able to do with the weapon before dismissing the notion. Whatever skill he had acquired and whatever power he drew from the spells of the hunt were nothing compared to the spell she possessed. That knowledge did little to quell her nerves.

As the noise came closer, she cast the spell of the hearth, and the top of the branch erupted into flame. She handed this to Yemerik and gripped her spear with both hands. Then she began her count.

What emerged from the woods moved too fast to be seen clearly. It was a blur of dark fur and muscle twice as tall as a man. It was nearly upon them before Alaji stepped back in time. "Throw the torch!" she shrieked as the creature leapt into the clearing. Yemerik hurled it at the animal, but it didn't even slow down. The creature's paw crushed the burning torch, singeing some fur, but it didn't flinch. Alaji stepped back and saw the scene play out once more. The creature snarled as it approached.

Alaji's count of five was of little use if she stood still. She charged at the creature and stepped back in time to increase her rate of approach. The creature saw her appear, and it leapt. She'd expected this. And she'd been waiting for something like this.

She stepped forward a single quickened heartbeat.

The creature was upon her. Or rather, she was right before it, less than a stride away from its chest. But her spear was outstretched.

Alaji had heard the sounds of animals taken by hunters and dogs. She'd killed a horse on the plains to spare the rider. The sound this made was like all those screams rolled together and magnified by ten. She felt the weight of the monster crash into her. They fell as one, and everything went black.

—

"Alaji!" Yemerik cried. A splash of water struck her face. She felt pressure over most of her body. She squinted, and the light of the sun blinded her. She looked down, and all she saw was red and black. A jumbled mess that looked like nothing and explained less. She was pinned from the chest down under the body of the dead monster. She worked one arm free and shielded her eyes from the light.

"Are you okay? Can you move?" Yemerik asked.

"Blood," Alaji replied, seeing her arm more clearly. It was covered. Coated. More than she'd ever seen. She suddenly became aware that her clothes felt wet. She touched her hair and found it the same.

"Are you cut? Are you hurt?" Yemerik splashed some water on her hand and rubbed it. To Alaji's relief, the blood washed away, leaving nothing but a few shallow scrapes and bruises. The blood hadn't come from her.

Her breathing relaxed, and she rested her head on the ground. "Get it off me," she said. Yemerik pushed against the monster, and Alaji crawled out from under its corpse, slipping in the pool of gore. She grabbed for the water, poured some into her mouth, and spit it out. She did this with mouthful after mouthful until her spit was no longer pink. Then she swallowed a few gulps.

"We need to move," Yemerik said, before she was even finished. She ignored him. It took everything she had to keep upright. Yemerik grabbed her shoulder and turned her towards him. "We have to go now," he said, forcefully.

The very idea was unimaginable. Alaji could barely stand, barely think. She leaned against a large boulder and took a deep breath.

"The spear. We should recover it," she said without making any movement to do so.

"Forget the spear! Didn't you hear it? We need to move."

Alaji didn't know what he was talking about and didn't feel like asking. She looked down at the dead body. The spear point protruded through its back at an angle, having snapped in the middle from the creature's weight. It was the size of a large bear, with longer legs and a head that almost resembled a wolf's. Only there was something wrong, beyond the wounds and blood. Something about the proportions was skewed in a way she couldn't identify. Its head and paws were too large for its body, and now that it was still, it seemed oddly fat.

Then came a howl. An answer to the death cry the creature had made. Only this was deeper and more distant. It shook the forest, and clouds of birds rose into the air. Alaji looked at the creature again, and the misshapen features took on new light. It wasn't the head of a wolf, but that of a pup. She looked down at her body, covered in the creature's blood.

In the distance, the crack of splintering trees echoed. It was coming from the south. Alaji forgot the pain in the back of her head. She started for the woods, and Yemerik followed. They neither discussed nor fully thought out their direction: the sound came from the south, so they went north.

The cliff petered off into a ridge jutting off to the northeast. They climbed, hoping to find easier terrain on the far side, only to discover that the north face of the mountain was no more hospitable than the east. They couldn't go back the way they'd come, which left few options.

Yemerik began speaking only to stutter and shake his head. Finally, he spat out, "We should make for the eastern peak." He pointed to the far-off mountain that lay past the river.

"It'll take us almost a day," Alaji responded.

"The alternative is to circle the mountain and hope that thing isn't waiting for us," he said turning. As soon as he looked back, his mouth opened. To their south a section of trees shook and toppled over as a mound of fur shuffled through. Clouds of dust rose into the air as the trees fell in its wake. As they watched, it reached the clearing where Alaji had killed the smaller one. The opening was barely large enough to contain this creature. It was far more immense than anything Alaji had ever seen – even the dragons she'd seen on the ocean were insignificant in comparison.

For a brief moment, it was still, then it raised its head into the air. In shape, it resembled a dog or wolf, though its shoulders were disproportionately wide. The beast let out a long, deep howl, a sound full of rage and pain.

It had found its offspring.

Then it shifted forward, shoving its nose into dirt, tree trunks, and bushes as it searched for their scent.

Yemerik turned to Alaji in a panic. She nodded, and whispered, "The eastern mountain." Then she started down the other side of the ridge as fast as she dared. She cringed as she heard another patch of trees come crashing down several miles behind them. It sounded as though entire trunks were shattering. They caught another flash of the beast when it crested the ridge, not nearly far enough behind.

They began dropping items from their packs, then some of the packs themselves. They kept their water, some food, and the clothes they wore. The shards of the talisman, of course, remained bound and tied at Alaji's side, and she kept a dagger. Yemerik kept his maps and coins, as well as a knife of his own. But most of their other possessions – blankets, large weapons, containers of salt and dried spices, objects and artifacts from different ages – wound up tossed on the ground to afford them a little speed.

Yemerik was soon exhausted, barely able to keep moving. Alaji was a little better. Using her count and stepping back, she could match his speed at a gentler pace or even hurry ahead and rest. They ran until Yemerik could no longer stand, and then they collapsed until the sounds of pursuit drove them on. Even with thousands of trees slowing the beast down, it was gaining on them. They reached the open stretch of uprooted trees they'd once mistaken for a road as the sky was beginning to grow dark. Now they saw it for what it really was: a path the monster had made to reach the lake.

As before, fallen trees lay among patches of upturned earth, alongside vines, bushes, and even the occasional sapling trying to grow out of the decomposing weave of logs. There were collapsed sections, often in the rough shape of massive paw prints. The land stank of death and mold and decay. The fallen remains of plants, animals, and men alike lay on the ground. There were few skeletons – mostly just bones, scattered and broken. Some were wrapped in remnants of rusting armor, bent or torn in half along with the body it was supposed to protect. There were weapons, as well. If she'd had more time, Alaji might have picked through to see if any were in good enough shape to take. But her spell warped time; it didn't command it. And the beast was coming.

Alaji started across first, stepping carefully to find a safe path, then moving back in time to increase her speed while she tested routes across. Some of the logs were slippery; others were rotting apart. If they went too quickly and fell through, they could potentially twist an ankle or even break a leg.

Behind them, the crashing grew louder, and a cloud of dust further darkened the sky.

Alaji used a branch for leverage and pulled herself over a raised cluster of logs. Instinctively, she stepped back in time before motioning for Yemerik to follow. She gasped as she peered down into a depression in the earth forming a large crater.

At first, she mistook the shapes for a patch of trees in the dimming light, but she quickly realized her mistake. They were the skeletons of two great creatures. She approached a few steps for a closer look: one was the skeleton of a beast, like the one that followed, and the other shape was that of a dragon. Only it was larger than any she'd seen.

She started to move on, but stopped when Yemerik cried out behind her. Briefly, she thought he'd simply caught sight of the skeletons, but he'd yet to climb over the stack of logs blocking the view. She turned back to see him kneeling on a log, pulling in an attempt to free his leg from a gap.

Something was pulling back.

Aided by her count of five, Alaji reached him almost immediately. She grabbed his arm and pulled. Together, they managed to get him most of the way up. The fabric over his shin was shredded, and he was bleeding. A sinewy green arm grasping his ankle fought to pull him back down. Around them, in tunnels beneath the wood, Alaji heard more goblins gathering.

The one latched onto Yemerik's leg began pulling harder. He was strong, and there were likely others bracing him. Alaji pulled as hard as she could, then restarted her count. She focused on that instant in place and time, and released Yemerik. He fell at once, caught off guard by the sudden loss of support.

"Alaji!" he called out. He screamed, as they pulled him a few inches deeper and jagged teeth ripped into his leg. "Wait! What are you doing?" What she was doing was drawing a dagger and aiming. "Stop!" he shrieked, as she drove the blade through an arc aimed at his knee.

Seconds earlier, she vanished and reappeared. Before Yemerik could fall, her blade stabbed into the goblin's wrist. The creature screamed and released its hold while Yemerik rolled onto the log, clutching his leg. It was bleeding where the goblin's nails had dug in.

"Get up!" Alaji shouted. Then she grabbed hold of two nearby trees, one in each hand, and uttered the spell of the hearth. They lit up at once, and she ran her fingers downward, extending the fire. She took a step and cast it again, lighting a larger trunk. Then a fourth and fifth. Smoke billowed around her and Yemerik, who coughed as he shifted away. Burning embers spilled into the maze beneath the logs, illuminating the naked goblins crawling back into their tunnels.

"It'll know where we are now," Yemerik said, as soon as he was far enough from the smoke to speak.

"It already knew," Alaji replied.

The goblins didn't trouble them again, though she noticed their shadows slipping through the tangled mesh of dead trees. She reached the edge of the forest just in time to look back and see the beast break through on the opposite side. It sniffed the ground and began across unencumbered by standing trees. It moved towards them, and logs collapsed under its feet like dried grass. It paused by the smoldering remains of her fire before continuing on.

"We're not going to make it," Yemerik said.

"There was a small hill ahead," Alaji said quietly. "Maybe a half day's march to the north."

"I remember it," Yemerik said. "What are you thinking?"

"I'll meet you there as soon as I can. Go!" she shouted, and vanished, reappearing five steps away. She flickered again and was five paces further, staying along the border of the road. In little time, she was more than a hundred paces ahead, and she was holding a piece of dry wood. She gripped the top, and it was burning brightly in the diminishing light. "Here!" she screamed. "I'm here if you want me!" She stepped back into the woods, torch firmly in hand.

The beast charged, tearing through the open stretch in seconds. Alaji ran, flickering like her torch light, blinking in and out of view. Behind her, the beast struck the forest full force, knocking down dozens of trees and shaking the ground.

The impact rattled the woods. Alaji stumbled, but retained her footing. Overhead, the trees shook, and small branches, leaves, and acorns rained around her. The beast was right behind, tearing at the net of trees holding it back.

Alaji ran, torch burning and cycle spinning. Behind her, the beast broke through the first line and continued forward, knocking trees to either side or tearing them out of the ground altogether and hurling them through the air. Just when she thought she might be gaining ground, an upended trunk fell directly at her. She leapt blindly back in time and ran as it crashed down behind her. Before she could breathe a sigh of relief, a branch swung down and struck her in the head.

Alaji struck the ground, skinning her palm. Her torch flew out of her hand and landed in a pile of dry leaves, which caught instantly. She ground her teeth and jumped back up. Her left leg was sore, but uninjured. She coughed against the smoke and ran on, liberally using her spell to try and regain a lead. She pulled a dead branch from a standing tree as she ran, and lit it between iterations of her count.

The beast was close, though, and it knew it. Alaji wasn't sure if it saw her, smelled her, heard her, or all three, but she knew the creature was aware of her presence. It howled, lunged, and fought for each step with even more ferocity than before. It struggled against the trees with abandon. When her exhaustion forced her to stop for a few seconds and look back, she could see its fur matted down with blood. If it felt any pain, it didn't show it.

Alaji pressed on. She ran through streams and stumbled over roots in the dark. She used her count to step back in time when she could, but she was losing focus. She needed rest. At least a few minutes to catch her breath and regain her composure. But the beast wasn't giving it to her. It was always close behind.

She was gasping for breath when she stepped unexpectedly into an open field. She froze for an instant, utterly spent. Billowing waves of long grass swayed in the moonlight to either side and as far ahead as she could see. A howl erupted from behind her, and she began to quiver. It wasn't fear but rage. Rage at the field for existing and the beast for not relenting. Rage at her exhaustion and every choice that led her here.

She cried out in answer to the beast and charged on, swinging her torch from side to side into the tall grass as she did. She ran forward, then darted side-to-side, lighting the grass. Then she used her count to step back. Her heart was pounding and her clothes were damp with sweat. She lit more grass and repeated the cycle, sacrificing distance and time to give the fire a chance to catch.

When the beast appeared, Alaji hurled her torch into the brush and waited. She was too exhausted to outrun it here, anyway.

At first, she thought she'd made a mistake. The beast's head was pointed directly at her. But then it shifted around. It lowered its snout to the ground and began sniffing. When it took in a gust of smoke, it coughed, and Alaji had to bite her tongue to keep from crying out in victory. It waded into the fires, smelling the ground. The ends of its fur on its face and legs caught and began burning. The creature snarled as the flames consumed strands of hair and bit its skin, but it didn't give up its search.

Alaji moved away slowly. She began her count, then took off in a sprint. The beast lunged after her. When she reached four, she dropped to the ground and stepped back to one. The beast was back where it had been, searching for her trail, but she was further away. She took another moment's rest, then ran again. Like before, the beast heard her and began pursuit; like before, she slipped into hiding and stepped back to a moment before it detected her.

Alaji was almost across the field before the beast finally picked up her trail. By then, she'd had time to catch her breath. She dashed into the woods with the beast charging behind her. She could hear its labored breathing and feel its feet strike the earth. At least it was tired, too. She knew she couldn't run forever, but she began to realize the monster couldn't, either.

As before, the trees slowed it down, and she managed to build up a modest lead while it tore a path into the growth. It bellowed in rage and frustration, and despite the pain and fear and exhaustion, Alaji felt a smile appear.

She struck thick undergrowth and fought through, briefly feeling a sort of kinship with the beast behind her. Thorns caught her sleeves and left small rips when she pulled through. The brush parted, and she stumbled out onto a rocky ledge.

The woods continued forty yards ahead on the other side of a gorge cradling a fierce river. It was twenty feet down to the surface of the water, and she had no idea how deep it was. Very, she guessed, since the river was relatively narrow here. That meant a strong current. She looked downstream and discovered the cliff only increased in height for the near future.

She'd hesitated too long as it was. With a deep gulp of air, she jumped. The roar of the beast faded as she fell towards the crashing river. She wondered if rocks waited for her just under the surface, if she'd be left with broken legs waiting for the beast to catch up.

She plunged into the black water, which grabbed hold of her and dragged her along as she pulled herself to the surface for a breath. It was colder than she'd expected, and the current was strong. She swam for the far shore, but found herself unable to control where the river tossed her. She caught hold of a large rock in the center of the river and tried to regain her sense of direction.

Cliffs towered over her on both sides. From the nearer side, the beast was looking down at her.

It had only to jump. Even with her count, she'd never outmaneuver it here, and whatever edge her spell gave her would only last until the waves or rocks or cold broke her concentration. Alaji pulled herself halfway up the rock and reached for her dagger. She knew it wouldn't help her with this creature, but she wanted it in her hand. Any cut she made would be lost among the hundreds left by the trees it crushed, but she hoped to leave her mark.

But the beast didn't jump. At least not at first and not the way Alaji expected. Its growling had ceased, and it began to search for footing. When a portion of the cliff crumbled beneath it, it scrambled back. For the first time, it seemed afraid. Then it backed out of view. A moment later, it charged and leapt the full width of the river to the opposite cliff, where it latched on for a moment, as if worried the entire cliff might collapse under its weight. When it seemed secure, the beast began to test that side, only to find it was no sturdier than where it had come from.

"So you don't like water," Alaji mused. Squinting, she examined the distance between the cliffs overhead. "And that's about as far as you can jump," she whispered. She kicked off of the rock and continued downstream. She treaded water to stay ahead, and kept an eye on the creature to make sure it didn't cross without her realizing. It followed along on the shore as the river's width increased, the cliff petered off to a gentle slope, and the current slowed.

Shaking, she pulled herself from the water. Every muscle ached from the strain of the chase and swim. "But I'm alive," she whispered, locking eyes with the beast on the opposite shore.

It tested the water but didn't wade in. Instead, it darted back the way it came. Alaji nodded and ran on, aided by her count of five. Then, when the beast was out of view, she turned back towards the river. She dove in and swam across, then began heading north again. With any luck, the beast might lose her trail for good. Even if it didn't, it wouldn't realize it'd been tricked until it circled back to the cliffs, crossed, then made its way to this spot. By the time it returned to the cliffs a third time, she'd have a real lead.

—

It was dawn before Alaji found Yemerik on top of the hill. He was covered in scrapes, he moved with a slight limp, and he was shivering. She was about to ask him if he was alright, but stopped when she saw his expression upon seeing her. She must have looked far worse than he did. She laughed for a moment and sat down in the dirt.

"I heard it," Yemerik said. "A few hours ago. It was… over there, I think."

"Near the river," Alaji surmised. "I tricked it. It won't go in the water for some reason. We can use that in a pinch."

Yemerik sighed and nodded. "I don't know where it is now," he said.

Alaji pointed to the woods on the opposite side of the river. "There's where I last heard it. By now, it may have pushed into the northeast or backtracked across."

Yemerik bit his lip. "We can't make for the eastern peak then.

It would bring us across the creature's path if it's still on that side of the river."

"But if it's crossed back, turning around will bring us right to it," Alaji reasoned.

"We can't do either. We need a different destination." His eyes followed the river north to the lake.

"If we stay by the river, we'll at least have a chance to get away if it finds us again."

"And we might be able to find assistance in the village. If anyone knows how to handle this creature, they will."

2

It was early morning, a full day later, when they reached the shore opposite the village and charged into the frigid water. Alaji could hear the beast panting through the trees. If she stopped and turned around, she was certain she'd have been able to see its head crest the river bank behind them.

The beast had pursued them without rest. It would have caught them by now, if not for the river, which they'd crossed four times the previous night. Each time, their lead diminished as the beast grew shrewder at guessing their location and boxed them closer and closer to the edge of the giant lake that now lay just north of them. They were beyond exhausted as they stepped off the shallow ledge of the river bottom and began swimming. Alaji wondered if this would be deep enough or if the beast would simply bound in after them and pick them off of the water's surface.

Alaji and Yemerik fought the tide, gasping for breath as they pulled themselves foot by foot across the icy river. As she swam, Alaji peered beneath the surface, all the way to the riverbed. There were no plants or rocks, just something long, smooth, and glistening.

And then the bottom of the river moved. Just slightly, it shifted to one side. For a brief instant she forgot the beast and looked down in wonder and horror. There was something down there, something alive in the river. And whatever it was, its girth took up a third of the distance from shore to shore. She could only have guessed at its length: a quarter mile, perhaps more, stretching north into the lake. A bit downriver, she caught sight of a fin, nearly extending to the surface, swaying gently from side to side.

Behind her, she heard the beast bellow, and her thoughts returned to their pursuer. She did not doubt that the thing beneath the water would devour them if it noticed their presence, but it did not seem to sense them yet. Unlike the beast, it was not hunting them.

Soon they reached the shore and crawled onto the muddy bank. They collapsed, struggling for air, and turned to watch the beast wade in to its knees. For a moment it seemed as if the creature would cross, and Alaji prepared to run, despite her exhaustion. But the beast tested its footing, stepped back, and bellowed again. Even after two days of hearing the sound, it sent a shiver down her spine.

The creature turned, lumbered away a half step, shifted over, and tried crossing in the new spot. It repeated this twice more before finally leaving the water. The black fur on its legs and underbelly hung wet and dripping. It didn't bellow now, but growled, a deep and spiteful sound that seemed to shake the ground. But it wasn't the ground shaking; just Alaji's legs, exhausted and terrified.

Briefly, Alaji allowed herself the luxury of pretending it was giving up. But she knew better by now. When it reached the top of the river bank, it turned left and ran. Clods of gravel kicked up behind its feet as it followed the river south.

"It will find a way across," Alaji said, forcing herself up. "Get up. We need…." She fell back to the ground. Two days without sleep. Two days without more than a few minutes at a time to stop and catch her breath. A few moments for a gulp of water or a handful of nuts. Two days of running.

And the beast still followed.

"We found the village." Yemerik was lying on his back. His head was tilted back, and he was looking behind him. He made a sound in the back of his throat, half a laugh and half a stifled cry. "City even. I'd say it's a city."

Alaji didn't acknowledge the sick joke. She turned to look at the structures they'd been moving towards since being cut off from the portal. Hours earlier, they'd realized that whatever this place had once been, it was now only ruins. But even if they'd had the energy, there was nowhere else to run.

"There could still be someone here. Or at least someplace to hide." She regretted saying it almost immediately and was about to correct herself before Yemerik cut her off.

"I'm sure they tried that," he said sardonically, sitting up. "Whoever lived here. I'm sure they tried hiding from that thing, too."

"There's only two of us. Maybe there's somewhere small enough it can't fit."

"It would just be waiting for us," Yemerik sighed. "Assuming it couldn't dig us out. It would probably just...." He snickered, picked up a rock, and threw it angrily into the river.

"Don't!" Alaji said. "There's something else down there! Something larger than that... thing."

Yemerik jumped to his feet, stepped away from the edge, and swallowed. "I was going to suggest following the shore. Perhaps even trying to swim across the lake."

Alaji shook her head. "It's too cold, and we're too tired. People used to die swimming Boars Lake when it was warmer than this, and that wasn't half as wide. How can water be this cold in the summer?" She looked to the wall of ice in the north and had her answer. "The village could have survivors. They might know how to trick it."

Yemerik just shook his head. "If anyone lived through that destruction, they'd have left ages ago."

"Then we have to kill it," Alaji said. She tried to sound brave, but her voice broke.

Yemerik laughed. "It would tear us apart in a fight."

"Then we have to die!" she shouted. Both her and Yemerik were silent for a moment. She breathed in deeply. "If we don't stop—"

"We'll collapse," Yemerik said. "And it will catch us anyway."

"So we have to kill it. Or die trying."

"There's another way." Yemerik said. "Just leave me to die and get back to the gate."

"I wouldn't make it. Not without rest. I haven't been able to concentrate. The count is difficult when I'm this tired. I'd never outrun it, not all the way back."

Yemerik nodded and looked towards the ruins. "Maybe there's something here. Some information about that thing and how to fight or escape it. If not…."

In the distance, they heard the beast howl. It sent another shiver down Alaji's spine. Finding some sort of salvation in this place seemed absurd, but there were no other options.

—

As she walked down the road into the remnants of the town, Alaji's legs were quaking, though she barely noticed. She was numb from the cold water that still soaked her clothes and still shaken by the massive creature she'd glimpsed beneath the river. Bones and long-dead corpses littered the streets: animal, human, and other things Alaji couldn't identify were strewn among debris from collapsed buildings and fallen statues she might have stopped to admire under different circumstances. As it was, she could barely find the energy to hold her eyes open.

"Hello!" Yemerik cried out. "Is anyone here?"

Alaji glanced over her shoulder, suddenly concerned with the attention they might draw. Caution was pointless, of course: the beast would find them no matter if they were silent. They might as well gamble on locating aid. But she felt exposed in the ruins. She shook her head to try and clear her thoughts.

"No one," Yemerik said after a few minutes of shouting. He seemed beyond despair. "There's no one here."

"Wait," Alaji said. "Down there." She knelt on the ground and examined the dirt road. "It's been disturbed. By... yes! There!" She pointed excitedly. "Those are footprints!"

Yemerik fell forward onto his hands and studied the tracks. He burst out laughing. There was no question: these were made by people. "There is someone here," he agreed. "They might kill us for bringing that thing, but there's someone here!"

Alaji laughed, as well, nearly on the verge of tears. "If they lasted this long, they must have a way of hiding. Or maybe even fighting back."

Yemerik nodded and gestured down the street. "They seem headed in that direction, don't they?" He stood up and dusted himself off.

"I think so," Alaji replied, slowly standing up. Her joints ached from the stress, but she hurried forward, following the tracks. More sets joined them as they went, crossing, overlapping, and splitting away. But the tracks seemed heaviest on a single path, and they seemed to grow heavier as they went towards some central location.

Finally, the trail came to an end in front of a large building near the lake that was mostly untouched by whatever had happened to the town. They studied the outside for only a moment, before Yemerik knocked against the door. He didn't wait for a response, but turned towards Alaji. "I'll go first. If whatever's behind that door kills me horribly—"

"I understand," Alaji said, focusing on her count. "Hurry. Before it reaches us." She glanced behind them, back towards the river.

Yemerik pulled the door open easily and stepped in. "Hello," he called out. He motioned for Alaji to follow behind.

It was dark inside and mostly hollowed out. The building had at one time had an upper floor, but this had fallen in, leaving piles of splintered boards on the ground level. There were signs of a fire, as well: charred planks and smeared ash. To their left was a large opening in the floor, where a staircase descended into some sort of cellar. The whole place smelled of death.

Alaji motioned, and Yemerik hesitantly nodded. Slowly, Alaji bent over and found one of the larger planks of wood and cast her spell of the hearth. Fire spread across one end of the board and illuminated the room. She started forward, but Yemerik stopped her. "I can't go back and save you," he said. She handed over the torch, and he started forward uneasily. Alaji lit a second torch and followed.

The stairs led down into a damp tunnel. Yemerik called ahead as he went, trying to put anyone down there at ease. But his voice grew more and more anxious. The odor of rotting meat grew thicker as the tunnel became wider and less structured.

"What is this place?" Alaji whispered.

"It might be where the survivors hide from the monsters," Yemerik replied, uneasy. "Or…." He shuddered.

"Or what?"

"It doesn't matter. We'll have a better chance hiding down here. Maybe this passage leads somewhere useful. A tunnel or something." He stopped abruptly. The passage opened up, and the ground dipped down into murky water. Floating on the surface were dozens of bodies. The nearest drifted just a few feet before them. There wasn't much left: more pieces had been torn out than remained.

"What did this?" Alaji whispered. Holding her torch close. The bites weren't like those of animals she'd known.

"Move away from the water," Yemerik said, quietly but with as much force as she'd ever heard from him. She did as he said.

"What is it?" she whispered.

Yemerik was shivering and staring into the water. "When you go back to save me, use the torch," he whispered. Alaji's eyes searched beneath the surface, and she saw movement. Milky white arms pulling a body forward. It took her a moment to realize what she was seeing, and when she recognized the creature, she almost screamed. "Use the torch, the fire," he repeated. "The knife won't—"

It burst out of the water, knocking Yemerik's torch aside as it grabbed onto his arm. Yemerik's scream drowned out the snap of bone, and the creature's teeth bit into him.

The creature was a man.

"Use the torch, the fire," Yemerik said, too focused on the body crawling towards him to realize that Alaji's position had shifted as she stepped back in time. "The knife won't—"

The creature lunged from the water as Alaji's torch slammed into its head. Its skull gave way, and it fell to one side as Yemerik leapt back.

"What is it?" Alaji shrieked, holding her torch out in case any more appeared.

"Look out!" Yemerik screamed in response, pointing at the fallen man. It stood up, somewhat uneasily, and turned to face Alaji. Then it hissed, as if it neither knew nor cared its forehead was caved in. "Run," Yemerik said. "Run!" he screamed, as he charged out the way they'd come.

Alaji's eyes widened as three more heads rose out of the water. One was a child, no more than eight. All had blank expressions in their eyes and bared their teeth. And none drew breath.

They came at her quickly, jaws snapping with enough force to chip their teeth. They met empty air, of course, as she fled, stepping back in time. They moved with little regard for safety or pain. They avoided fire, but it didn't drive them back or even keep them at bay: they simply sought to push it away.

"Quickly!" Yemerik cried, as Alaji hurried behind him. She caught up to him almost at once using her count, then turned to try and fend off the creatures. Yemerik tore up the stairs while she skipped in time and batted at the pale bodies from different angles. She struck the first one's head again, caving it in completely. It collapsed in convulsions, still animate but now without direction. It wormed on the floor while others crawled over it. More had appeared – Alaji wasn't sure how many – and they clawed and scratched at each other to vie for a chance to get at their fleeing prey.

She followed Yemerik up the stairs with the creatures just behind. Their seemingly endless will ran out, however, when they stumbled into the slivers of sunlight cutting in through the cracks and windows. The creatures shrieked in pain and raised arms to fend off the light. Whiffs of smoke appeared on their skin where it was illuminated.

But the creatures behind these pushed ahead, forcing those nearest through the net of light. Alaji ran beside Yemerik, who stood ready at the door. "Vampirism. Some form of – never mind," he stammered. One of the creatures charged them, and he threw open the door. Alaji and Yemerik ran out as the screeches turned to shrill screams, and foul-smelling smoke billowed out behind them.

Alaji pushed herself away from the building, as the screaming intensified. "We should burn it down," she whispered.

"Alaji," Yemerik said, stoically. She looked over and saw him staring down the street. She followed his gaze to that of the beast, which stood a quarter mile away, staring back. Its muscles were taut and its fur was matted down with blood. Tree branches were tangled in some spots; others were raw where clumps of hair had been pulled out. The beast's chest heaved, and its eyes widened. Its nostrils flared, and it howled loudly.

"Get out of here," Yemerik said. "Get to one of the gates, and go back. Find me when I arrive, and take us somewhere else."

Alaji shook her head. Her energy was too far gone. She'd never manage to outmaneuver the beast long enough. She looked around frantically, considering the lake, various ruined buildings that might slow the beast down, and even glanced back at the building they'd just emerged from. The tunnel, even with its horrors, seemed an enticing option.

But before it came to that, her attention was drawn to a hill to the southeast. Standing not far off were a group of riders watching the scene play out. Their weapons reflected the morning sun. They were at least a dozen strong; maybe more.

"Yemerik," she said, pointing. "You need to reach them."

"I'll never make it," he said, turning back to the beast.

"You'll make it. Get out of sight as soon as it's distracted," Alaji said. Then, staring directly at the beast, she screamed. "Come at me!"

She charged the beast, and the beast charged her.

3

It hurt to run. It hurt in her chest every time she inhaled and every time her heart beat. It hurt her feet to strike the ground and her heels and knees to bear her weight. Her eyes ached just to stay open, and her palms ached as her fingernails drove into her wounded skin.

But she knew what would happen if she stopped, so she locked her teeth together and accepted the pain. Briefly, Alaji was worried the beast would ignore her and go after Yemerik, but as soon as she looked it in the eye, she knew better. Once she was dead, it would gladly hunt Yemerik down and tear him to shreds. Then, for all she knew, it might slaughter every animal for a thousand miles. And every plant, too, perhaps. But while she lived and while it was close, it wanted her. She saw this in its eye, and did not doubt it.

It was exactly what she needed, but the notion didn't bring her much relief.

It was as close now as it had ever been. She turned and darted down an alley too small for the beast's width. This didn't stop it, of course: the beast plowed ahead, just as it had in the forests and fields. The already crumbling ruins broke before it into clouds of dust and falling debris. The beast lumbered on, leaping onto the disintegrating pile of rubble. It dug through, throwing massive pieces of breaking buildings into the air as it went.

Alaji narrowly dodged. There were too many collapsing walls and pieces of stone masonry sailing through the air for her to keep track, so she used her count of five sparingly to limit her chances of materializing in front of a falling object. She coughed against the cloud of dust. The beast coughed as well. It wheezed and spat and snarled as it limped through the ruins towards its prey.

—

The ground shook beneath the footfalls of the beast and the destruction it unleashed, and Yemerik scrambled towards the rise. He was no less exhausted than Alaji and no less desperate. It had occurred to him that the riders might be ambivalent or hostile to their predicament, but it hardly seemed worth considering. If they weren't willing or weren't able to help, he was no better off than if they hadn't appeared. Whether they killed him, took bets on how long he could elude the monster, or simply waited to die beside him seemed academic. If they lacked some power over the beast, he was as good as dead. But, unless he missed his guess, so were they, which gave them some incentive to try and offer assistance.

As he approached the hill, the riders spurred their horses down towards him and all the commotion below. He could see they had spears strapped to their horses. Two were women, one armored heavily and another with only a sword.

Yemerik continued towards them, though they seemed less interested in him than in the monster. This was probably for the best, though he decided it would be safer if he didn't appear to be fleeing from them.

The first of the riders flew by him so close, Yemerik was almost knocked over. The second went by a bit further off, but not enough for comfort. One by one, they passed by. The last was the largest, and he came a bit more slowly. As he approached, he steered his horse directly towards Yemerik, who shifted to try and run. At the last moment, the horse veered and the rider leaned out of his saddle. With one hand, he took hold of the back of Yemerik's shirt and swung him off the ground. The force alone was enough to knock the wind from Yemerik, and the next thing he knew he was on his back across the horse. He was looking up at the rider, whose hand was the only thing keeping Yemerik from slipping off to be trampled. And the rider was howling with laughter.

—

Alaji stood with her back to the river while the beast wriggled its way through the pile of rubble. She had her knife in one hand and a torch in the other, though she knew neither would help. She considered going for the river and trying to reach deep water before it caught up with her, but she didn't trust her concentration if she was exposed to the icy currents again, and without her count of five, the beast would get her before the water covered its ankles.

To her left, she saw some motion in the distance. The riders, if she was lucky; creatures like those she'd encountered below, if she wasn't. The cloud of dust was too thick to make out forms, but this was no time for caution, so she ran towards the movement.

Behind her she heard the beast break free and hurl itself towards her. She used her count of five to prevent it from overtaking her and pressed on.

The dust began to thin, and she saw the riders ahead of her. Their mounts were still, but all but one held spears and seemed ready for a fight. The last, a tall woman with dark brown skin, had dismounted and was staring intently at Alaji.

She might make it to them before the beast caught up with her; she might not. Rather than risk it, Alaji turned to face it once more. She charged at it. They would collide in a matter of seconds, and the beast would simply catch or crush her. She cried out for the monster and leapt off of a broken beam as she came close. Then, just as the beast reached out its head to catch her midair, she stepped forward five heartbeats in time.

The risk seemed immaterial: anything she might try was likely to end in her death. But even if the beast figured out what had happened, Alaji guessed it wouldn't be able to stop fast enough to make much difference. And if it did, if it managed to spin around in time for her to reappear in its body, she didn't think it would end any better for the beast than for her.

She appeared right where she'd vanished, but the world had moved forward. The beast, now behind her, was slowing down and growling, but it was confused, inhaling the thick air and coughing out billows of black dirt. It craned its head from side to side, as it slid to a stop.

Alaji fell to the dirt road and landed on arms and knees. It was hard to see and harder to breathe, but she was alive for the time being. She sat very still, certain the beast would see her as soon as she started to run, and choked back a cough so it wouldn't hear her.

Then she saw the first flash and heard the creature cry out in pain. A plume of fire engulfed the beast's head, then faded out just as quickly. It reeled back, and Alaji caught sight of spears pinned in the beast's forearm. It leapt forward, away from Alaji, and swept the ground with its head. A horse careened end-over-end into the air. It would have almost been comical if not for the animal's cries. These met a sharp end when the beast leapt up and snapped its jaws shut around the horse's torso. What hadn't broken off, the beast spat out, then reared up, swiping at something before it. Somewhere, a man screamed.

A pair of spears caught the beast, one in its left cheek and another in its belly. The beast lashed at the road, and there was another scream. Alaji found herself grateful for the plume of dust near the ground that made it impossible to see clearly.

But the beast's head rose above the worst of it, and it looked around frantically. In the corner of one eye, it caught sight of Alaji and lost interest in everything else. The beast lumbered around, though it moved more slowly than before and without growling. Then it started towards her.

Alaji nodded and looked to her right. There was a building, or the remnants of one, not far off. The roof had fallen in, but the walls were mostly intact and made of wood. She ran for it, using her count to pick up time. The beast moved after her, but she had the advantage. She reached the doorway and lit the wood on fire as she ran in. There were several holes along the far wall, and she cast the spell of the hearth near one of these, as well, before running out. The flames spread quickly behind her.

The beast burst through the front and the wooden beams snapped and splintered around it. It stumbled and fell head first into the far wall, then broke through. The fire scorched its face as it clawed after Alaji.

For her part, she was trapped. The alley she was in was blocked at one end. The only other way through would bring her within range of the beast's claws, and they were coming closer. She swung a burning board in a futile attempt to fight off the monster, but the beast's paw splintered it as it pulled itself nearer.

Then, just as it was about to reach her, the beast yelped in pain. A huge blond man wearing blackish furs had slipped in beside it and stabbed the beast in the left ankle with a blade longer than any Alaji had seen. The beast lashed out with its wounded leg, but the foot hung limp. The attacker was thrown back, but he kept hold of his sword. He landed on his feet in the alley with a smirk on his face.

For a moment, the beast seemed unsure which of its foes to go after. It drew back its head slightly, though its body was wedged in the ruin of the building. Alaji took the opportunity to cast her spell of the hearth on what remained of her board. Once it flared up, she threw it at the beast's eye with a shout. The beast blinked to avoid the object, which glanced off the edge of its face. When its eyes opened, they were fixated only on Alaji again, and it dove towards her, snapping.

She leapt back, just out of range, while the warrior raced forward. He thrust his blade upward as the beast's head lunged down, and metal met flesh at the creature's neck. The beast's eyes widened in panic, as the warrior gripped his sword hilt and turned it upward, forcing the monster's head down. Then he completed the arc, cutting through to the air and leaving a deep cleft in the beast's neck.

A mist of red sprayed onto the warrior's furs, skin, and hair, and left a smear across the alley onto the building behind him. Alaji avoided the worst of the gore, but even she was covered in spots of blood.

The warrior looked at her, at his arms and body, and at the twitching beast. And he bellowed with laughter and joy.

PART 4: ULITHAINE, THE WARRIOR

1

Against his better judgment, Yemerik threw up. He knew it was likely a breach of etiquette, but between running for two days from a gigantic creature intent on devouring him whole, nearly being torn apart by ravenous undead monstrosities, getting grabbed by a man who was nearly seven feet tall, being pinned to a galloping horse, getting dropped onto the ground to watch helplessly while men and horses were slaughtered horribly, and standing downwind of the monster when it released its bowels in its death throes, he found the situation entirely beyond his control. Besides, he hadn't vomited on the rider who'd dragged him back to the edge of the fight, so there was certainly a chance they wouldn't kill him for this display of weakness.

He wasn't entirely sure how good of a chance that was: these were, after all, the sort of men who seemed to consider trying their mettle against titanic beasts great sport.

Yemerik choked out the last of the meager contents of his stomach, which was mostly water, anyway. The warriors weren't paying much attention to him, so he began crawling towards the river. Perhaps he could wash himself off before they realized what had occurred.

He'd almost reached the river when he felt a hand grab his shoulder and turn him around. It was the dark-skinned sorceress, and she had a look of disdain on her face. She said something he couldn't understand – his pendant hadn't picked up their language yet. It would help, of course, if they spoke more than a few words or curses at a time. He simply shook his head while she sneered. She spoke again and gestured at the river.

He nodded and turned back towards the water. She responded by grabbing him again, spinning him around, and striking the top of his head with the back of her hand. It clearly wasn't meant to injure him, but it was a stark reminder that desperate times breed strong people: the blow was excruciatingly painful, and only in part because he was already exhausted and worn thin.

Yemerik fell back and cringed. The woman reached down, untied a waterskin from her belt, and threw it to him. He reached for it, and she caught his arm. Then she pointed back towards the river and shook her head. He nodded, picking up two key concepts: he wasn't supposed to go near the river and – more importantly – she didn't seem to want him to die of thirst. Or maybe she just wanted him to wash out his mouth, so she wouldn't have to endure his breath. Either at least implied they weren't intending to use him to practice their archery, which was fairly comforting. Not quite as comforting as the water in that instant, but still a good sign.

He rinsed out the foul taste then splashed some of the extra water on his face and hands. Yemerik did his best to make himself seem presentable, though he imagined the effect would have been more convincing under better conditions. He stood up and began back towards the ruins propping up the beast's corpse.

He still didn't know what had happened. It had rushed in after Alaji, and one of the riders who'd survived the initial assault had dashed down an alley after it. Then there were screams, roars, and a fairly grisly sound culminating in the beast collapsing, twitching, and fouling the ruins of the town. He had no idea whether Alaji was alive or not. If not, it made matters much more complicated. He'd have to reclaim the shards of the talisman, get away from the marauders (or whatever these people were), then try to go back in time to before they arrived and wait for her to appear. Between the two jobs, he'd have preferred to be brutally killed by the beast. He was relatively sure he would have been capable of managing that.

Fortunately, his concerns were unfounded. The warrior who'd gone after the beast emerged, coated in gore, and Alaji followed behind. As soon as the warrior appeared, the other survivors ran to meet him alongside the dead monster. The largest of the men, the one who'd carried Yemerik down the hill, clasped his arms around the warrior and lifted him into the air, laughing. The large man laughed again when he set his companion down and looked at himself, now stamped with red. The others seemed content to clasp the shoulder of the one who'd killed the beast. Finally, the sorceress approached and looked at him somewhat blankly. They traded quick words, and she pointed to Yemerik before beginning a spell of some kind.

Alaji stumbled away from the beast and sat on the ground. One of the men set a pack beside her, but beyond this, they seemed willing to give her some space.

Yemerik was working up the energy to walk over to her, hopefully without fainting or vomiting again, but the lead warrior, still covered in blood, left his men and came to him first. "Phaesha says you can't speak Okrilian," he said.

"No. No, I can speak," Yemerik stuttered. "I hit my head earlier. Nothing made sense for a moment, but I'm alright now."

"Good," the warrior said, looking him over quickly. "When the girl didn't speak, I was worried we'd have to postpone introductions. Did she… hit her head, too?"

Yemerik wasn't sure what he was implying. Was he mocking him? Testing him? "No. Alaji can't speak. No language from these parts. She's from.…" He gestured to the east, since there was more land that way. "She was brought here after her parents were killed. It took me several years, but I've learned to communicate with her."

"Several years," the warrior repeated. Then he smiled, though it did little to make him less imposing. At more than six feet, he towered over Yemerik. He was broad-shouldered and muscular: the sort of person bred by bad times in history. It was difficult to determine his age beneath the coating of blood, but Yemerik guessed late twenties. "I'm Ulithaine," the warrior added, clasping his own shoulder with a cupped palm.

Yemerik mimicked the gesture. "Yemerik," he said, nodding. "Thank you for your help. That… thing… came at us. I'm sorry it's cost you." He motioned to one of the fallen men.

Ulithaine's smile faded for a moment, looking at the body. "Treinile. A bowman like no other. But his death's not on your head, nor are the others. We've hunted Krishind's hound for weeks. The girl's presence here was a welcome diversion. I think we'd have lost more if we'd caught up to it under different circumstances."

Yemerik pulled his cloak close as the wind picked up. Above him, the sky began to darken. He looked around to discover wisps of clouds spiraling towards them. Ulithaine glanced towards the sorceress. "Is she the first Tythalian Enchantress you've met?" He asked.

"I… yes. I saw one once, but I've never met one before. Not really," Yemerik said, as casually as he could manage.

Ulithaine nodded and laughed. "Don't let her frighten you. They're all like that." Droplets of rain began to fall from the conjured cloud onto the building and creature. "When the fires are out, we'll pry the teeth free. You know to stay out of the river, right?"

"I do now."

"Good. The hound's nothing to the eel," Ulithaine said. "You'll explain it to the girl?" He motioned towards Alaji, who was walking towards them.

"Yes, of course," Yemerik replied.

"It's good we met here, Yemerik," Ulithaine said. He whistled sharply, and his horse trotted to them. "There's some food and water in the saddlebag. I'd pull it down for you, but…." He opened his arms to display the grisly mess covering him. "I've got some work to attend to, but I'd like to speak with you again once I'm through." Yemerik thanked him, but Ulithaine just nodded and hurried away, pausing only to pet his horse on the side of its neck, leaving a red print behind. Then he continued towards the sorceress. His men had already started gathering their fallen comrades, at least those the beast had left intact enough to be recovered.

—

"The fires will be gone soon," Phaesha said. "The brutes can take it from there."

Ulithaine smiled. "I'm just one of the brutes. I'll lend a hand."

"You should leave it to the others. You did your part already."

"Are you worried I'll dirty my shirt?" he joked.

Phaesha looked past his shoulder at Yemerik and Alaji, sitting in the road and trying to clean the dirt and blood out of their clothes. She sneered again. "I saved the man's life," she said. "Hardly worth the effort. He was about to dive into the mouth of the serpent."

"It's probably asleep, anyway," Ulithaine replied. "It didn't eat them when they swam across last time."

"They crossed the river?" she asked, surprised.

"There were tracks," Ulithaine pointed. "Your father would have caught them. That's not all. Did you see the smoke as we came in? They've been into the caverns. I assume the dead took one look at them and decided they weren't so hungry after all."

Phaesha laughed, then looked away. When she turned back, her stiff, statuesque demeanor had returned. She noticed Ulithaine kept glancing at Alaji, so she said, "Bait for the hound," and snorted. "Another girl in distress. You waste your time on them."

"You think so? Let's hope she does, as well. Don't tell them," he motioned quickly to his men. "Let them think I killed it, and there was no more to the story."

"That isn't what happened?"

"I put it out of its misery. But it was more than half dead by the time we got here. It'd been running for days without rest. That's why we missed it at the cliffs. Damned thing's been after them since we heard it over the peak. The hounds weren't bred for that kind of stamina. Krishind made them to slaughter and feast. To run down their prey quickly. They weren't intended for a long hunt."

"How did they escape it for so long?"

"The girl has some sort of magic. I saw it as we rode in and again in the alley. She vanishes and reappears nearby."

Phaesha shrugged. "My mother knew spells like that," she said.

"This was no mere invisibility. This was something else. I'd like to talk with her about it, but it's too soon for that. The man's speaking now, though," Ulithaine added, matter-of-factly.

Phaesha tilted her head, as if this was another joke. "He was dumb a moment ago."

"Well, now he talks just fine. Better than fine, he speaks like a duke at court in one of the old romances. Not the girl, though. She's from a far off land to the east. Only knows a mysterious language we've never heard of."

Phaesha blinked at him, confused. "Land? What land? Amnithil? Wesrivith?"

"I had the distinct impression it was farther than that. Somewhere hidden in the mists of forgotten knowledge. Why, it took him years to learn to speak her language."

Phaesha stared at Yemerik and Alaji. "Are they mad?"

"Before I forget," Ulithaine went on, "Do me a favor and tell the others, if you introduce yourself to them, touch your shoulder when you say your name."

"Is it something they do?"

"It is now, I think. Also, I told him you were a Tythalian Enchantress, so just ignore him if he uses the word."

"What's a Tythalian?" she asked.

Ulithaine shrugged. "Something I made up to see how he'd react. I suppose it means you're black."

"Who are they then? Where are they from?"

"Who knows? Another world, perhaps? Or something equally strange." He smiled widely.

"Is such a thing possible?"

"No idea," Ulithaine admitted. "But I can't wait to find out. I'll be able to learn more if I get them alone. The sight of you lot can't put them at ease. They don't seem used to gangs of brutes. Or Tythalian Enchantresses."

"If you want them at ease, bathe and change your shirt," Phaesha said. "If you travel with them, I'll stay at your side. In case the girl is as dangerous as you think, you'll need magic." She held her hand up to display the snake's tooth she wore around her wrist.

"With your talents for diplomacy, they'd run off the moment our backs were turned. When we've finished here, take our prize across Harbil's Pass and cut across the river. Take Brithol and Thirove north with you, but leave the others under Geffe's watch at camp, then meet me at the Breaking Falls."

"You want to meet with the wizard with only three at your back? What if he picks a fight?"

"We'll have Yemerik and the girl, as well," Ulithaine answered, nonchalantly. "If they're not what I expect, we'll send for aid before traveling on."

"You mean to test them," Phaesha said, irritated. "The Burrows?"

"It will be easy enough to steer them that way," Ulithaine replied.

"They'll be torn apart."

"Possibly. I thought you'd be happier at the prospect."

"You'll be torn apart, too."

"There can't be more than three families of apes in those hills. I don't expect to live forever, but it will take more than a handful of apes and their pets to bring me down."

"I still don't like it." She looked over at Yemerik and Alaji. "How do you know they aren't his? How do you know the necromancer didn't send them?"

"He'd send a scrawny man with no knowledge of the world as an agent?" he scoffed. "No, they're something else. From somewhere else. I don't know where, but you saw the sky between the mountains. That wasn't the necromancer's doing. Wherever they're from, it's somewhere tame, by the look of Yemerik. Not so sure about the girl, though. She's got fire in her. Your rain hasn't countered her spell, yet."

"If we crossed, I'd leave nothing of her," Phaesha replied. "Whatever tricks she's learned, they are nothing to my sorcery."

Ulithaine shook his head. "Your sorcery couldn't run one of Krishind's hounds halfway to its grave. But it doesn't matter. I don't want you fighting her. Dead, she's worthless."

"Mark my words. She's worth less alive."

Ulithaine looked Phaesha in the eyes for a moment and grinned. "Save your fire. Before long, we'll reach the Ice Halls. You could actually come in handy there if things go poorly."

"If you don't reach the Falls, if the girl or the man who forgets how to speak stabs you in the back, don't think I'll avenge you. I'll collect the reward for the hound then take command of your men."

"If that happens, you're welcome to fight Geffe for control. I'm really not sure which of you would win."

"I'd win," she snapped, perhaps a bit too quickly. "He's always feared my magic."

Ulithaine just laughed and shook his head.

2

"Why are they helping us?" Alaji whispered.

Yemerik looked over at the warriors who were emerging from the alley with teeth nearly as long as their arms, stacking them, then returning for more. The armored woman was helping, though the sorceress stood apart, somewhat between the group of butchers and him and Alaji. She occasionally glanced at the two of them, usually with a disdainful expression. That seemed to be how she looked at the warriors, as well, so at least she wasn't singling them out. As far as Yemerik could tell, she hated everyone and everything.

"I don't know," he said, sipping a bitter wine he'd taken from Ulithaine's saddle. He offered some to Alaji, who gulped down a mouthful. "They weren't so friendly when I met them on the hill." He rubbed his shoulder. He'd be sore for days, if not weeks.

"Then they want something," Alaji replied. "They want us off guard. Like Minot-Rin."

"What?"

Alaji shook her head. "I'm sorry. That wasn't this version of you. It's hard to remember sometimes. Minot-Rin tried to make us comfortable to get information. Before he turned on us. It was difficult. I had to stab one of his guards in the stomach."

Yemerik nodded slowly and shifted. "These don't seem like royalty. They seem more like…," he trailed off.

"Like northmen, you mean," Alaji said. She drank down another mouthful of the wine.

"Maybe. I don't know. Hollik could be kind, too. He'd joke with his men and share his food. But he'd do anything for power."

"These men didn't kill my brother," Alaji replied. "But I suppose they've killed someone's brother."

Yemerik sighed. "The sooner we can get out of this era, the better. Giant wolf-bear monsters, even bigger things in the water, and vampires… it's a wonder the world survives times like these."

"I have so many questions," Alaji said. "That thing at the bottom of the river was horrible."

"Well, I don't know anything about that. I didn't even notice it. But I can tell you about the vampires. Or I can try to. They're complicated. It's a disease, sort of. Family of diseases would be more accurate. It can arise naturally from unrefined magic and bad conditions, but usually it's created by a wizard, either as a weapon or in an attempt at eternal life. The worst part is that it's actually a fairly effective means towards that end. Provided you don't mind the cost, they can live thousands of years. Longer, in the right environment."

"They weren't people. They weren't even like animals."

"Well, that was a primitive form of the disease. There are ways to improve it so it leaves the mind intact. Even ways to reverse the hunger and reaction to sunlight. If you're looking to live a thousand years, there are worse paths to take. Like trying to extract a magic potion from a time-traveler."

Alaji watched the warriors move the collection of teeth onto a wagon they'd found and repaired. "Do you think they'll let us go?" she asked.

"I'm not sure," Yemerik said. "They seem more interested in the monster. Maybe they'll be content to go their separate way. Assuming that's even what we want."

"It's certainly what I want," Alaji said.

"No, I mean… we don't know what else is out there. When that thing was on the hunt, the woods were empty, but who knows what'll come out now that it's gone?"

"They do," Alaji said, considering the dilemma.

"Looks like we're about to get some answers. Or have to fight for our lives again." He said this while maintaining a cheerful expression, so Ulithaine, who was strolling towards them, wouldn't infer the direction their conversation was heading in.

The coat of blood covering the warrior was thicker than before, though he was wiping his arms and face with a large rag as he approached. "Are you feeling better?" he asked.

"A little. Thank you."

"My men and I are almost through here. I wanted to see if there was anything you needed before we left. It's a dangerous land," he added.

"We were just discussing that," Yemerik answered. "Though it seems you've made it less so." He motioned towards the gigantic corpse.

Ulithaine nodded solemnly. "I hope so. Though I shudder to think of the damage that will be done before...." He trailed off and shook his head. "I'm sorry. It's foolish. You're heading northeast, aren't you? You should be well enough as long as you don't linger in these lands."

Yemerik swallowed. "We weren't sure where to go next," he said, not wanting to reveal their destination. "But we're generally heading south."

Ulithaine grew pale. "You'll want to give the valley a wide berth. He turned to the east. Do you see those peaks? You'll want them on your right if you're going south. There's a pass that cuts through the range. Just follow the water until you reach the eastern edge of the lake and keep going. You'll find it. There are better times of year to risk it, but it'll be safer than staying here."

Yemerik stared into the distance. The mountains he was referring to would take weeks to reach and, by the look of them, weeks more to cross.

Ulithaine was studying them, as well. And he looked thoughtful. "I don't think it will venture that far. And it certainly won't be able to cross after you," he added. "Assuming all goes as planned, we should be able to mount a final expedition this fall. Wait to hear word, then, if you're ever able, come back with a guide and a team of men. The arch is something you should see up close, once the way is clear. It is a thing of beauty." He turned to gaze on the gate in the distance.

He knew he shouldn't, but Yemerik couldn't stop the words from leaving his mouth. "What are you coming back for? What should we avoid?"

"Its mate," Ulithaine said matter-of-factly, motioning to the dead beast.

"Of course," Yemerik replied, dryly. "I'm sorry," he added. "I've been awake for too long."

"Just don't sleep here!" Ulithaine said. "We'll be riding out soon, and we'll take you a few leagues outside of the town. There's quite a few hours until nightfall, but you'll want to be as far as possible before then. You know of the curse?"

"Rumors," Yemerik replied.

"The dead don't stay dead here. Not all of them. They emerge in the darkness to feed. The lucky are devoured. The others...." He grimaced. "We'll take you both out of the town and drop you off to the east. You can make for the pass. I'm sorry, but I have too much business in these lands to accompany you. I'll leave you weapons. I trust you can handle goblins and their kin. If you see giants, you should kill the girl then yourself. They've been known to toy with their prey first, and you won't be able to fight them off. I don't think you'll encounter them, but it's best to be prepared."

"I'm not sure we can go that far east," Yemerik said, slowly. "We were told to venture due south of here. Is there a quicker road?"

"Where are you trying to reach?" Then, before he could receive an answer, Ulithaine raised a hand and said, "No. Never mind. Don't feel you have to answer. It makes little difference. The west is perilous if you don't know the land. You'd be taken by the necromancer's birds if you crossed into his realm." He considered for a moment. "I may be able to help, though, if you'll accept. I can't offer the protection of my men, but if you'll accompany me north to conclude some business, there's a path to the west of here, just before the necromancer's domain, where we might find safe passage. We'll need to watch for signs, but, unless I miss my guess, the second hound will stay to the southeast, which will only leave its young. Still nothing to be taken lightly, but we'd have a chance of outriding the whelps. Or fighting, if it calls for that. It'll be dangerous, but it's your best chance of reaching the sea. Assuming that's where you're heading."

"We're in your debt," Yemerik said.

"I only wish I could do more," Ulithaine said, bowing his head and clasping his left shoulder with his right hand. Yemerik, of course, repeated the gesture.

3

"It's what you hoped for, isn't it?" Alaji asked, after Yemerik had explained the conversation to her. He left out the part about the monster's mate, just saying there were dangerous creatures they'd be better off avoiding.

"A little too close to what I wanted," Yemerik replied, brooding. "I don't like it when people are kind to me. It usually means they're planning something."

"I'll remember to treat you worse in the future then."

"Don't be absurd. When we first met, you almost killed me several times over. You only stopped when you realized you needed me alive. That's how I know I can trust you."

"We could ask Ulithaine to try and kill you."

"He'd almost certainly succeed," Yemerik said. His tone had shifted, and he almost sounded serious.

"We could try to get away first," Alaji suggested.

"Why risk running from all eight of them when we'll only have to escape one tomorrow? Assuming the plan isn't to separate us and take us before then. But why not just grab us now? Why give us food and time to rest?" He shook his head. He couldn't think straight: it had been too long since he'd had any sleep.

"Then that's the plan? To wait until tomorrow and take off in the night?"

"Yes. Maybe. I don't know. If he's telling the truth about… about the danger, it doesn't make sense to leave at all. If he's really going to take us back by the gate…." Yemerik shook his head. "I think the plan is to pay attention, stay together, and watch for danger."

"Then run if we have to?"

"If there's a chance. But if it looks bad, if it's not safe to take me, just go. They can kill me or torture me or do whatever they like. Just get away, reach the gate, and go back to when we arrived."

"I still don't like that plan."

"You don't like it? I'm the one who gets tortured to death. But you can outrun them, and I can't."

"I don't know if I can outrun their horses," Alaji said.

"You'll think of something. Besides, maybe they're actually just trying to be helpful."

"Or maybe the food's poisoned," Alaji muttered, biting into a piece of dried meat.

———

"I'll ride with the squirrelly one." It was the largest, the one who'd plucked Yemerik off the ground earlier in the day. He had long dark hair and a thin beard and mustache.

"You'll ride with Ishta," Ulithaine replied. "Lend the two of them your horse."

"Why don't you lend them your horse?" the large warrior replied.

"Because Ishta insulted me the other day, and I'm a petty man. Make it quick, or I'll have you walk back."

"You'd leave me to the dead?"

"Don't be dramatic," Ulithaine replied. "You'd be fine. Your stench would drive them off. Ishta! Gritle! Hurry up with that. There'll be time to pray once we light the fires."

The two warriors mouthed a few more words then tied a fur blanket over the cart carrying their dead, along with the teeth of the beast. They mounted and joined the others. Before he climbed onto Ishta's horse, the large warrior brought his horse to Yemerik and thrust the reins into his hands.

"Sorry," Yemerik stuttered, unsure what to say. The expression on the warrior's face suggested annoyance but not anger. That was something to be thankful for, at least. Yemerik and Alaji climbed onto the back of the horse, while Alaji tried her best not to look surprised at the sophistication of the saddle.

"At least they're not separating us," Yemerik whispered in Alaji's language. Once again, his tone and words didn't match, at all. He actually might have felt better if the warriors had been more threatening.

As they began to move, Phaesha rode up alongside them. She matched their pace and studied them, as if daring them to question her. "Huh," she mused. "You've cost me money." She paused, but Yemerik didn't reply. It was obvious she was baiting him. After a moment, she delivered the punch line anyway. "I bet Ishta you'd fall off or ride in circles. I bet her you wouldn't be able to ride, at all."

"Sorry," Yemerik said, again. His apology wasn't as sincere as it had been with the warrior, though. It probably should have been, since he suspected Phaesha was at least as dangerous, but he couldn't muster the energy to be more careful.

She snorted. "You're holding the reins wrong," she added, demonstrating the correct method. Then she hurried ahead, presumably so she wouldn't have to look at him. Yemerik knew the correction was intended as another insult, but it made the horse easier to control.

"I don't like her," Alaji said.

"It's much worse if you can understand her," Yemerik replied.

"She called rain from a clear sky. It's unnatural."

Yemerik chuckled. "It's a common family of spells. I was more impressed by the conjured fire."

"I only caught the edges of the fight. What did she do?"

"She pulled fire out of the air and threw it at the monster. Again, it's nothing unusual, but it made for an impressive show."

"Did she hold it?" Alaji asked, somewhat animated despite her exhaustion. "Without it burning her palms?"

"I suppose so. She kind of created it then threw it quickly. She used a few variations, I think."

"The old woman did that, too," Alaji said. "The one who broke our talisman. She caught fire and manipulated it without it hurting her."

"Again, none of this is all that rare. Unless she bears a striking resemblance."

"No. The old woman's skin was like mine. Could you ask her to show me her fire magic? I want to see if it's the same."

"Better not. She might take it as an invitation to burn us alive. Unless I miss my guess, we'll be better off putting some space between us and her."

—

Phaesha caught up with Ulithaine at the front of the party. She rode alongside him for several minutes silently, but he did nothing to acknowledge her presence. Finally, she grew impatient. "You are being reckless." She glanced behind her to make sure Yemerik and Alaji were well out of hearing. Even so, she spoke softly when she said, "We should just kill them and be done. To hell with their tricks and spells. Leave secrets to the wizards. Those are your own words."

"This is a rare change. The dark sorceress telling me not to chase after knowledge and power. I never took you for the timid sort, Phaesha."

"Bah. I'm not afraid! I'm cautious. And you're behaving like a fool. It's your hide I'm trying to protect."

"I never took you for sentimental, either." As if sensing he'd crossed a line, he flashed her a smile. "Those two aren't a danger to me. Look at them. They've been terrified ever since we took them on. Just meet us at the falls like we planned. Bring my heavy furs and others for our new companions. Nice ones for the girl. And extra equipment for the climb."

Phaesha continued at his side for a while. Finally, she blurted out, "If you take her in Wuerra's place, I'll have to kill her." She glared at Ulithaine with a fierceness that kept him from laughing.

"That's not for you to decide," he said firmly. "But, for what it's worth, she's too small for me. I might as well take you to my bed, Phaesha." He cracked a half smile and laughed.

She laughed, too, but she dropped away after that and rode on by herself.

—

They rode for several hours, and Alaji and Yemerik each caught the other falling asleep and saved them from slipping off the horse. The group stopped at the top of a small hill near a pool. After watering the horses, the warriors prepared a pyre for their fallen companions. They gathered around the fire, laughing, drinking, and telling stories, while Alaji and Yemerik found a spot to sleep.

4

Yemerik was asleep when Alaji woke to the smell of roasting meat and eggs. It was morning, and the sky was clear. When she stood, the muscles in her legs and back ached, and her joints popped. She was dehydrated, dizzy, and part of her wanted nothing more than to fall back to the ground and sleep for several more hours.

It was painful to move or stand still, to breathe deeply or shallowly. It was painful to exist. But the pain was a reminder of life, something she'd won and the beast had lost. It was a luxury to stop and experience the bruised knees and skinned palms the last two days had left her with. And, in a strange way, she relished it as she looked out on the horizon.

Everything was still. No monsters or dead bodies clawing for her flesh. No beasts larger than buildings or bulbous creatures lying in the water. Not even something mundane, like a pack of wild dogs or a hunting dragon. She knew these things were out there somewhere. She knew this era was more fearsome than any she'd yet experienced. But for now, the world was a sunrise of red and orange, a warm fire, a wall of ice in the distance, and the smell of food cooking.

She saw Ulithaine was watching her. There was nothing threatening in his look or his posture – he was sitting back, far more focused on three birds roasting on spits than on her. Still, he smiled and motioned for her. She walked to the fire and sat on the ground.

Beside the birds, he had the contents of a half dozen eggs cooking in a small pan which he'd placed in the embers. She stared at the pan, a piece of round, dark metal. They'd had versions of such things in Elsimi, in the inns of Hathari, and even on the ships of Minot-Rin, but this was different. Iron, she suspected, based on descriptions she'd gotten from two versions of Yemerik.

There wasn't even a sign left of Ulithaine's companions. The warriors and sorceress were gone, as were all of the horses. It was just her and Ulithaine sitting by the fire, Yemerik snoring nearby, and three packs leaning against a tree. Another indication Ulithaine planned on keeping them alive, she decided.

Ulithaine said something, but of course she couldn't understand. She shook her head. "I don't speak your language." She spoke slowly, despite the fact it wouldn't make any difference. He nodded in some sort of understanding and gestured around him. Alaji decided he was trying to look confused. She pantomimed drinking, and asked, "Do you have any water?"

He considered for a second, then reached for one of the packs, fished out a bottle, and offered it to Alaji. She examined it quickly. She'd seen these in the village where they'd brought the pilgrims but still wasn't comfortable opening them. She grabbed the cork stopper and struggled with it until it came loose with a loud pop. Then she held it beneath her nostrils and inhaled a sweet odor. It was familiar and enticing, but she knew better than to start with it. She shook her head. "Wine," she tapped the glass bottle. She worked the stopper back into the mouth of the bottle as best she could, then tried to hand it back, but Ulithaine simply set it on the ground between them.

Alaji brought her hands to her mouth, as if drinking from a stream. "Water," she said, again.

Ulithaine nodded in understanding. He grabbed a waterskin from the side of the same pack and handed it over. He patted the side as she took it and asked, "Water?"

She untied the clasp and drank deeply. "Water," she said, handing it back. He replied with a word in his own language, which Alaji tried to repeat, with considerably less success. He laughed and tried to correct her, but the sound was too foreign for her to duplicate accurately.

Yemerik shuffled over while they were trying to work out the pronunciation. He sat down slowly, wincing with each movement. He addressed Ulithaine first. "I'm sorry. We don't usually sleep so late."

"Don't trouble yourself," Ulithaine replied. He talked past Alaji, who was sitting between him and Yemerik. "We were all tired after yesterday's adventure. You'll be happy to know there hasn't been any sign of the other hound, or their offspring," he added. "My best guess is that he's still on the west side of the river, likely somewhere beyond the Elk's Spine." His finger traced a line along the further of two ridges cutting behind the mountain where the west side of the gate stood. "I saw a bear on the south side of the hill, though. I don't think he'll trouble us, but it would probably be best if we stayed to the north and east." He moved the roasting birds, swiftly shifting the one nearest to the center of the flame to the outside, the one in the middle to the center, and the outside to the middle. "I'm sorry I couldn't catch us larger game," he added. "The meat of the hare in this country is unlike any I've tasted, but they're quick and clever. I suppose they've had to be, with the hounds."

Yemerik turned to Alaji. "He said there was a bear down there." He pointed to the south. "Keep an eye out."

"He said more than that," Alaji replied.

"The rest didn't matter." Yemerik addressed Ulithaine again, and his mouth reformed around the new language. "She said she'd be grateful for anything hot. We both would be."

"Ah. The words of new friends. The type who have never experienced my cooking. When I met Phaesha, she was a cordial sort. Then I made her breakfast. You see what she's like these days."

"Where is she, anyway?" Yemerik asked.

"They've gone west already. If all goes well, we'll meet up with them in a week or so." Ulithaine moved the eggs out of the fire to cool, then handed two of the birds to Alaji, who passed one to Yemerik.

Yemerik blew on his bird to cool it, then nibbled at one end. "It's good," he said. He nodded to Alaji.

Alaji bit off a piece, chewed, then paused to pull a small feather from her mouth. "Better than nothing," she told Yemerik. She nodded and smiled as she spoke, though, to conceal her ambivalence.

"She agrees," Yemerik told Ulithaine.

"I think you're both being kind," he responded. "I've always thought of spices as one of the mystic arts. I'm no more capable of seasoning meat than I am of calling lightning from the clouds or making a quail grow tusks."

"We'd be happy to take over the cooking in the future," Yemerik said.

"I hate to ask it, but I suspect we'll all be happier if I catch the food and you two prepare it."

"Alaji is actually a capable hunter," Yemerik added, before realizing he should have kept that quiet. Ulithaine didn't seem surprised or particularly interested in the details, however. Alaji heard her name and looked up. "It's nothing," Yemerik whispered.

She shrugged and reached for the bottle of wine resting on the ground. The cork was loose and came out with a light tug. She held it to her lips and sipped it. As soon as it touched her tongue, she recognized it. "Verow's Brew," she said, gazing at the bottle. Memories of her brother flooded back, of the last morning they'd spent together, when he'd shared this same drink with her. She'd never had anything like it before or since.

This seemed to catch Ulithaine's attention. He spoke quickly, and Alaji only recognized a single word, "Verow." She assumed he was copying her, so she told Yemerik, "It's our name for the drink. Well, not our word. The northmen's." She drank again, and handed it to Yemerik.

Caught between two conversations in two languages, Yemerik stuttered for a moment. "That's his name for it," he said to Alaji, pointing to Ulithaine. "When did... wait. Let me...." He turned back to Ulithaine to find the warrior was studying his expression carefully. Yemerik feigned a smile. "She's had this before. Where is it made?"

Ulithaine pointed towards the east. "Verow's Crest," he said. You can almost see it from here. There are fields on the mountain filled with grapevines and a flower. It's like...." He leapt to his feet and scoured the hillside around them. Within a few seconds, he found and plucked a small flower with a dozen tiny, white petals. "Like this." He held it beneath his nose briefly, then handed the flower to Alaji. "It's not the same, but it's close."

Yemerik summarized, "He said – he said it's from around here. It's a similar – it's the same flower as that one."

Alaji looked at the flower. "Theojin said the flowers it was brewed from grew in the north. The woman he got it from – she was a trader of some sort traveling with Hollik. She called it Verow's Brew. Hollik's homeland was a lot like this, I think. Cold most of the year. It makes sense the flowers would be the same, doesn't it?"

Yemerik shook his head. "Not after all this time. Even if they'd started the same, they'd have changed by now. Besides, I traveled with Hollik for weeks. I tried every kind of beer and wine they had, and I never tasted anything like this." He handed the bottle back to Alaji, who stared at it closely.

"It's the same," Alaji said again.

Yemerik nodded, concerned. "I wish it wasn't. It means

someone's tracking us – both of us – in time. They know where we were and where we are. And they want us to know that."

Ulithaine simply watched the scene unfold. His expression varied from neutral to concerned in response to the tone of the speaker's voice or the look on their faces. But his eyes darted back and forth between them, and he hardly breathed.

—

They picked up camp soon after and headed into the east, keeping the lake nearby but never quite moving to the shore. Ulithaine told stories about his adventures, most of which Yemerik assumed – or at least hoped – were inventions. He had tales from his youth, when he'd spent several years as a thief in a city called Felrue. He seemed unconcerned relating tales where he'd stolen from churches and nobles. Then, he spoke briefly of his time as a mercenary. "I am not ashamed of what I had to do, and I learned a great deal. But, between the two, I found far more honor in theft than war." He went on to talk favorably of his time at sea after that, though his descriptions were so vague, Yemerik was left unsure if he'd been a pirate, a merchant, or simply a passenger.

"When I was shipwrecked in Trall, I was without employment. I spent a time wandering the old lands, taking odd jobs, before I discovered there were better uses for a sword than war. I'm certain you've heard of the serpents there, at the sea. They appear at midday, for some reason. It lacks poetry. I've always thought monsters should come at night. But they climb the beach and go into the fields. The young farmers try and fight them off; the older ones just avoid them. They take sheep mostly, or chickens. Sometimes they even make themselves useful and grab a fox. But other times they find a child wandering alone or a farmer trips while trying to protect his flock, and that's that. I discovered I could make a fair wage by the beach. After three months' time, I booked passage on a freighter with a chest of coins. I was robbed, of course, but I had something better than money. I'd found a living and a use for my sword my stomach could abide."

"That's why you hunted the... the hound," Yemerik surmised.

"That's part of it. But it was also a personal matter. There was a woman I knew, another hunter of such things. We traveled together for a time and... more. She tried for the hound not long ago. She took a dozen with her, and they weren't enough."

"I'm sorry," Yemerik said, softly.

Ulithaine shook his head. "Don't be. Life is dangerous, and the end is set. I liked Wuerra and enjoyed our time together well enough, but she was not my true love or anything so dramatic. She told me once I wasn't her favorite lover, so it's no betrayal to say the same of her. But I once saw her fire two arrows through a leaping cheetah's eyes before it landed. She deserved vengeance. A man who can't give his woman that isn't much of a man. Even if she wasn't really his." Ulithaine's demeanor had darkened a bit as he'd spoken. He shook off the mood and grew more upbeat. "Don't think I'm all sentiment, though. There's money in the deed. We wouldn't have bothered with the teeth otherwise. A wizard in the north has offered a fortune for proof of the kill. I'm sorry – I feel like I've been talking for hours. Tell me something of your travels, how you met the girl or how you found yourself pinned down by the hound in those forsaken ruins!" He laughed and slapped Yemerik on the back.

Yemerik forced himself to smile. "I'm afraid there's not much to tell. We were exploring the forests when we heard that thing approaching. We ran for the town trying to find somewhere to hide. I saw you on the hill and ran towards you, hoping you'd help us."

"And received less hospitality than you were due. I should apologize for Wray'tol. I asked him to collect you in order to keep you safe. I didn't expect him to be so zealous."

"You saved our lives," Yemerik said. "I'm not going to quibble about manners."

"I won't ask after your business in the north, but surely you've a few tales to tell from your travels. Or perhaps the girl does, if you don't mind translating."

Eleven years as a storyteller had given Yemerik some experience substituting himself into various tall tales and anecdotes he'd known from his travels or learned in his studies. For once, the fact he was displaced by eons and lost in a timeline that shouldn't exist was an asset, as there was no real danger of Ulithaine being familiar with any of his stories. He was even able to adapt a few events and misadventures from his time in Hathari, though he steered clear of anything that would likely be anachronistic. His stories may have lacked specificity, but they seemed to do the trick. Ulithaine laughed so hard he had to stop walking when Yemerik described a drunken oaf whose stool was pulled out from under him by a toddler just moments after boasting there was no one in the tavern who could best him.

Alaji was content to keep to herself, though she resolved to later ask Yemerik what he had to say that was amusing enough to elicit that sort of response. She'd traveled with versions of him for months without hearing him say anything that funny. She saw Ulithaine nibbling on some pale white berries and plucked a handful herself. They were sweet, though the taste turned bitter if she bit into the seed. She started biting just softly enough to break the skin, then spit out the seeds. She was surprised Ulithaine wasn't doing the same.

They went on until dusk. The lake was still to their left, though they'd turned partway north now. Ulithaine and Yemerik continued speaking, while Alaji started a fire. At Yemerik's suggestion, she went out to hunt, and quickly returned with two squirrels, a wren, and a large hare, which seemed to excite Ulithaine to no end.

Yemerik prepared the food while Alaji sat watching the fire. Their camp was on a hilltop overlooking the lake. She gazed out and saw a flicker of light in the distance, just beyond the northern shore. Alaji stood and moved a little closer, positioning herself so there were no trees obstructing the light. Her eyes adjusted, and she realized there were at least three fires across the water. She waved to Yemerik and Ulithaine and pointed. Ulithaine shook his head and said something in response

Yemerik translated, "He's not sure. Thinks they could be traders passing through. We should know tomorrow, assuming they stay put." The two men returned to trading stories and jokes.

Alaji continued eyeing the flames, trying to judge their size and distance. It was impossible to say for sure, but they were either not far or very large. She considered Ulithaine's lack of concern. Was it because he knew the lay of the land, and could tell they were too far away to notice their smaller fire? If so, these could be large encampments – shouldn't they alter their plans and avoid them? Alternatively, if the fires were smaller and nearer, shouldn't they be quenching their own flame to reduce the chances they'd be seen? Whoever was out there could come at them in the night.

Behind her, she heard them continue to laugh. Their words were a jumble of sound to her, but the tone carried through. They spoke like old friends sharing secrets. She trusted Yemerik to keep his wits about him: this was the tone an older iteration of the same man had used to lure in Imn Orith, after all. But what of Ulithaine's tone? It was similar, friendly, trusting. And sometimes she glanced over her shoulder and found him looking at her. He was studying, learning. And, stranger still, he seemed to be listening. He always grew silent when she spoke, despite the fact—

"You understand me," she said, turning around. She met his eyes directly, and he waited a moment too long to reach for the water or the remnants of wine or to look around in confusion.

He chuckled. "Well played," he said, speaking the tongue of her people. It was jumbled, with a strange accent and warped intonation. But it was intelligible. Yemerik's mouth hung open, but Ulithaine didn't seem interested in him, anymore. "You were testing me, right?" he asked Alaji.

She drew her knife, and her count began. Ulithaine leapt to his feet, as well, though his expression was playful. Slowly he took the knife from his belt and caught the fire's light in its reflection. Then he threw it, blade first, into the dirt near his sword. He stood back, away from his weapons, and showed them his hands, as if daring them to act. His eyes locked on Alaji's, and they studied each other.

"What now?" he asked.

Alaji motioned for Yemerik to move out of Ulithaine's reach, which he did slowly. Stuttering, Yemerik said, "An artifact of translation. You have one?"

"An artifact of…." Ulithaine shook his head and chuckled. "You mean this bauble? He pulled back his shirt to reveal a small metallic disk with a blue rune painted in the center tied around his neck. "What fool would travel alone without one?"

"Why did you lie?" Yemerik demanded.

"Because I figured you'd be more open if you thought I couldn't grasp your words. And because I was fascinated by a man who walks with an—" he paused, raised his head, then mimicked Yemerik, "An artifact of translation." He shook his head and continued, "One that works quicker and better than any I've ever heard of, yet its wearer assumes he's the only one who's ever heard of such a thing. Are they really so rare where you're from?"

"Whose fires are those?" Alaji demanded, motioning to the distant lights. "Are they your men? Is this a trap?"

"They're not mine," he replied. "Truth be told, I'm not sure who or what's out there."

"You haven't given us much reason to trust you," Yemerik replied.

"Don't be foolish. If I'd meant you ill, I'd have stabbed the girl on the road when her back was turned. Through the chest, if I'd wanted her dead, in a leg otherwise."

"Why her?" Yemerik asked.

"Because she's the one with power. She killed the hound's whelp and ran the monster ragged across the countryside. She lured it into the alley. And I'd bet my life she was the one who got you out of the catacombs intact."

"How long were you watching us?"

"I didn't have to watch you. The trail you left stretched back to the arch, whose majestic opening you never thought worth remarking on. The night sky appears between the mountains at midday, and you fail to notice or consider it beneath mention. For what it's worth, your discussions of ancient lakes, lost cities, and eons of time barely qualified as validation. It's a portal, isn't it? In time, to the different ages of the world. I always wondered why the wizards fight so fiercely over this worthless stretch of land."

"We don't know a thing about your wizards," Yemerik said, forcefully.

"The first thing you've said today I believe," Ulithaine answered back.

"Yes, it's a damn portal." Yemerik moved closer to Alaji in case this turned into a fight. "But your wizards can't use it."

"No. But you can." He smiled. "I'm curious what brought you to this cursed age. Weren't there temples of gold filled with riches and wine and women in times past?"

"I seriously doubt it," Yemerik snapped. "Was your plan to sell us along with the teeth? To hand us over for a chest of treasure?"

"Of course not. You're worth more than everything the wizard owns. More than all their power and wealth put together. To hell with them and their fights! Even if there are no towers of gold, I'll wager there are times and places worth exploring. Let conjurers and necromancers battle for the scraps left by their wars! I'd have something greater."

"And if we refuse?"

Ulithaine laughed heartily. "I haven't decided yet. Maybe I'll try to convince you with steel or pain. Or maybe a share in the treasure."

"And if we run off in the night?"

"I'd be tempted to let you go," he replied. "Do you really think you'd make it back with what's out there?"

"We made it this far," Yemerik pointed out.

"Barely, and only with my aid. You're in a strange land, full of strange creatures. And by now the hound's mate is seeking blood."

Alaji's eyes widened at that, but Yemerik barreled on. "I don't think the hound has a mate. At least not one alive. That thing wasn't exactly subtle, and I haven't heard anything from the south."

"Well, then. Why not kill me and find out? I'm unarmed. No, wait," he reached behind him and took out a second knife, which he tossed to the ground near the first. "There. Now I'm unarmed." He stared at Alaji. "If you're sure I'm lying about the hound, go ahead. I've seen how you move. Like a spirit." He tilted his head up to bare his neck.

Yemerik turned to her. His mouth was slightly open and moving, as if resolving then abandoning what he was going to say. Alaji simply stared at the warrior as her count ran in her head.

Ulithaine lowered his head. "If murder doesn't appeal to you, I could offer another option. Come with me to the north. There's a hefty prize waiting for us, and you've a claim to a piece. After, I'll see you back to your gate with my men. Give us passage to a better time. Then go on your way in peace or join my company, whichever suits you."

Yemerik breathed in to speak, but Alaji cut him off. "Deal," she said, sheathing her knife. "If you bring us to the portal, we'll take you somewhere else. But I want one of those." She pointed at Ulithaine's pendant.

Ulithaine laughed. "You'll have one! When we reach the wizard," he promised. "Now then. I'd like a drink."

PART 5: THE APES OF THE NORTH

1

Alaji found it difficult to sleep, even after she looked over and saw Ulithaine slumbering quietly. It was madness. She should slip over and cut his throat. She looked around and saw Yemerik awake and watching the warrior, no doubt thinking the same thing.

The absurd thing was that she was growing to like Ulithaine. He was strong, energetic, and handsome. And of course he was clever. But he was dangerous, as well. Not in a way that was exciting. When she was around him, even now, when he was unconscious, it was like she was a part of his story. She could think about murdering him, but she couldn't really imagine doing it. It was as if he owned the woods and lake and hills. It was impossible to imagine him dead, because he was the one who would survive. She didn't feel as secure.

—

When Yemerik shook her awake, she got halfway to her knife before realizing there was no need. A second later, she felt the weight of the morning hit her. Her head ached, and she was dizzy. She wiped her eyes, coughed, and rubbed her forehead.

Ulithaine was already gathering his belongings and singing

softly as he did so. He saw Alaji and smiled at her, as if he'd never known discomfort. The idea of stabbing him in the neck seemed less impossible than it had the night before.

She ignored Ulithaine's pleasant demeanor and Yemerik's fidgeting. Ulithaine offered them a handful of nuts, along with a bulbous plant he promised was edible. She accepted reluctantly after Yemerik did the same. Of course, Ulithaine had already refilled the water and scouted the next leg of their journey. They left before the sun had fully risen over the mountains.

They continued along the lake, still keeping their distance from the edge. They saw the tracks of deer, wolves, and small animals, along with something Alaji initially thought was a bear. Ulithaine examined them carefully.

"Boreal apes," he said, looking back to see if the others offered a hint of recognition. "Brutish and cruel, they raise our kind as slaves and livestock. Most live in caverns at the glacier's cliffs and only leave to hunt. Some burrow into hills instead of ice, but it's rarer. We'll need to be cautious." He readied his sword, then looked at Yemerik and Alaji. "Your knives would barely scrape their skin." He removed the two blades he'd shown them the night before. "These will serve you better. If it comes to a fight, stab hard and fast. Go for the neck or groin or beneath the arm. An eye socket, if they leave it open. Don't let them get a hold of you: their grip is a vise. Fight to the death. You don't want to be taken alive. And don't run, because they'll catch you." He looked at Alaji. "Maybe not you," he admitted. "Their sight is bad, and they tend to flinch in a straight fight. They're strong but cowardly. Show them something they've never seen, and they're likely to recoil."

"Anything else?" Yemerik asked, taking the smaller of the two knives.

"When they take captives, they'll either eat them immediately or pair them off and breed them first. Either way, they never leave them alive longer than it takes to get children. Those, they raise like dogs. If they have slaves, size them up quickly. If they can speak or show reason, cut them free. But if they're feral, cut them down. Even the young."

Yemerik shifted uneasily while Alaji took the remaining knife, a curved weapon more than twice as long as her own, and tested the edge. She swung it a few times to get a feel for the weight and balance. It wasn't as heavy as she'd expected, certainly less so than smaller stone blades she'd grown up using. The hilt was larger than she'd have liked, but the blade itself was sturdy, strong, and sharp; it would cut into flesh easily enough, she decided. It was by the far the best blade she'd ever held, even surpassing the one she'd gotten from Yemerik and lost in Hathari.

"I don't like this," Yemerik whispered, once Ulithaine was too far ahead to hear them. "It could be a trap. It feels like a trap."

"He had plenty of chances to kill us. In the town, when we were with his men, on the road, even in our sleep. Why bother with games? Why arm us before leading us to danger?"

Yemerik couldn't think of a response, so he just concentrated on keeping up. Ulithaine was pushing ahead harder now, almost sprinting through the wood. Occasionally, he'd stop, give them a chance to catch up, then stay put long enough to point out additional tracks. "These are apes, all right," he muttered, pressing his hand against an indentation in the mud. "See the claw marks?" He measured the depth with his fingers. "They're bred for climbing ice. Digging in, as well."

"The fires we saw yesterday," Yemerik began, "they belonged to the apes?"

"It's likely."

"If they can use fire, they're probably capable of reason. If we can communicate—"

"If they let us pass, it would only be to hunt us down at night. Besides, if we cross their path, I have a responsibility. They could have women down there. Elderly. Sometimes they keep them around for a few days before butchering them." Ulithaine considered for a moment. "If it comes to it, go north until you hit the cliffs, then turn west and travel until you find a waterfall streaming through a rift in stone and ice. If it's less than the most spectacular sight you've set eyes upon, you are likely in the wrong place. Keep going until you find a falls that takes your breath away. You'll find Phaesha there. Tell her what happened. She'll send others to kill the apes. Tell her I said she was to take you to the archway." He dug into a pouch and handed over a silver ring. "Give her this. She'll know you speak the truth." With that, he charged ahead into the forest.

Alaji hurried behind him while Yemerik looked at the ring skeptically and dropped it into a coin purse. Cautiously, he followed, trying not to fall too far behind.

Ulithaine's pace slowed enough to allow Alaji to catch up. They went on in silence, until – without warning – he spoke. "Why five?" he asked.

"What?" she asked, startled by the suddenness of the question.

"You nod your head when you run. Not always, but often. Constantly since we discovered the tracks. Four short nods punctuated by a fifth. I was wondering if it had some significance."

"No. Just something I do," Alaji said. As she spoke, she could tell her words were too fast and her tone was too defensive.

"Never mind then. I suppose we all do such things without thinking. Tics and the like. I'm sorry for bringing it up."

—

They reached the outer boundary of the apes' encampment in mid-afternoon. From beneath the trees, they peered down a hill into a cleared valley. They could see a number of burrows in the side of the hill. Several apes were gathered near these openings. Alaji had seen similar creatures in the markets of Hathari, but none so large or with this coloration. Their fur was a mix of white, grey, and light blue. They were beautiful, the color of ice.

But even from afar, she could see the bones. They littered the ground, and not all had come from animals. Worse yet, in the bottom of the valley were a number of men and women chained to stakes in the ground.

Ulithaine, Alaji, and Yemerik slipped back into the forest, so they wouldn't be spotted. Ulithaine whispered, "I'm going to circle around to attack from the east. Even if I can't overpower them, they'll likely be drawn that way. Make for the west, and try to sneak by next to the lake. But don't step in the water unless it's absolutely necessary. There are things beneath that surface I'm loath to speak of. If you come across one of the apes on your way, kill it quickly. After that, make for the north and Phaesha's encampment, as we discussed."

"Be careful," Yemerik said, and Ulithaine hurried off.

Alaji watched him disappear towards the encampment. "We should help him," she said.

"He didn't ask for our help," Yemerik pointed out. "Which means he either doesn't need it, doesn't want it, or he's testing us. Or this is all a bizarre and convoluted trap. None of those situations leave us better off for charging in."

Alaji crept back towards the edge of the clearing.

"What are you doing?" Yemerik asked as loudly as he dared.

"I want to see," she said.

"This is… come on. We need to go while we can. If he wins, he'll find us. If not, he's one less concern."

"We still don't know the land," Alaji pointed out. "We don't know how to survive here. Besides, there are people down there. He seems to be trying to help them."

"We know he's lied to us every step of the way," Yemerik said. "We should go now." But he joined her, crouching in the brush, to watch. "This is what he wants us to do. You realize that, don't you?"

Alaji shrugged and scanned the east for a sign of Ulithaine. She spotted him walking slowly out of the woods towards the camp. Then she heard a shrill scream. A moment later, two massive apes holding wooden spears charged towards Ulithaine, who raised his sword in response. The other apes scattered, grabbing an assortment of spears, clubs, swords, and stones. The captive humans charged as well, though their harnesses caught them and pulled them to the ground before they'd gone more than ten paces.

Ulithaine cut down the first of the apes, then lopped the head off the next. The other apes ran at him, hurling rocks and bones. He had little trouble dodging the projectiles, though the apes closed in. One swung a long sword, which Ulithaine batted aside with his own two-handed sword before cutting into the ape's belly. It hunched over with a pained scream.

Ulithaine readied himself for the next wave, but, stepping back for better footing, his foot slipped on a stone, and he fell to the ground. The apes rushed him.

"We need to leave now," Yemerik said. "While there's still…," his voice trailed off as Alaji vanished. He looked over to see her disappear and reappear closer to the fight, then again. "Oh, no," he whispered, though there was no one close enough to hear him over the clamor below.

2

When Alaji charged towards the fight, Yemerik grabbed her arm, but his grip wasn't strong enough to hold her. She tore away, and he stumbled out from under the trees. In the valley below, one of the naked human slaves saw her and screeched a warning. Two of the apes nearly upon Ulithaine turned to meet her.

She reached five in her count and stepped back, and none of it had happened. She glanced back to see Yemerik still in hiding – had he even grabbed for her? The apes were back where they'd been when she'd left the shelter, and the slaves hadn't noticed her. That changed instantly, as their shrill call sounded just after she appeared. The apes broke away once more, and she ran forward, counting. She hit five just feet from where she'd have collided with the apes.

This third time was different. The slaves' yell was sounding as she reappeared, and the apes had already turned towards her. But that meant they'd also seen her vanish and reappear. As Ulithaine predicted, they didn't react well to this. They froze for an instant, then began backing away.

It suited Alaji when her foes retreated. She focused on where the closest had been, charged forward to that point, stabbed her knife into the empty air, then stepped back in time to when the air wasn't so empty. The ape was dead without ever having a chance to raise its guard. The next turned to flee, and Alaji was upon it just as fast, her knife severing its spine at the base of its neck.

Nearby, Ulithaine swung his sword and body simultaneously. The motion turned him upright and brought him to a kneeling position. It also allowed his sword to bite into the leg of an ape, who stumbled as the warrior rose. The ape's spear struck the earth and snapped. Ulithaine caught the ape's throat with one hand while he worked to free his sword from the creature's leg with the other. The beast fought back, clawing at Ulithaine's shoulder and tearing through fur, cloth, and skin. Its mouth opened wide, revealing jagged teeth and incisors each the length of a man's thumb. Ulithaine didn't flinch but tightened his own grip. The ape was stronger, but every inch it gained put that much more pressure on the sword wedged in its wounded leg. Eventually, the pain was too great, and it fell backwards. A moment later, Ulithaine's weapon was free, and he brought the hilt down into the ape's face. Once. Again. A third time, and it gave up its assault to try and shield itself. The opening gave Ulithaine a moment to leap to his feet and cut into the side of another ape nearly upon him. He finished these two quickly: the first before it regained its footing, then the second before it reached the ground.

The next wave kept their distance. They scavenged the ground for rocks and bones, which they threw at the intruders. Their aim was poor, but the sheer number and speed of projectiles made pressing the attack even more dangerous.

Ulithaine ducked behind a boulder and scooped up a smaller stone. He threw it and struck the largest of the beasts. Then he laughed and taunted them, mimicking their language and movement. They concentrated their aim at him, and he responded by charging ahead.

It was madness – he'd be struck any moment – but it gave Alaji an opening to charge as well, stepping back to reach the fight quickly. As she darted past him, she heard Ulithaine grunt as a stone caught him head-on. She stepped back, and the ape about to throw that stone stopped and turned towards her. It aimed for her instead and hurled it towards her. Most of the other apes did the same.

She never learned if any might hit, because she stepped back in time before they could reach her. The apes had only had time to realize that she'd appeared nearer to them; they hadn't had time to aim, let alone throw the deadly projectiles. Now she was nearly upon them.

If they'd understood what was happening and had time to prepare, perhaps they might have assembled a meaningful counterattack. She wasn't invincible, after all, and they would only have had to strike her once to throw off her concentration.

But to them, it was as if she vanished and reappeared as she chose. So they did as others had before, as the sailors had on the island to the far west, as the two men on the road to Hathari, and as the guard in Minot-Rin's palace: they retreated to buy time to think. But, as always, it was time they gave to her to choose her angle of attack, to close in. It was time she stole from them, stepping back before they could ever use it.

The next to die saw only the point of her knife, and then only for the split second it took her to drive it through his eye. She tore her blade free from his head, and – to the rest of them – vanished before the body collapsed in the dirt.

The apes did the only thing they could. They scattered in all directions. Some held onto their weapons; others dropped them, perhaps thinking she'd be more likely to go after the armed ones first. A few apes found themselves running straight towards Ulithaine, who met them with bloodied steel. Alaji chased down some of the others, particularly those heading in Yemerik's general direction, but almost half their number escaped. The survivors were mostly the smaller ones, and they made for the woods.

With a thrust to the chest, Ulithaine finished off an ape who lay dying beneath him. Then he looked around, seeming pleased with himself and even more pleased with Alaji. She wiped some of the blood from her face and hands, then found a place on her belt to sheathe the knife. "The hound. In the village," she said, still a bit out of breath. "We're even now."

Ulithaine laughed as if it was the funniest thing anyone had ever said.

3

"What about them?" Yemerik stood just outside of the circle where the slaves were bound. None of them were of the civilized variety Ulithaine had hoped to find. These were born here, raised like animals. Scattered around their feet were bones etched with the teeth marks of men and apes both. Even a cursory glance was enough to verify they'd been fed – and eaten – their own kind. And, judging by the way they looked at him, Yemerik doubted they'd hesitate to tear into him if they could escape their bindings.

They were nude, save the chains. A number of animal skins were strewn about nearby, but they seemed warm enough without them. They bore old scars and bruises, and two of the four limped from broken bones which had healed improperly.

Ulithaine stood just beyond the length of their chain. "They aren't human," he said. "Not really. They don't speak or act like men, and they lack reason. If we were to cut them loose, they'd come at us. If we leave them here, they'll either be reclaimed by the survivors or the last will starve to death after devouring the others."

"They are human," Yemerik said. "And those sounds they're making are a form of speech. Do you want to know what they're saying?"

This caught Ulithaine's attention. "You can understand them? After only a few minutes?" He pulled out his own disk that translated speech, glanced at it, then shook his head. "To answer your question, I doubt I want to know what they're thinking."

Yemerik looked at those in the circle. He stretched his mouth then spoke in a jumbled, guttural voice. The sounds he made did not seem like words, but the slaves froze and looked at him. Then, without warning, they charged towards him until their chains ran out of slack and pulled them down.

Ulithaine shook his head. "I told you, there's no reason left."

"I asked if they'd be able to leave in peace if we let them go," Yemerik responded.

"I guess they interpreted that as weakness. Weakness is food."

"So it's leave them to suffer or execute them?" Yemerik asked, dryly. "I don't much like your era, Ulithaine."

"Nor do I," Ulithaine responded. "But perhaps now we understand each other. Go back to the woods with Alaji and keep watch in case any of the survivors are close enough to attack. I'll handle this work."

—

Yemerik and Alaji sat just out of sight beneath the trees. Alaji drank some water. She wanted to wash herself, as well, but they didn't have nearly enough for that. She doubted it would be long before they reached another stream, though.

"I thought I'd know by now at least," Yemerik mused sardonically. "Whether it was a trap or not."

"It was a bad one, if it was. He almost died out there."

"Did he?" Yemerik wondered. "I'm not sure. I couldn't tell if he was playing with them or fighting for his life."

"When they were throwing stones, one would have crushed him. If I hadn't gone back, he'd have died. And there's no way he could have known...." She stopped mid-sentence and wrinkled her brow. "There's no way he'd have known," she repeated, doubtfully. Then, from the valley below, they heard as a human voice cried out briefly. Another followed, then a third and fourth. The first group dead: there were two more, at least.

"He told us he didn't know whether these were out here. Said they must have moved into the region since the last time he came through. But he seems to know these woods well."

"And the piles looked like they've been forming for a long time," Alaji added, remembering the scattered bones and shredded remnants of fabric. "Should we ask him?"

"Do you really think he couldn't think of a lie to cover a few discrepancies?" Yemerik asked, and she shook her head.

Another scream rang out as Ulithaine reached the next group of slaves.

—

They kept close together after that, in case they came across any of the surviving apes. After a few miles, they crossed a stream with several pools and took the opportunity to clean the blood out of their clothes and tend to their wounds. The only one seriously injured was Ulithaine, who didn't seem concerned. He began bandaging his shoulder with a handful of large leaves he'd plucked while walking through the wood.

"Wait," Alaji said, hurrying towards Ulithaine. Yemerik caught up with her and silently nudged her, then gave her a concerned look. She shook her head. "Does it really matter?" she asked, speaking loud enough for Ulithaine to hear. He tilted his head, intrigued. "I can heal it," Alaji explained. "My skills are limited, but it doesn't look deep or infected."

"A healer," he said, seemingly impressed.

Alaji rolled her eyes. Then she shoved his bandages aside, not trying to be gentle. "It'll hurt, most likely." He didn't seem concerned, so she chanted the invocation and moved her palm over the cut, never quite touching the tissue, but coming close.

His expression made it clear her warning was merited, but he didn't seem overly bothered. When she'd finished, he examined the flesh. "Astonishing," he said. He looked her in the eye. If he was lying now, it was a believable one. "I've seldom seen this performed, and never in such conditions. Those with such power are retained by kings and paid handsomely."

Alaji shrugged. "You'll still want to bandage it. I can't close it completely, but it should help. We should get moving if we want to open some distance between us and that pit," she motioned back towards the site of their battle.

"Thank you," Ulithaine said, sounding sincere. "Both for this and your help back there. It was a great deed. Many will be better for it."

"It was still horrible," Alaji replied.

"Great things usually are. But I saw you on the field. When you slew them, you felt it. You were alive in a way few men will ever know. And fewer women, by far. I think we share things in common. I think we are both warriors at heart."

The fact he seemed to believe it made the words no less sentimental. But Alaji couldn't help but be moved. She shrugged, concealing the emotion, before realizing this, too, seemed like something he'd do.

Ulithaine finished bandaging his shoulder then led on, into the wild north towards the distant cliffs of ice.

4

The terrain gradually shifted into swampland broken up by the occasional hill. The air grew cooler as they went, and the trees withered until they were only surrounded by low brush bearing small blue-green leaves. They traveled through bogs where patches of plants would sometimes collapse beneath their feet, plunging into icy-cold pools formed from the approaching glacier. The water was murky and white, almost like milk.

There were plenty of berries and several plants worth eating, but beyond that food was sparse. The birds near the ground were small and subsisted on berries and insects. Like the few rodents they saw, these weren't large enough to bother with. They saw a handful of birds of prey, as well, circling the sky and picking off smaller animals. But these never ventured close enough for Alaji to consider hunting.

She managed to catch a few fish, which made for a more substantial meal, though she found the fatty meat and strange texture unpleasant. Ulithaine revealed a store of nuts and some dried meat he'd been saving. It kept them alive but hungry, and they were in poor spirits when they finally reached the Breaking Falls.

Alaji had seen too many marvels to hold it as the most spectacular, but it certainly stopped her breath. A pair of mountain peaks had been pressed nearly together by the encroaching ice wall. In the center, a chasm carved by the melting snow cut deep, and in this crack a waterfall thundered from the top to the ground below. To either side of the cascade, rivulets of ice had frozen, almost like falls themselves. Underneath, a thick mist formed above the pool where the water broke. The air here was fresh and cool, and droplets of water mixed with flakes of snow blowing off the cliffs far above.

Phaesha and two men were camped on the far shore of the river flowing off the rocky ledge. One called out to Ulithaine, who yelled back, "Hail, travelers!" Laughing good-naturedly, he charged into the frigid water and waded across. He embraced one of the men, who clasped his shoulder. The men struck their foreheads together and howled like wolves.

"I suppose we should cross," Yemerik said, feeling the water with his fingertips and cringing as he did so.

Alaji waded in, doing her best not to react to the blistering cold.

"You're not like them," Yemerik said after her, speaking softly so it wouldn't carry. She turned to look back at him with a confused, irritated expression. He held his palms in front of him. "I didn't mean it like…. Never mind. It's just…. I'm sorry. Never mind. Forget I said anything."

She turned away and fought through the rough current towards the other side. More than once, a piece of still-frozen ice brushed by her. She emerged shivering to find Ulithaine catching up with his companions. They spoke their own language, so of course she couldn't understand them. But one of the two men Phaesha had brought looked at her and nodded. It was a look of admiration and approval, the sort one man might give another. She wasn't sure why, but it filled her with pride.

Phaesha's attitude was unchanged from their last encounter. She gazed at Alaji with a mixture of annoyance and disgust. But Alaji also thought she detected a hint of fear. And, for the first time, Alaji really looked at her. Phaesha's skin was darker by far than her own, which was already darker than Ulithaine or any of the men she'd seen traveling with him. Phaesha was also taller than almost any woman Alaji had known, which gave her a fearsome presence.

But she was young. Almost as young as Alaji. She dressed to conceal this, covering herself in decorations of war and carrying herself like a master of her craft, but underneath that, she was no older than twenty. Perhaps not even that.

She saw Alaji staring and said something in a bitter tone. She motioned with a jerk of her head, conveying that she wished to be spared Alaji's presence. Alaji shook her head and wandered off to pick at the small brush that grew by the edge of the shallow river. The plants were small, damp, and cold to the touch, but their roots were short and gave up their grip with only the slightest hesitation. It took her a while to gather enough, and she was even colder by the time she had.

At some point, she became aware that she was being watched. She turned to realize Ulithaine's men were interested in what she was doing. Words were exchanged and Phaesha laughed, likely amused Alaji would need a fire after so trivial a thing as climbing through a river of freshly melted ice. One of the two men she'd brought chuckled as well, but Ulithaine just watched silently. The third man, the one who'd nodded at her when she arrived, looked on, intrigued.

Alaji was too cold and too tired to care. She piled the damp vegetation and looked for the largest piece. Then she began her spell of the hearth, ignoring Phaesha's snickering behind her. A puff of smoke erupted beneath her fingers, and she felt the exploding flame singe her thumb. She pulled that hand away with a yelp, then plunged the burning stick into the pile. She sucked on the burned digit for a moment and steeled herself for the coming laughter.

But no one laughed. Instead, Phaesha appeared beside her a moment later and knelt to look at the fire. Her mouth was open the slightest bit, and her eyes squinted, as if she didn't believe what she was seeing. She made a gruff sound in the back of her throat, climbed to her feet, then hurried away to the group of warriors. A moment later, Yemerik took her place.

"She's impressed," he said.

Alaji shook her head. "She's mocking me. She called rain and hurled fire at the beast. She thinks this is funny." Alaji motioned her hand over the small fire.

"The fire she created didn't really last," Yemerik said. "It was good for a scare, but it's not the same. Getting heat – real, lasting heat – takes skill. That's what I've heard, anyway."

Alaji put her hands over the tiny flame and soaked up its

warmth. She looked back at Phaesha, who seemed irate once again, this time at one of the men who'd plucked some brush from the ground and was waving it at her.

"I gave Phaesha that silver ring. The one Ulithaine told us was a message."

"And?"

"She recognized it. She said they used them to communicate. If we'd come back without Ulithaine, the ring would have saved our lives. Or at least saved us from a fight. It would have meant he'd trusted us."

"That's what he said," Alaji pointed out. "More or less."

"I know. I was just surprised. I'd have bet a hot meal he'd just said that as some sort of game."

Alaji shrugged. "It doesn't matter, anyway, does it?"

"No. Though I suppose we'd be on our way back to the gate if we'd left him to die. I don't mean that you shouldn't have—"

"I don't trust him," Alaji said curtly, "but I trust him more than I trust her." She motioned towards Phaesha, who was still fending off the taunts of one of the warriors. "How long will it take the others'… magic necklaces… to start working?"

"The translation charms? I'm not really sure. I'd guess a day or less, assuming they work like Ulithaine's. And that they have them at all."

"You weren't expecting those things to exist here," Alaji said.

"Well, no. I mean, translation magic should have existed all along, but only because there should still be civilizations carved out of the ruins of the Hatharian Empire. Not the one we saw, I mean—"

"The real one," Alaji interrupted. "I know."

"It's not that the sorcery needed to construct something like that is impossibly complex, it's just… not the kind of thing you expect to find in an era this primitive."

"You should try expecting less," Alaji said. She watched Phaesha rip the plant out of the warrior's hand, cast a quick charm, then throw the branch against a rock, where it shattered like ice. Phaesha shouted something back at the man who'd taunted her, which seemed to terrify him. Ulithaine and the other man almost fell over laughing, though Alaji couldn't tell who or what they were really laughing at.

—

Ulithaine half dropped, half threw a pile of furs beside Yemerik. It was late afternoon, and the rest of the group were drunk, having finished the last of the wine Phaesha had brought. "For the night?" Yemerik asked.

He responded with his characteristic laugh. "If you need them to sleep, certainly. But you'll want them tomorrow for certain. We leave for the wizard's palace with the sunrise, as long as the weather cooperates. If we're lucky, we'll reach it before sundown. If not… you'll be glad you've the furs."

"Where is this palace?" Yemerik asked, somewhat hesitantly.

A smile greeted this question. "Not to worry. Just a bit more to the north."

This answer caught Alaji's attention. Her head turned in tandem with Yemerik's and they stared at the darkening cliffs before them. "The glacier," Yemerik said, as the blood drained from his face. "You mean to travel over the glacier?"

"You'll be wanting these, as well." Ulithaine dropped thin metal chains. "Wrap them around your boots. Helps keep you from slipping off." He snickered as he used two fingers to pantomime a man slipping and falling from a great height. "I'm kidding! We'll tie ourselves together, so no man goes over. Unless…." More snickering. "Unless all do!" He laughed out loud, then repeated the joke at great volume in his native language. Across the camp, his two men howled with laughter.

"We need specialized equipment," Yemerik said. "If we're to climb the ice—"

"We have knives! But there'll be very little climbing. Look at that cliff face. See the indent? It's a path cutting up the rock."

"It must be coated in ice," Yemerik responded.

"Several feet deep," Ulithaine replied. "But don't worry yourself. I've walked the glacier before and lived. Brithol and Thirove have, as well. That's why I asked them along. And I asked Phaesha...." He raised his voice again and switched languages, "I asked Phaesha along in case we fall!" More laughter from the other two men. Phaesha, for her part, looked no more or less annoyed than when they'd begun.

"Sleep well," he said. "It'll be a long day. But if we live, you'll have seen a sight. Actually, if we all die, you'll still see quite a sight. Just faster. And from a different angle." He laughed so loud, his men began laughing, too, despite the fact they hadn't been close enough to hear the joke, nor would they have been able to understand the language if they had been.

He left Alaji and Yemerik alone, staring at the cliffs before them. "Is it possible?" Alaji whispered, half in fear and half in awe.

"Yes, it's possible," Yemerik replied. "But right now I'm wishing you'd listened to me when I said to leave him to the apes."

"That isn't funny," Alaji snapped back.

Yemerik opened his mouth to object, but he seemed to think better of it, sighed, and shook his head. "We should get some sleep. Assuming we live through it, tomorrow will be a long, trying day."

PART 6: WIZARD'S JUSTICE

1

The sky was still dark when one of Ulithaine's men – Alaji still wasn't sure which was Brithol and which was Thirove – approached her and Yemerik. She was already sitting up, though Yemerik remained asleep beneath the oiled deerskin they'd propped up to keep out the wind. Alaji was so still, the warrior didn't see her until he was nearly beside them. He stepped back quickly, then recovered his composure, grunted softly, and motioned towards where Ulithaine and the others were gathering their supplies. Alaji nodded, crawled over to Yemerik, and gently punched him in the shoulder.

"What?" he muttered, opening his eyes. "It's pitch black. They said we weren't leaving until daybreak."

"Ask him," she suggested. She walked to the shore of the river, dipped her hands into the cool water, and cupped them together. Then she brought the water to her lips and drank it in.

"You should boil it first. Even up here."

Alaji realized with some surprise it was Phaesha's voice. She turned to find the woman bound up in several layers of furs. Her expression was cold and uncaring, as ever.

"It won't hurt me," Alaji said. "I'm protected."

"Magics," Phaesha said. "So I hear. You're a healer, too."

Alaji shrugged.

"I distrust healers," Phaesha said. "They shelter themselves in cathedrals and guard their secrets. They are like whores who ask too much money."

Alaji stood to face Phaesha, who towered over her. "I'm not sheltered," she said. "And if it's any consolation, I'm not that good a healer. I'm not sure that will be as comforting if you're wounded."

Phaesha snorted. Her expression was like one Alaji had seen on Ulithaine several times in the swamps. "You may be of use to us after all," she said. "Tie the furs tight and don't fail to ask for help. You'll see the fate of those who don't soon enough."

Alaji nodded and hurried back to Yemerik, who was still half asleep. Alaji looked down at him. "Hurry up," she said. "You're embarrassing us."

—

The path up the cliff face was even worse than it looked: a steep climb up a thin, winding trail coated entirely in ice with nothing at the edge but an increasingly large drop. They traveled single file, connected by a long, thick rope. Yemerik wondered if it would offer any real protection if he fell, or simply snap under the weight. The chains wrapped around his boots were certainly better than nothing, but he still slipped and landed on the icy surface several times. Ulithaine led, followed by Phaesha, then Alaji, Brithol, Yemerik, and finally Thirove, who unrolled a separate rope behind him that stretched several hundred feet to the crate below containing the teeth of the beast. Occasionally, they'd run out of rope and have to stop to haul the crate up to their current location, fix it in place, then move on to the next stopping point. It was slow going.

They reached the top before noon without catastrophe, and Ulithaine expressed annoyance that it had taken so long. The top of the cliff was slightly higher than the surface of the glacier. As soon as they stepped over the crest, they were exposed to fierce winds burning against their skin. But the sight was extraordinary.

"That's the castle, I presume," Yemerik said. In the distance stood a massive structure of carved ice.

"That's Oriv's Keep," Brithol said. "Built of magic and maintained by its creator, the youngest of Orthim's six sons. There. In the distance. You can make out Misji's home, as well."

"Another of Orthim's sons?" Yemerik asked, sarcastically.

"No. Misji's older than—"

"Never mind," Yemerik snapped, still angry he'd been tricked into this predicament. "I don't really care."

They stopped briefly to rest, but it was already late in the day. Between the cold and wind, Yemerik understood Ulithaine's desire to make the city by nightfall.

The other side of the cliff dipped slightly to the glacier's surface, which stretched out between them and their destination. It wasn't far to the ice, though transporting the hound's teeth down was no easy feat. Once they reached the surface, they stopped again to convert the crate into a sled. Then they began across, still bound together, with Ulithaine in the lead.

—

Alaji's head and eyes had begun to ache from the brightness of the ice and the constant count in the back of her mind. It had been going since they'd started up the cliff, and she found it difficult to stop even when she wanted to. Nothing about the glacier felt safe.

She was soon grateful for those instincts. About an hour after they'd started, she heard a loud crack ahead of her, and Ulithaine vanished into the ice, along with a sizable section of the ground. Phaesha cried out as she was pulled off her feet and dragged towards the hole. The rope snapped tight, just as Alaji stepped back in time.

"Wait!" she screamed. Ulithaine froze in place immediately, though Phaesha stumbled forward and looked around.

"Stop!" Ulithaine hissed, partly at Phaesha and partly for Brithol and Thirove, neither of whom had a translation charm. Everyone stood still, as commanded. He turned back.

"Step back," Alaji said to Ulithaine. "Slowly." He did as told, and motioned for Phaesha to do the same. Once they were nearly to her position, she pointed to where the ice had not given way but would have. "It's hollow." She held her hands together, flat in front of her, fingertips touching. Then she folded her fingers downward.

Behind her, she heard Brithol say something. Ulithaine translated quickly, "He said you vanished and reappeared. You should probably re-tie your harness, though." He motioned to the rope, which had dropped away when she'd stepped back. "Is it safe over there?" Ulithaine asked, gesturing to the right.

"I don't know yet," Alaji said, honestly.

Ulithaine shrugged. "I suppose you'll warn us again if it isn't," he said.

They continued on, and the ground felt sturdy. After a hundred paces, Phaesha called for the group to stop. She turned and looked back at the spot they'd been minutes before.

"You don't believe?" Ulithaine asked.

"I want to see for myself," Phaesha responded. Then, with a quick chant and flick of her wrist, a tiny spherical fire flew towards the ice. It struck with a small explosion, and the ice cracked a bit but didn't break. She repeated the spell, and this time the pocket was exposed with a shattering sound and a cloud of snow. She nodded to Ulithaine, who simply shook his head amusedly, then led on.

As they went, Phaesha's pace decreased, until she was right alongside Alaji. "You look into the future?" she asked.

"It's more that I live it then come back."

"Then it's true. You are from a different time." She spoke solemnly. "I have a question then. There are those who say we near the end of things. That each generation there is less and less that grows and more that hunts, and that before long the last living things will devour each other. A few hundred years, or perhaps less, is what they say."

"Yemerik says things get better. He told me time works in cycles, like the seasons. There'll be good times and bad ones. But I don't really know. I come from a time so far in the past, I'm not even sure how to count the centuries. It was better than this in some ways, and worse in others. This time isn't more than a fifth of the time between my people and Yemerik's. Not even a fifth of a fifth, if I understood him right. It's still… I guess you'd say it's all still early."

Phaesha's gaze lingered on the ice palace in the distance. "That's… that's terrifying," she said. Then she laughed – not brashly, like Ulithaine – but merrily, the way Alaji might have laughed with Theojin.

Alaji laughed, too, not knowing what else to say. Phaesha was right: the idea was terrifying.

Once they'd calmed down, Phaesha adjusted her outer cape. "Your time. Tell me about it."

"It's different. Things are more…." She stopped herself before saying it was more civilized. "It's smaller," she said. "The beasts are smaller, our homes are smaller, we have fewer spells, and there is nothing like that." She motioned ahead to the buildings of ice in the distance.

"But no gods walking the earth?" Phaesha's voice was stern once again, though she almost looked like she might smile.

"We had five gods. They mostly just threatened us if we learned more magic. Or that's what our seers claimed." Alaji looked over to see Phaesha raising her eyebrows in puzzlement. "They gave us ten spells: five for men and five for women. The rest were supposed to be reserved for themselves. It seems silly now."

"They sound as worthless as our gods," Phaesha declared. "But ours were less stingy. I worship Crithe, the lord of snakes. I would show you my talisman, were it not buried beneath these furs. Do you know what kind of god Crithe is?" Phaesha asked, sounding more serious. Alaji shook her head, and Phaesha grinned. "The best kind. He is a children's story. A lie. There is no Crithe." She laughed again loudly.

"Yemerik told me they were all fake," Alaji said.

"If only," Phaesha said. "I met a god once, in the desert. Lit-Reen-Dor, the ancient. Do you know of him?" She paused, and Alaji shook her head. "He is a thousand years old, and his skin is like sand turned to stone. He is twice as tall as Krishind's hound. My father was taking us through the wastes, my brother and I, and we came across one of Lit-Reen-Dor's groves. We did not know, so we stopped to drink. A day later, the god came for us. His footsteps shook the ground and a storm of sand accompanied him like a shroud. We tried to outrun him, but how do you outrun a god? When he found us, he demanded a sacrifice as recompense. I thought my father would choose me, but he chose my brother instead." Phaesha brushed the side of her nose. "I asked him why he'd given up a son for me, but he never told me. Perhaps my brother was not truly his. I don't know."

Alaji was silent. She thought of her own brother, of course, and tried to picture her father choosing to spare her life over Theojin's. She was unable to imagine it.

"Some say the river serpent is a god," Phaesha said, abruptly changing the subject. "Do you know what I speak of?"

"The thing in the water beside the dead town," Alaji said. "I saw it when we swam to avoid the hound. It was slick, like a fish, but it was immense. I couldn't see head or tail, but it had a fin that moved side to side. The fin was the size of that dune over there." Alaji pointed to a nearby mound of snow.

Phaesha shook her head. "I would not cross there to escape the hordes of hell. I have heard stories of it pulling boats of men down in whirlpools to swallow them whole. You are lucky it slept. It is a foul thing, but it is no god. It is like the hound, I think, given life by one of them," she motioned towards the distant castle. "One of them or their kind."

"Why?" Alaji asked, disgusted.

"For war or vengeance. It is one and the same to the sorcerers. They fight each other and war against the kings. Oriv desires trade with his neighbors. If he is refused, he unleashes beasts upon them. If he is given what he wants, Krishind breeds hounds of hell and sets them loose, so the villagers can no longer aid his foe. So Oriv creates the bats, and sets them upon Krishind's lands." Phaesha pointed to the east. "It is no better there. None live within fifty miles of the caves. Beyond that, the villagers lose chicken, cattle, even their own lives in the night. One of the bats is large enough to carry off a grown man."

Alaji looked at the ice castle, horrified. "The wizards are worse than the monsters, aren't they?"

"Worse than the monsters or the gods," Phaesha agreed. "But they hold great power. And great wealth. So we bring Oriv the hound's teeth to collect our reward."

"Aren't you worried about Krishind? If he learns you're helping his enemy—"

"We fear no wizard!" Phaesha snapped. "Let him rage! Let him send dogs or assassins! We will send them to hell!" She said this loudly, and her eyes focused on Ulithaine's back as she spoke. But he did not turn around.

Alaji swallowed. "I wouldn't want to meet another one of those things."

"What? The hounds? There are no more, save its pups. And most of those are dead."

Alaji noticed Ulithaine turn his head. He caught her gaze and smirked. Briefly, she considered confronting him, but then she looked around and remembered where she was. What could she do? Instead, she bit her tongue and returned her attention to the ice, so she wouldn't slip. It seemed Phaesha was done speaking for the time being, as well. She rarely relaxed her jaw, so she always appeared angry. But the longer Alaji spent near her, the more Phaesha just looked tired.

A few minutes later, Phaesha broke her silence. She spoke quietly, in almost a whisper, and she did so with even more intensity than before. "When this ends. If we survive it. I will teach you to hold fire as I do, if you'll teach me some of your magic." She watched Alaji carefully, as if daring her to laugh.

"I'll show you what I can," Alaji said, quickly. "I don't know how to teach you how to… step back in time. But I can try to teach you my other spells."

To Alaji's surprise, Phaesha looked relieved. "I would like that," Phaesha said. "If it is agreeable, I would like to see how you make fire. Your technique is quite impressive."

2

Long before they reached the city, they came across the dead. Travelers who'd come unprepared for the journey or who'd simply met a string of bad luck littered the path, their bodies preserved by the bitter cold and harsh winds. Some sat alone; others huddled together for warmth which had long since left their bodies. Some lay calmly on the glacier's surface, as if they were simply stopping to sleep. Others were partially submerged in the ice, in which Ulithaine claimed they would slowly sink, like a sailor drowning over years. Most of the dead held packs, or leaned on them. Some had carts or sleighs like their own, though any belongings of value had been pilfered long ago.

These were the traders, the travelers, and madmen who'd died by chance or foolishness. They'd broken bones or gotten lost in a blizzard. Now they lay in the frozen plains, because no one had cause to move them. These were only dead, though: they were not the damned.

"The forest," Phaesha whispered. They were near the city when they came upon it. The sun was dipping on the horizon. Ulithaine paused so the others could catch up. The ropes connecting the group were removed and collected. Here, the ice wouldn't crack or give way. Here, the enchantment started.

"Behold how wizards mete out justice," Ulithaine proclaimed.

Before them stood dozens of metal stakes driven into the ice. To each of these was chained a man or woman, now frozen solid. A glimmer of light emanated from the ice below the bodies. Yemerik stumbled forward. "Jar's tears," he muttered softly, peering through the surface. Beneath their feet, shimmering forms slipped through the ice like fish underwater.

"You know what they are?" Ulithaine asked.

"Yes. I know," Yemerik replied. "She doesn't though," he motioned to Alaji. "Probably best it stays that—"

Ulithaine cut him off. "These are the spirits of the dead. Those the wizard decreed betrayers. He keeps them from the halls of the dead for all time. Hell would be a preferable fate."

"Hell!" Yemerik choked back a sickened laugh. "Save your antiquated notions of…" He cringed, squeezing his eyes closed. When he opened them, he seemed calmer, though no less disgusted. "I'm sorry," he said. "They won't stay here forever. That sort of power can't be controlled by men: building it requires more time than time has to offer. They'll stay here until his spell breaks. Maybe until he dies, or maybe not until this sheet of ice melts into the sea. But they'll get free." He met Ulithaine's gaze, and – for the first time – Ulithaine seemed at a loss for words. "What? If you're really going to accompany us through time, you should have some idea of what you're getting into. This. All of this! It was land once, and it will be again. The glaciers appear, flow through the lands, then recede. Time passes, and it starts again. They're barely getting started here. Unless something changes, they've got thousands of miles further to travel south before diminishing to almost nothing. It will take tens of thousands of years." He stopped, looking down again at the ghastly forms flowing beneath him. He stood and shook his head.

Ulithaine nodded slowly. "We should go," he said. He turned and began marching across the ice at a faster pace. Yemerik, Alaji, and Phaesha followed, while Thirove and Brithol dragged the sleigh in back.

"Are you okay?" Alaji asked Yemerik.

"I'm sorry. I'm getting caught up in the politics of an era I barely understand. It really doesn't matter, anyway, since...," he trailed off, remembering that Phaesha was close enough to hear them. "It just doesn't matter. We should finish this and move on. Get back to the gate and find a safer time. When we reach the Citadel, the Assembly can deal with all this."

—

The sun was setting as they reached the crystalline walls of Oriv's city of ice. In the dusk, the surface shone red and violet. The outer wall was curved and divided into segments by massive towers. They were two hundred feet tall, Alaji estimated, and then only a fraction the size of the central tower beyond.

A trail approached the wall of ice, but there was no opening or doorway. There was nowhere else to go, so Ulithaine cried out, "Hail! Hail, Watchman!"

A man appeared at the edge of the wall. He leaned down and called, "Who is there? What business have you?"

"We are warriors from the south, come to claim our reward! We have slain the great hound of Krishind!" Ulithaine motioned to Brithol, who began to pry open the crate.

The guard watched silently. "You have proof of this deed?" he shouted. "Have you the head?"

The lid popped off, and Ulithaine removed a tooth, which he held up. "I could not have dragged the head up the cliffside if all my company survived the battle. We brought the teeth plucked from the monster's jaws. If another finds the corpse and hires an army to haul it here, you can ask them why the teeth are missing!"

"How do we know they are the hound's teeth, and not some dragon's?"

"I'll wager your sorcerer can tell the difference," Ulithaine shouted. "Now let us in and bring us some hot food! We've done a service, and deserve better than to listen to your prattle!"

The guard vanished for a moment, then returned. "We'll let

you through!" He shouted. "Stand back until the ram has cleared the doorway."

Another moment passed, then the ice before them grew red and began to crack. Slowly, a shape took form through the thinning barrier. The remaining ice shattered, and a metal rod seven feet thick extended through the wall. Immediately, it was drawn back, and a voice inside called out, "Hurry! Before the wall freezes once more!"

They dragged the open crate into the enclosure. Several guards worked to turn the rod around and slide the end into a fire roaring in a massive furnace of stone and iron that rested in a shell of ice. Behind them, the opening in the wall began to close. In a few minutes, it would be as before.

"It's warm," Alaji remarked. The room was indeed far warmer than it should have been, even with the furnace.

"Temperature manipulation," Yemerik whispered. "A kind of magic. This is somewhat advanced."

Six other soldiers stood ready with swords and a weapon Alaji had never seen before that looked like a miniature bow and arrow set on top of a wooden grip. None of what anyone said made sense to her, so she occupied her attention with the strange device.

Yemerik stood back, as well. He understood what was being said but doubted he'd have much to offer. Besides, he still wasn't convinced Ulithaine wouldn't try and sell them to the wizard, and he wanted to be ready to act if necessary.

"Your weapons, there!" One of the guards demanded.

"What hospitality is this?" Brithol demanded. "We have accomplished a great feat!"

"That isn't for us to say," the guard said, aiming his crossbow at Brithol's chest.

Ulithaine stepped slowly between the two men with his hands raised in front of him. The smile he'd lost at the forest of bodies had returned, and he reached up slowly to remove his sword from his back. He lay this where the guard had indicated, then took out several knives, which he set beside his sword. "As he says," Ulithaine commanded. Then he turned to Alaji before Yemerik could think to do so and said, "Leave your knives with ours."

Alaji did as instructed, as did the others. When they finished, the guard said, "You will need to be searched. Remove your furs and hand them over." Once again, Ulithaine translated and did as they asked. The guards inspected his robes for hidden daggers and the like, then searched his person.

They made their way through the group, doing the same, until they came to Phaesha. She tossed them her fur cape and held her arms to either side. But when one approached her, she stared him down. "If your hand touches me, I will break it off."

The guard watched her carefully, unsure how to proceed.

Another guard stepped towards Alaji, but Phaesha blocked his path. "Touch her, and you can keep your hand. But you'll wish I'd taken it instead."

"Perhaps you can find a woman who might help resolve this?" Ulithaine suggested.

They wound up forgoing a thorough search of Alaji and Phaesha, though they insisted on inspecting their belongings. This included Alaji's pack containing the shards of the talisman, which left her uneasy, though the guards weren't interested in those at all – after a quick glance, they handed them back to her. Phaesha's snake-tooth charm was met with more controversy: it made an older guard uneasy, and there was a great deal of screaming and threats, the vast majority from Phaesha. Ulithaine managed to calm her, and she reluctantly turned it over with their weapons, though not before informing several guards in detail what would happen to them if it was kept from her upon their departure. No one translated any of this to Alaji, and for once she was grateful to remain ignorant.

They were told to leave other items, as well: their rope, the chains they'd brought for the ice, extra cloaks, and various tools. These were piled up in a room just to the side of the entryway.

As they were led onward, the head guard glanced at Phaesha, Alaji, and Yemerik. "We are aware there are magicians among you," he stated, and Yemerik translated for Alaji. "Make no mistake, you are in the domain of one far wiser and far more powerful. The archmage, Oriv, whose power and generosity sustains this city, welcomes friends but does not suffer challengers. His is the only power permitted here, and his retribution is fierce and quick." His words were polished and practiced, and as he finished speaking, he stepped into an opening in the hallway. Inside were several blocks of ice containing robed figures. Some held staffs or wands; others' arms were raised in a defensive posture. The ice was crystal-clear, and the bodies perfectly preserved. The expressions they wore – defiance, rage, regret, or sorrow – were lifelike.

"Over the years, our lord has welcomed guests who thought themselves above his law. Those you see here believed they could unravel his spells. They believed they could hide their magic from his gaze. They thought to undermine him from behind closed doors. You see what became of them. In an attempt to prevent such tragedies from occurring needlessly, he offers this room as an exception. If you would like to test our lord's power, you may try to melt these statues. Be assured, many have tried their magic and none have gotten so much as a drop of water to appear."

Phaesha began to step towards the nearest encased body, but Ulithaine stopped her. "Thank you," he said to the guard. "But we understand your rules and don't need proof they can be enforced. None of my people will cast a spell without permission," he said, forcibly. "Now then, we are hungry and thirsty, and there is a matter of our reward."

"You will be given food and drink," the guard said. "Your reward will need to wait until morning, when our lord can examine your claim. If you speak true, you will be given all you were promised. But he is not one who can be deceived."

Ulithaine smiled. "Give us our food then! And bring wine befitting hunters and slayers!" Brithol and Thirove cheered this. Phaesha looked back at the frozen bodies and stayed silent.

3

They were taken through a series of tunnels. The walls, ceilings, and floors were formed out of ice, though the surface wasn't slippery beneath their feet. Rows of tiny bumps provided texture, and despite the temperate conditions, there wasn't a drop of water present. No torches adorned the walls, but sections of ice glowed a strange blue, like moonlight breaking through the surface of a lake. Tapestries with sections cut out hung in front of these areas, and they created beautiful patterns of shadow and light. Alaji gazed on in horror and awe, but Yemerik seemed unimpressed.

"What is it?" she asked in as quiet a whisper as she could manage.

"What's what? Oh, the light. Just magic," he replied. "Probably runic." He flipped one of the cloth tapestries up as he walked past, revealing a strange pattern etched beneath the surface of the ice. "See. Just as I thought." A few of the guards looked back but said nothing.

Soon, they reached a set of heavy, wooden doors. Their frames were embedded in solid ice, but the doors themselves swung open with ease. Inside, a pair of long tables were butted together. On top sat several loaves of bread, three massive pitchers of wine, another two with clear water, and a stack of clay cups. The guard motioned for them to enter. "If you have need of a privy, you'll find one through the far corridor, past the curtain," he said. "You may rest here, but may not leave this enclosure until bidden. More sustaining food shall be brought when it is prepared." He stepped out of the room and began closing the doors.

"See that you send for roast pork and goose!" Ulithaine shouted, as the doors closed completely. He smiled, grabbed a cup, and plunged it into the nearest pitcher of wine. "Let none say our host isn't gracious!" He threw back the cup, emptying it in a single, quick gulp. Phaesha, Brithol, and Thirove joined him, while Yemerik began looking around. Alaji, meanwhile, stood back. Phaesha brought her a cup of wine and went over what the guard had said.

Alaji took a sip of the wine then waved her hand through the rippling light flowing out of the walls. "I can't decide whether this is the most astonishing place I've ever seen or an abomination. I knew someone once who believed in a world beneath the ocean. I wonder if this is what she imagined it would be like. It's terrifying and beautiful."

Phaesha shrugged. "They are usually one and the same. I went once to the Catacombs at Arilforge. Skulls of men and beasts are inlaid in the walls and ceiling. Entire hallways are built in the skulls and spines of dragons, and those of giants mark important places. I was a child then, and it made me sick. It still makes me sick to think of it. But I have always wished to return and walk those paths again. The world seems full of such places, if one has the will and luxury of finding them. Is this true of all time?"

"I don't know. I've only seen a small portion of it. For what it's worth, this is the most striking age I've visited. Hathari didn't have anything like that hound or this castle."

"Hathari? I do not know this. Was it a place?"

"A city. A nation, is more like it. I thought maybe you'd have heard of them. They were a powerful civilization long ago."

"I know of no kingdom before the Trythians. They were said to be the first civilized people, more than five thousand years ago. In your travels, have you been to their empire? It is written the gods cried on the day their gardens burned."

"I've never even heard of them. Five thousand...." She instinctively shifted her fingers to better feel the numbers. "That's just a fraction of the time between Hathari and here. I'm sorry. We probably just jumped over it."

"Jump over Trythe?" Phaesha's mouth was agape. "It was the

center of all knowledge, the birthplace of culture. And you missed it?" For a moment, Alaji thought she was angry, but then she cracked a smile and started laughing.

Before long, the guards reappeared with food. There was no roast pig or goose, like Ulithaine had demanded, but there was mutton, fish, stewed vegetables, and ripe pears, which Alaji quickly discovered a fondness for.

Their stomachs full and their furs returned to them, the warriors, sorceresses, and the sole constructive historian specializing in theoretical pre-history set down as comfortable a padding as they could and prepared to sleep.

—

Alaji was awakened by a bright light. The pale blue glow from the prior night had been replaced with a bright yellow one. The others were sitting up around her, likewise trying to make sense of their surroundings. Before they could speak, the door to their chamber swung open and a dozen new guards appeared. The leader addressed the room.

"Honored guests. Our lord, Oriv, has agreed to an audience in two hours' time. We will show you to the baths." The guards roused them quickly but politely. Ulithaine finished off one of the pitchers of wine before leaving, tipping the massive container overhead. Then they divided the men and women, and led them to separate rooms, where they were left alone.

The inside was full of steam. The floors were wood, though the walls were opaque ice, cool to the touch, but – like the rest of the castle – they seemed impervious to the warm air. Next to the door was a slab of ice extending from the wall containing several pieces of clothing, neatly folded.

The wooden floors ended in a series of pools of water held in ice basins. Phaesha hurried to these and began checking the different temperatures. "What are we supposed to do with these?" Phaesha asked, exasperated.

"I hoped you'd know," Alaji replied. "I'm used to bathing in lakes and streams."

"This one isn't overly hot or cold," Phaesha said. She knelt and loosened her clothing. Then, thinking for a moment, asked, "Are there robes there?"

Alaji dug through the fabric and chose a few long pieces. "I'm not sure what these are," she said, handing one to Phaesha.

Phaesha examined it for a moment. "I think it's a dress," she decided. "Who would wear such a thing?" She pulled it open, around her. "Do as I do. This is a wizard's castle. Who knows where he has eyes?" She wrapped it firmly around herself, slipped off most of her clothes underneath, then set these aside. Alaji did the same, and they knelt over the pool, cupping warm water in their hands and washing themselves under the cover of the dresses, which were soon thoroughly soaked.

After, they dried themselves with the robe-like dresses they were wearing, then searched the pile of offered clothes for something practical. Alaji found a decent enough shirt, but nothing fit Phaesha. Finally, she grew irritated and gathered her own clothes. They dressed beneath the dresses, then peeled off the wet garments, folded them, and placed them as neatly as they could at the bottom of the pile.

They left through the door they'd entered, and waited along with the guards for the men to emerge. When they were all present, the only one of the group who looked measurably cleaner was Yemerik.

The guards herded them through more hallways and down long, winding staircases. Gradually, the light from magic was replaced with natural light, seeping in through thinning sections of ice and eventually through open windows. Looking out, they began to get views of the city itself. The architecture was similar to that they'd seen already: spiny towers and curved surfaces were all but universal. These were all interconnected by a series of arches and bridges, though they were clearly unsuited for travel.

Beneath those structures, the hole in the ice cut through to the earth. And there resided a paradise. As they were hurried through, Alaji caught glimpses of green fields full of livestock, groves of trees bearing fruit, gardens draped with vines, pools of water, and flowing streams. At last, they reached the bottom and stepped off the icy floor onto rounded stones. The air was fresh and warm.

It was a place like no other, a marvel surrounded by towering walls of ice. All the buildings were connected by arches of ice the same shape as the gate they'd passed through to reach this age. Structures were rarely square or rectangular: almost everything was curved and smooth. Statues and intricate carvings were an exception, breaking the pattern with the form of a dragon or a beautiful woman growing out of the side of a tower or simply emerging from the ground.

The people, however, were like those Alaji had known in her village and every other land she'd visited. They harvested grain, tended sheep, and raised children. If they differed from others she'd known, it was only in a general sense of contentment. Only the guards carried weapons. Only the guards had need of such tools. It was plain in the people's faces: they were secure. Wars were fought elsewhere.

"This way," the head guard said, leading them onward. They followed a stone path towards the middle of the city, where the massive central tower stood. It was taller by far than any other building, and it alone rose higher than the exterior wall.

They reached the foot of the tower and found two dozen guards standing ready. Ulithaine yawned as four of them joined the guards who'd brought them this far and led them inside. Ulithaine followed, with the rest directly behind him. Finally, four more guards brought up the rear, and the massive company marched down a long hall, then continued up a short set of stairs. Briefly, Alaji feared they'd need to continue in this way all the way to the top. She was relieved when they reached a metal doorway almost immediately, and one of the guards hurried in to announce them.

Alaji leaned over to Yemerik and whispered, "Tell me if there's anything I need to do. Otherwise, I'll just copy you and try to stay quiet. This is too similar to Minot-Rin's court for my comfort."

The guard's voice bellowed out, "Ulithaine of the southern wilderness. You may enter with your company."

And with that, they went in to meet the wizard, Oriv.

4

It was less a throne room than a banquet hall. There were a handful of guards and women who might have been courtesans, as well as a musician, but no advisors or the like. The decorations were minimal, designed mostly to emphasize and play with the light flowing through the enchanted ice. A massive rug with strips removed had a similar effect to the tapestries they'd seen the night before, albeit at a larger scale.

There was a massive table laid out with a plentiful amount of food. In the center of the floor, beside the table, was a chest overflowing with gold and silver coins.

And behind the table, seated on a throne of ice, was the wizard himself. He was old and thin, but not frail, and was dressed in red robes embroidered with golden thread. His hair at least paid homage to his surroundings: it was white as winter. In one hand, he held a tooth from the hound, and he was smiling.

"Tell me, who leads this company?" he asked, though the question was clearly a formality. His gaze had already fallen on the man in the center of the warriors.

"I am Ulithaine."

"Ah. I've heard of you. Good and bad alike, your reputation travels far. I have lived three hundred years, and I can count legends like yours on a single hand. Tell me, how was the monster felled?"

"It was tricked. Worn low by my companion, Alaji," he said, motioning at her. She flinched at the sound of her name and bowed as soon as she realized the room was looking in her direction. Ulithaine continued. "My warriors and I rode down on it. At great cost, we drove it between ruined buildings with spear, spell, and the lives of our comrades. I myself plunged steel into the creature's skull and spilt its blood and brains. Is it so?"

Ulithaine's men cheered. Thirove clasped his leader's shoulder. "It is so!" he shouted.

"Krishind swore his hound could never be beat," Oriv said. "He swore no fire or magic or weapon of man could do this. He boasted no power but his own could end its life. But you have done so." He motioned to the food. "Let us eat. Let us celebrate an end to Krishind's terror and the rise of the Land of the Crescent Shadow!"

Ulithaine bellowed, and his men did the same. Yemerik applauded politely, and Alaji mimicked him. She continued to copy him as he retrieved a glass made of ice that was full of wine. Oriv toasted them, and all drank. Then Ulithaine reached out, grabbed hold of a leg of a large, roasted bird, and tore it off with a twist. He bit into the meat greedily, and his men, Phaesha included, grabbed food from the table. Alaji held back, wanting neither attention nor competition. Besides, she still felt full from the previous night's meal, and Yemerik didn't seem interested in battling for the food, either.

Oriv ignored the meal, as well, though he watched the warriors carefully. With a gesture of his hand, the musician raised his lute and began playing softly. Oriv motioned for him to stop when his guests slowed their gorging, then proclaimed, "You see this chest before you? It is everything promised and more."

"We're grateful," Ulithaine said, downing a second glass of wine. "If it is not too much to ask, I promised Alaji a Speaking Stone. If you've one to sell me, I'd trade back a few of those coins."

Oriv smiled, stepped to the nearest wall, and placed a hand upon it. The spot he touched seemed to shimmer, and he reached through. The area around his hand was nothing more than water now. "The third alcove," he said, shifting his stance. A few moments passed, and his hand emerged with a small wooden box. He opened this and sifted through a number of medallions until he found one similar to Ulithaine's. He withdrew it, and handed it to the warrior. "Do not trouble yourself with the coins. This will be a gift."

"Thank you," Ulithaine replied. Then he turned and tossed it to Alaji and shouted, "As agreed."

He spoke her language, which caught the wizard's attention. "What speech is this?" he asked, now looking at Alaji. She'd caught the pendant and immediately placed it around her neck beside the necklace holding a small shard of the talisman.

"That one? We're still working out where she's from. Useful to have around. Invaluable against the hound."

"Where did you find her?" Oriv asked. Alaji still couldn't understand his words, but his interest, coupled with the look of concern on Yemerik's face, left her on edge.

"We met in the south," Ulithaine replied. "She's something of a hunter."

"A woman hunter. Not unheard of in the south." His eyes darted to Phaesha, before returning to Alaji. "But her skin... it is closer to the Du Gerid of the west. Only her hair is all wrong for the Du Gerid. Perhaps her blood is mixed, bred of western and eastern lineage."

"I think that must be so," Ulithaine replied.

"Perhaps you will remain another evening. By that time, her charm should allow us to communicate more freely."

"Certainly. If you'll feed us." Ulithaine laughed and reached for a serving fork. He speared a cut of veal, and began chewing on the meat.

Oriv feigned a laugh, though it was obvious he was disturbed by the warrior's manners. He smiled and nodded. "It's settled then. You'll remain as my guests. You will be honored here as the champions you are." He motioned to one of the guards, who nodded then stepped away to make arrangements. Then he sipped his wine thoughtfully.

Ulithaine paused his meal to turn to Phaesha and his men. He raised his glass high and said, "To our host!" His men toasted, drank, and refilled their glasses.

"To those lost," Thirove said. "To Treinile! Urjim! Rithile! And Portmire!"

"And to Wuerra," Ulithaine replied, solemnly.

"To Wuerra and those who rode with her," Thirove agreed. Once more, they drank.

Oriv watched, silently. He waited for a moment to pass before speaking again. "Tell me, Ulithaine, what will you do with your treasure? With the money you've earned, a man could build a great keep and fill it with artisans, minstrels. And women." He grinned broadly. "There is a great deal a man could accomplish with such wealth."

"It is a start!" Ulithaine proclaimed to cheers from Brithol and Thirove.

"Indeed," the wizard said, thoughtfully. "It is a great sum. Great enough for a keep. But not a kingdom." He spoke the word pointedly. "A man of your strength and cunning, aided by companions who value camaraderie could accomplish that or more. Given the right patronage," he added.

"Are you offering to make me a king?" Ulithaine asked.

"No man can make another a king. Crowns may be passed around, but a king – a true king – makes himself. If you had such ambition, I should think you could achieve it. And there are ways I could assist."

"Have you more monsters you need slain?" Ulithaine asked.

"No, not exactly. You've slain the hound of Krishind, but while its master lives, I worry about the land it stalked. Its master will be angry, and his attentions will be drawn back to the Land of the Crescent Shadow. And to those who killed his sentry."

"I'm not afraid of him," Ulithaine answered, slapping his chest. "Let him send pets or mercenaries."

"Well spoken," Oriv said, raising his glass. "But a man like Krishind can be a dangerous foe. He is patient and clever. If he sees a chance to strike, he will take it."

"I won't run from the likes of him," Ulithaine replied.

"Nor would I have you do so. You have performed a great feat, Ulithaine. One worthy of song and celebration. No, I would not have you run. I would have you do what you've always done. I would see you triumphant. You've slain the monster; why not its master?"

Ulithaine's mouth and eyes widened. "You would have me challenge a wizard?"

"Why not? Krishind is ancient, but he is mortal. His powers are great, but they have limitations. I have watched him for centuries, even met with him on occasion. I know his weaknesses, Hound-Slayer. Killing him would not be easy, but I should think it a simpler task than the one you've already accomplished." He tapped the tooth he was holding. "It is only a matter of getting near enough to strike. And I have secrets that would aid you in this quest."

"It is madness," Ulithaine replied.

"It is opportunity," Oriv answered. "Opportunity for us both. For you, it is a chance to take revenge on the mad wizard once and for all. For me, it is a chance to free these lands from his tyranny. With him gone, we could see the south returned to greatness. Then, by my hand, a vengeance will be lain upon those cities that aided him. One so fierce as to make his hounds seem trivial. And for you, the rewards would be great. Tenfold the contents of this chest for Krishind's head. I pledge and swear it will be so."

Ulithaine turned to those present. "Phaesha. What say you?"

"It is death to challenge Krishind," she replied. "But we did this when we killed his hound. If you agree, I will be with you."

"Brithol? Thirove? How about it? Will you stand with me before glory or death? Will you fight by my side against one who controls powers untold?"

"If you'll have us," Thirove said.

"And if you supply us with wine," Brithol added.

"Heh," Ulithaine chuckled. "Then it is all but settled. Alaji," he said, shifting languages. "Alaji. When I finish speaking, no matter what, nod. Then, when you know the time's right, deal with the guard to your right."

Alaji and Yemerik grew pale, but she nodded nonetheless. Yemerik began to stutter, "Wait," but Ulithaine ignored him.

"She's agreed!" Ulithaine proclaimed. He leaned over the table and extended an open hand to Oriv, who clasped his wrist tightly. "Brithol, Thirove. It seems we'll be killing a wizard!"

Oriv smiled. Then, with a splintering crack, his expression changed to pain, horror, and rage, as Ulithaine's grip shifted from wrist to hand and crushed the bones in his fingers.

"Alaji! Now! Phaesha! The bowmen!" Ulithaine yanked the wizard forward even as he called out his instructions. The old man's thin body landed against the table in front of Ulithaine. Plates of pork and boiled eggs overturned and broke against the frozen floor. The courtesans screamed and retreated to a far corner.

Alaji's count was only on two.

Still holding her wine glass, she darted to one side, feigning weakness and fear as her mother had taught her. She watched the warrior go for his sword and step forward. She focused on that point in space and time and waited. This was three. Behind him, six guards posted by the door raised their crossbows. Phaesha was quicker, though. She swung her arms in an arch and called forth waves of fire, which washed over the guards. They were barely singed, but they flinched away from the coming flame, buying time.

Four. The guard pulled free his sword. The wizard struggled with his free hand, while Ulithaine pummeled him mercilessly. Oriv gestured, and a wild, frigid wind filled the room. The tapestries whipped away from the walls, and pieces of food, cloth napkins, and decorative objects rolled and bounced along the floor. They were at the heart of a storm.

Five. The guard stepped forward, shielding himself with his free arm. He ignored Alaji, and she dove behind him. She reached out with one hand and swung her glass with the other. Then she stepped back to three.

The wineglass shattered against the startled guard's face, as Alaji grabbed the handle of his sheathed sword. Her count started once more: this was one. The guard stumbled, and Alaji pulled on the handle of the blade. He lashed out with one hand, grabbing her arm, while he clutched his face with the other. Blood trickled between his fingers.

Alaji neither gave up her grip or her count. The angle was wrong for her to pull the sword from its sheath, but she didn't need to free it. She shifted, and he moved to counter, stepping away. This was two.

With the hilt in hand, she stepped back to one. The wizard's spell was just starting. The guard was where he'd been, but Alaji was a step away holding his sword. Not realizing the blades were one and the same, he clutched at the empty air above his sheath.

Now this moment was one.

The weapon was heavy. Alaji swung it with all her might. The guard leapt straight back, easily avoiding it. Two. He stared Alaji in the eye as she pointed it directly at him. He ducked to one side, testing her. But it was futile, because she wasn't holding the blade in front of her to keep him at bay.

She was aiming to kill him.

She stepped back to one, before he'd jumped to one side. The man's body merged with metal in an explosion of blood, and the swirling winds spattered the icy walls red. The guard's body went limp, its weight pulling against the tip of Alaji's sword, trying her strength. She stepped forward now, two heartbeats into the future, and the sword, though chipped, was free. The body lay at her feet in a pool of blood.

The fight had skipped ahead, as well. The wizard's second hand was broken. He called out, and shards of snow and ice materialized in the winds. Thirove and Brithol had charged the startled guards and were fighting for their lives, while Phaesha was throwing small spheres of fire at the ones they couldn't reach.

Yemerik, wisely, was huddled in a corner beside the courtesans and musician.

Ulithaine grabbed the serving fork before it could slide off the table. "As you say!" He shouted. "The hard part is getting close enough to a wizard to strike!" He drove it downward into Oriv's chest, splintering bone and piercing organs.

The wizard howled. "You think I am so easily felled?" He cried out a word, and the table began rising from the ground. Ulithaine brought his two fists down together against the wizard's head, driving him and the table back down to the floor. "Even if you win, you will be damned," Oriv shouted, through a broken jaw. "My spirit will hunt you to the ends of the earth!"

Ulithaine held up his open palm, as if expecting to catch something. Then, laughing, he shouted, "Hunt all you like! I think you'll be disappointed." Then, "Alaji! The sword! Two seconds ago!"

Alaji stepped back and threw the sword, just as Ulithaine raised his arm to catch it. "Hunt all you like! You'll only be disappointed!" Then he swung the blade downward, severing the wizard's head.

PART 7: ASH AND FIRE

1

Ulithaine did not run. His was a swagger, sword in one hand, head of the wizard dangling by the hair in the other. The guards were speechless. They were terrified. The wind inside the room had died down, but echoing through the halls they could hear the whistle of cold air swooping off the glacier and spilling down into the city. The mystical lights which had illuminated the halls went dark.

One of the men charged forward, screaming obscenities at the man who'd killed his master. Ulithaine's expression was a mocking one. He held the wizard's head in line with the warrior's initial swing, forcing him to stop short or slice into it. Then Ulithaine half turned and batted the soldier's sword away with ease.

"Do you throw your lives away?" He demanded. "Are you without families? Friends? Do you not see what is happening here?" He held his arms out to either side and motioned around him. "Sorcery upheld this. Sorcery gave this place life. And I have severed that magic's head. If you think yourselves mighty, come take revenge! If you think that your pampered lives in this oasis have prepared you to match arms against one who wrestled serpents. Who slew Krishind's hound. Who killed the ice-wizard!" He shook the head at them. "Then face me! If you think your aim is true, try and see whether your bolts are faster than my companions' magic! Otherwise stand aside!" He bellowed this at them, and the guards fell back, tears in their eyes. The nearest turned and made for the door. He almost tripped over the others who dropped whatever weapons they carried and did the same. The courtesans and musician followed closely behind.

"Tell any you see to flee if they value their lives! Tell them they may make it if they hurry. But to hinder us is death! And if any take those things we left at the gate, we will hunt them down and feed their bodies to crows!" He turned to his people. "Arm yourselves!" he motioned to the guards' abandoned weapons. "Thirove! Gather some of this food. Brithol! Bring our reward for the hound's teeth. Phaesha! The wizard's box looks to contain other treasures our host has no further need of! Make haste, all of you! It will be chaos out there, and I'd have this city behind me before the worst of it!"

Yemerik was grinding his teeth. He poked at the corpse of the guard near him and found a dagger strapped to the body's leg. He removed it, wiped some of the blood off its handle, and found a spot in his belt. Then he offered some help to Thirove, who was trying to convert a tapestry into a makeshift sack.

Alaji, meanwhile, was trying to make sense of what was happening. She'd fought and killed alongside Ulithaine and his men, but she still had no idea what the fight had been about. She assumed she'd have had a better understanding if she'd been able to hear what they were saying.

In less than a minute, they started for the exit. At first, Ulithaine led cautiously, stopping to peer around corners before proceeding. Eventually, he called Alaji forward. "I could die any moment. Stay behind me and shout out to me before I do." He didn't wait for a response but nodded and hurried ahead. Alaji's count started, but they met no opposition as they charged through the building.

"What is happening?" she managed to ask Yemerik, as they neared the exit leading out of the central tower.

"I believe Ulithaine wanted one last story before leaving his time," Yemerik responded angrily. "And because of that, we have to race for our lives."

"But this will help, won't it? It will make things better." There was a great deal Alaji didn't know, but she had seen the forest of the dead and the room of frozen mages. And she understood that Oriv had created things as bad as the beast, even if that particular monstrosity had been the work of his rival.

"It's not that simple," Yemerik muttered, following the warriors into the sunlight. All but two of the guards outside the tower had abandoned their posts, and the pair that remained didn't look ready for a battle. They were as terrified as anyone Alaji had ever seen, but they held their positions to either side of the doorway. The gardens hadn't frosted over yet, nor had the streams and ponds turned solid. But they would. It was only a matter of time.

Meanwhile, the land before them was full of men, women, and children trying to find loved ones or reach shelter. Some seemed confused; others were terrified. Alaji heard shouting, crying, and even anxious laughter. One man sat silently on the ground ten paces from the stairs with a blank expression on his face.

Ulithaine stared the nearest guard down as he passed, but said nothing. They didn't move to stop him, nor did they speak.

Yemerik, carrying a smaller sack, paused. "This isn't some test of loyalty. This is happening. Get your families, get something warm and some water, and make for the surface." The guards traded glances but didn't move. "Dammit! I don't know how long all of this will stand without him. Do you understand?" He shook his head, frustrated, and ran to catch up with Alaji.

"Are we in danger?" she asked, keeping an eye on three soldiers who seemed to be trailing them.

"Of course we're in danger." Yemerik looked at Ulithaine, who had drawn several yards ahead of them. "He destroyed everything these people had. It will be a miracle if a tenth of them survive. We need to get out of here and hope we make it back to the cliffs before anyone catches up to us looking for blood."

"Let them come!" It was Phaesha, who Yemerik hadn't realized was close behind them. "They grew fat in the wizard's shadow while kingdoms burned. We are bred in that fire! We are what comes of it!"

"Phaesha!" Ulithaine shouted, having caught the edge of the conversation. "Leave it! Look around. We're being stalked." To either side, about forty yards out, bowmen were edging towards them. "Give them a fright!"

She chanted quickly, weaving a spell in the air, then swung out at the first group, and then the second. An explosion of fire erupted on either side.

"Hear me!" Ulithaine cried out, waving the wizard's head wildly. "We are bringers of death! Come and claim it!" One of the men loosed an arrow, but it missed its mark by a good five feet, sailing over their heads.

Phaesha glared at the man who'd fired and pointed two fingers directly at him. She concentrated and began to cast, but before she finished, Alaji shoved her hard. Phaesha spun back angrily, but froze as an arrow shot directly between the two women. Alaji nodded and pointed at the second group, right at the man who'd nearly killed her.

With a cry of rage, Phaesha began hurling fire at both groups. A few flames struck, lighting clothing and scorching flesh.

Ulithaine turned to his right, while Brithol turned to the left. They readied their weapons for battle and prepared to charge.

"We don't have time for this!" Yemerik screamed. "We need to leave before the walls collapse!" He was speaking as much to the guards as to Ulithaine, but no one seemed interested.

"If they want death…." Ulithaine snarled. He started forward, but froze when he heard Alaji's voice.

"Forget them. Keep the others at bay," she commanded, then immediately vanished, reappeared, vanished. She closed the distance between herself and the men in front of her before they could regroup.

Phaesha turned to focus her magic on the other group. Brithol and Thirove concentrated their attention in that direction, as well, in case any arrows came their way. But Ulithaine watched the fight.

It was less than one-sided. Alaji did not give the soldiers a target to strike. She moved swiftly, without weapon drawn or plan. Her foes reacted as she'd come to expect. Their bows were nothing. Most dropped them at her impossible approach; the ones who didn't became her first priority. One guard fitted an arrow and drew back his string, only for Alaji to appear at his side. With a touch, her spell of weaving snapped the string, and she was gone again. Another held a knife and swung it wildly. She appeared in front of him, and he swung for her, unaware the blade was gone. She vanished again, and he fell over, the knife now lodged in his leg. A dropped bow was in Alaji's hands, and one end burned brightly.

The men scattered like rabbits. She let those who'd lost or abandoned their bows go. The others, she hunted down, taking their weapons or wounding them. It took only seconds for her to dismantle the group. Seconds later, she was back on the path, panting.

Phaesha dealt with the others quickly enough. She called the winds to toss the few arrows they loosed off course, then hurled flame until they gave up and ran off. She turned to Ulithaine, but he was already focused on their goal. As they charged forward, a cracking sound echoed through the city.

No one else tried to stop them until they reached the stairway leading to the surface. Five guards blocked the way, swords drawn. Ulithaine displayed the wizard's head to them as if it were some sort of pass. They responded by charging ahead.

Ulithaine answered in kind. With a grunt, he gripped his sword with both hands, and swung. Oriv's head, still held by the hair, followed behind awkwardly, but it didn't throw off his aim. Metal clashed, and the blade of the nearest soldier was turned away. Its owner spun, exposing his back, and the edge of Ulithaine's sword whipped back, biting through leather and flesh. The wound wasn't deep, but it was enough to send him reeling, clutching at the cut.

The next two attacked together, but one fell back as a blast of fire shot towards him. Ulithaine made short work of the other: he dodged the guard's clumsy swing, stabbed him through the gut, then stole the dying man's sword to replace the one left in the guard's belly. The next came at him, swinging, only to be knocked back. He blocked Ulithaine's blow, but the force threw him to the ground. Before he could regain his footing, Thirove knocked him unconscious with a kick.

The remaining two fell back, withdrawing into the stairwell.

"We haven't time for this," Ulithaine said.

Phaesha motioned towards them, spoke an incantation, then jerked her hand back. A blast of wind rushed out of the opening, carrying the guards with it. They fell, sprawled on the ground like fish knocked from the water. They tried for their swords, but Ulithaine made short work of one and Phaesha the other. Brithol started towards the surviving guard, who was still nursing the cut on his back, but Ulithaine raised his hand. "He was foolish but brave. If he can escape in time, let him." With that, he ran into the tunnel.

The stairway spiraled up the height of the glacier, and almost the entire way was in darkness. Phaesha conjured a sphere of light and held it above her head. All around them, the ice creaked. Echoing cracks reverberated through the hallways, and drove them on despite fatigue brought on by the seemingly endless stairs.

They passed a pair of refugees a third of the way up and another small group around the halfway mark. The first two were a young couple, huddled together in the dark, making their way up step by step. As the warriors approached, they held each other and pressed up against the ice wall. Ulithaine let them be, though he sneered at the sound of their whimpering.

The second group consisted entirely of men, and – unlike the first – had something he wanted.

"The torch," he said. The men looked at each other, then at those confronting them, as if sizing up their chances. "The torch. Now," Ulithaine added.

"Wait. We have an extra," one of them said, removing an unlit torch from his pack. "I just… I need to light it." He held the torches together until the second flared up. His hands were shaking as he handed the first torch over.

"That one, too," Brithol said.

"No. They dealt fairly," Ulithaine said, before turning to the men. "I'd tell you that you could follow us up, but if you couldn't outrun us with a lead, I doubt you'll be able to keep pace with us the rest of the way." With that, he hurried on with his men, Phaesha, Alaji, and Yemerik close behind him.

—

They were exhausted when they reached the top. Even Ulithaine leaned against a wall to catch his breath. Ulithaine's torch had burned out, so Phaesha pulled a tapestry from a nearby wall, rolled it into as tight a cylinder as she could manage, then lit one end. She handed this over then conjured her own light again.

The smoke was bitter, but at least the flames shed some additional light around the room. They'd reached the opening where Oriv had kept his trophies – those enchanters and conjurers who'd dared use magic in his domain. "Don't," Ulithaine said, good-naturedly but still forcefully, when he saw Phaesha eyeing one of them. "I don't think all of us would enjoy the sight if it melted." He cast a quick glance at Alaji.

"I wasn't going to," Phaesha replied. "I already proved his rules didn't scare me."

"I think our guest has come far enough," Ulithaine said. He tossed the wizard's head on top of one of the frozen pillars. "And now the collection is complete!" Brithol and Thirove chuckled. Yemerik simply looked away. Ulithaine snapped his fingers to get Yemerik's attention. "What's the matter? Troubled by a little cold? Or would you have preferred we bowed low to the great Oriv, master of the northern ice and all below him."

Yemerik breathed deeply, visibly trying to contain himself, but his rage boiled out. He spoke in Alaji's tongue, so only Alaji,

Phaesha, and Ulithaine could understand. "It was dangerous and pointless. We could have all been killed."

"No point? We rid the world of a maker of monsters. We freed lands of his control and saved countless from the fates of his enemies." He motioned around the room. "You saw the forest of dead: how much larger would that grove have grown? How many more would have died as he moved against the lands Krishind loved? Or his other rivals, for that matter?"

"And what of the people here? How many of them will be crushed when this city collapses or freeze to death on the ice fields?"

"They brought it on themselves!" Phaesha said, stepping in.

"They did what they had to in order to survive," Yemerik said.

"At whose expense?" Phaesha demanded.

"Some of them will likely live," Ulithaine added. "The strong, the smart, the ambitious: there's time."

"Not for the old," Yemerik said. "Or the young."

"I have no patience for this," Ulithaine said. "You know nothing of this world or its troubles. You come from a soft time. This era is not one for soft people."

"Obviously!" Yemerik replied. "Which is why I've been trying to get out since the moment I realized it was inhabited by monsters and madmen!" He was standing now, yelling directly at Ulithaine.

The warrior stared down at him. His muscles tensed, and he ground his teeth. Then, he laughed. "I think I was wrong about you, Yemerik! There's some strength behind those eyes, after all!" He patted Yemerik on the shoulder, nearly knocking him to the ground. "Come on. There'll be guards ahead, followed by a long trek back across the frozen wastes. And then we've still a cliff to contend with." He started onward, and his men followed after him. Phaesha paused to glance at Yemerik briefly, though he couldn't tell what was going through her head. When their backs were turned, he shivered.

"Are you alright?" Alaji asked.

"Not really," he muttered. "I can't tell whether he let me live because he likes me, feels obligated to do so, or because he knew you'd turn on them if he cut off my head."

"We should hurry," Alaji said.

They moved on cautiously. The makeshift torch had burned out, and they went on in darkness, save the dim light from Phaesha's spell. Before long, they arrived at the gate room, which was mercifully lit with a number of torches and by a shaft of daylight pouring in through the jagged remains of the wall that had stood there. The rest of the ice lay scattered just beyond the opening, likely the final act of the battering ram.

The room had changed since they'd last come through. It was colder, of course, but no more so than the corridors they'd just left. The furnace was gone, as well. It hadn't simply burned out, but melted down into the ice. In its place was a massive slick of re-frozen water.

There were a dozen guards in the room and, from the sound of it, more outside. There were also a handful of refugees who must have run up the stairs at the first sign of trouble. The guards saw the warriors approach and readied their weapons, but they didn't look likely to start a fight. Ulithaine glanced down at the sword he'd brought from below. "This isn't fit for a training blade," he said, tossing it on the floor. It slid towards the soldiers. Then he walked past them towards the room they'd left their equipment in. No one moved to stop him.

He pulled on the door, but it was stuck in the ice. Thirove set the sack of stolen food down and helped him, while Phaesha began chipping away at the ice with small darts of flame. Finally, the seal shattered and the door opened. They hurried in and gathered their belongings, strapping on layers of fur, chains to help them traverse the ice, and other items. Phaesha located her charm and tied it around her wrist, and everyone armed themselves with their old weapons.

As they emerged, one of the guards spoke up. "What's happening down there?

"Death," Ulithaine replied, plainly. "The city is dying, and anyone who stays will suffer the same fate."

"That's impossible," one of the other guards said. "Oriv would never—"

"The wizard's dead," Ulithaine said, then added casually, "I left his head down the hall with his friends."

The guards tensed up at this and raised their weapons, though none charged. "Our lord is eternal," one said. "You blaspheme!"

Ulithaine laughed at them. "Go have a look, if you don't believe me. Or better yet, look around you. The enchantment is gone from this place. Listen to the breaking of ice. The city is fallen by my hand. Come and try to claim vengeance if you like, but you'll fare no better than those before you. We bring magic and strength beyond understanding. If your wizard fell to us, what chance have his servants?"

The men stood their ground, but still none approached. They traded quick glances, as if trying to determine their best choice of action. One glanced at a crossbow set nearby only to see the string catch fire and snap.

"I would kill you all for delaying us," Ulithaine said. "But I am not without sympathy. There will be others coming up soon. This place" – he stomped his foot – "this place is not safe. When the cliff gives – and it will – this will all spill into the hole below. Any who would live should make for the glacier's edge. Most will die on the way. More will die trying to descend the cliffs. But all who stay here will be buried. Tell them and give them what you can. Or take what supplies you have and leave the rest to die. It is the same to me!" With that, he started towards the door, and the guards parted to let him through.

2

Once more, they tied themselves together in case the ice gave way. They took no break; it was already late morning, leaving them little time to reach the far cliffs by nightfall. Behind them, the occasional crack sounded, like lightning beneath their feet. Ahead of them lay the forest of the dead.

"There," Ulithaine pointed, as they approached. A form of light and mist walked slowly across the surface. "They are free, at least." He turned to Yemerik, but didn't seem to be mocking him.

"After decades imprisoned, I wouldn't count on them retaining enough reason to understand which side we were on or to care. When they were trapped, they weren't dangerous."

"I don't fear the dead," Ulithaine retorted, though he seemed less confident than usual.

"Well I do," Yemerik said. "Ghosts operate on inconsistent principles when they're improperly bound. I don't like fighting things you can trust to bleed, let alone those you can't."

"You've crossed them before?" It was fleeting, but for an instant there was almost a hint of respect in Ulithaine's voice.

"Not like this. Not in the open. But I've studied a little. And a friend of mine was a specialist in spectromancy. That means... I assume you can figure out what that means." He turned to Phaesha. "If it's hostile, do you have magic that can turn it back?"

She shook her head. "I do not know. I have heard the dead fear flame."

"Not all of them," Yemerik replied. "We should steer clear of the apparition if possible. Otherwise, if it comes over, I'll try conversing with it. If it attacks, try... anything. Fire, wind, arrows, blades... anything."

"What good is steel against a spirit?" Ulithaine asked.

"That depends on the spirit. They're more emotion than reason. If it thinks a sword through its chest will rip it apart and leave it a quivering mass, it might revert to that state for a while. Maybe even pass outside of the physical realm to reenter the cycle, the way it should have the first time. Of course, it's just as likely all that's left will be rage and hunger."

"And if that's so?" Ulithaine asked.

"If that's the case, we better hope it can't figure out how to touch physical objects. The only positive part of this is that it probably didn't learn too many tricks while it was trapped in the ice."

They pressed west to try and avoid the specter. It seemed to drift towards them anyway, though it moved slowly. They picked up their pace and continued southwest.

"There," Phaesha said, pointing to their left. "Another one." A second spirit hovered a few feet above the ice, arms raised above its head, as if held by some imaginary shackles. It was drifting slowly parallel to them, carried by the wind.

"It's mimicking the pose its body was left in," Yemerik said.

"Is it content there?" Brithol asked, gripping the handle of his battle ax tightly. "Or will it come for us as soon as we cross some unseen boundary?"

"I have no idea. But if we stay here, his friend will catch up before long." Yemerik pointed back towards the other spirit. "We could circle back. Look for another way around."

"We've wasted too much time as it is," Ulithaine responded. "We risk more by staying on the ice longer than necessary. We press on, straight ahead. If our way is blocked by man, beast, demon, or spirit, we will do as we've always done. And if this is to be the day we are brought low, let us die rejoicing in the deeds we've performed." His men offered their normal round of cheers, but they were far less enthusiastic than usual.

The floating ghost simply drifted on as they walked past. The other shadowed them for several hours, sometimes gaining and sometimes losing ground, until finally they looked back to discover it was gone. None of them could say whether it sank into the ice, flew into the air, or simply faded into nothing, but they seemed to be free of it at least.

The rest of their journey was cold and unpleasant, but otherwise uneventful. It was early evening when they reached the cliff and falls, leaving them with two unpleasant options. Either they could descend the steep path down in the dark or camp on the glacier and chance survivors from the ice city catching up with them in the night. Despite the edge they'd have in combat, even Ulithaine seemed wary of facing an unknown number of assailants who'd lost countless friends and family and were half frozen. There comes a point when pain and loss have stripped away so much, someone has nothing left to fear – only a fool confronts such adversaries.

So they began the descent down the icy trail. They used their ropes as best they could, looping them around frozen outcroppings they hoped would hold, then started down, sliding along the path. They went single-file, with Ulithaine leading, as always, Brithol next, then Alaji, Phaesha, Yemerik, and Thirove in back carrying the treasure.

To one side, the cliff towered over them, casting a dark shadow that blotted out the moon and stars. On the other side, there was a sheer drop to the next switchback, if not all the way to the ground. The wind snapped at their capes, as if trying to flick them over the edge, and what little light found its way to them merely left them with a sense of vertigo. The world gave them few gifts: the occasional patch of bare rock where the ice had been melted away by the sun, a few sections of rough snow offering a bit of traction, and sometimes an outcropping to grab hold of.

They went slowly, often skidding into each other. Then, when they were passing around a bend a third of the way down, Thirove propped himself up against an icy ledge to change direction, and it broke apart under him.

Alaji's count had been cycling the entire time, and she immediately stepped back a few seconds. "Look out!" she cried, trying to warn him.

His body jerked to attention, and he fell against the ice. He kicked out to balance himself, but only succeeded in striking the ice, which split off. He slid off the edge, snapping the rope like a bow string. Alaji leapt for his location and stepped back a second time. Her hands grabbed the rope an instant after he fell off, but it tore free of her grip. Once again, it went taut, and Yemerik and Phaesha were pulled off before the rope broke.

Alaji pulled her knife free and swung it at where the rope had been. Then she stepped back in time as far as she could manage, just after she'd failed to catch Thirove. The rope broke off there, and Thirove fell alone with their treasure, shouting briefly as he tumbled twenty feet to where the path crossed below them. He struck hard and went limp, as his momentum carried him over that edge and the next. Then the night swallowed him, and all that was left was the sound of a body bouncing off of ice, followed by a long pause and the thud of him striking the rock below.

"Murderer!" Brithol bellowed, lunging towards Alaji.

Ulithaine caught him and forced him against the cliff. "Easy!" the warrior commanded.

"Why did you cut him free?" Phaesha demanded. "We were tied! The rope would have caught him!"

"Quiet!" Ulithaine demanded. "She tried that. Didn't you?"

Alaji nodded. "The rope snapped. A few feet past Phaesha. The cliff took her and Yemerik, too."

"You could have saved them!" Brithol said.

"I couldn't!" Alaji said. "I can only go so far, and only if I'm ready."

"It's true," Ulithaine said, patiently. "I've been paying attention. She has a few seconds to act, that's all. Then what's done is done."

The fight left Brithol after that. He slumped down, tears welling in his eyes. "He was like a brother to me," he said to Ulithaine.

"He was more than that," Ulithaine replied, then shrugged. "Don't look surprised. I have eyes. I'm sorry." He released the massive fighter. "He'd be grateful, though. That Alaji's quick thinking kept us from losing anyone else. He wouldn't want that on his soul, the guilt of taking his companions down with him."

"It's true," Brithol said. He turned to Alaji. "I ask your pardon. It was a moment's madness, nothing more." He glanced at her. "You've slipped your rope," he added.

Like before, it hadn't come with her when she stepped back in time. "I'm sorry," she said, while knotting the loop back through her belt.

"I guess the wizard's speaking stone is working," Ulithaine said. Alaji realized he was right: she was speaking their language and hadn't even realized. She nodded slowly. It hardly seemed important.

—

It was late in the night when they reached the ground, but they didn't sleep. First, they went in search of Thirove's body, which they found on the rocky floor. Alaji expected Brithol to weep when he approached, but he simply knelt beside the corpse and began cutting the bindings that held the chest of treasure. He removed it carefully and handed it over to Ulithaine. The chest was intact, though a corner was splintered.

Then he began gathering plants. He pulled up dozens of small brushes and reeds, then laid them around the body. Finally, he removed his outer furs and set them down, as well. Ulithaine and Phaesha did the same.

Alaji took off hers, as they had, but Yemerik stopped her. "We may want these again," he reminded her. She pushed him away, pulled off the extra coverings, and set the furs around the body.

"Phaesha," Brithol said. "Would you light it?"

"Alaji's fires burn hotter. Let her do it. She fought beside us. She's the same right as I."

Brithol nodded to Alaji, who knelt down and cast her spell of the hearth on the capes and hats, which caught immediately. She shifted around the pyre, casting several more times, so even if one section burned out, there'd be others to keep the fire going.

It was a fire her mother would have been proud of. The magic burned hot and deep, and despite the pitiful fuel, it consumed the body, casting a plume of black smoke into the air. Brithol stood directly in the smoke and inhaled, choking back a cough. Then he stepped aside and Ulithaine did the same. When he'd finished, Ulithaine said, "Thirove performed many feats and went on many adventures at our side. And countless more before that. But he has reached his end on this journey. Would that we all could die after so great a deed."

Phaesha stepped into the smoke and inhaled while Brithol spoke up. "In song, they should remember him for the battle in the palace of ice. The slaying of the wizard and the felling of the guards. He should have died there or battling the dead. Not a misplaced foot on a path of ice. When I tell this tale, I will tell it different. I will say he died fighting a dozen soldiers, the dead wizard's wine in his throat, a concubine on his arm. That's how I'll tell the tale."

"That's how we will all tell it," Ulithaine said. He looked to Alaji once Phaesha stepped out of the smoke. "It's an old custom. Perhaps a barbaric one. Our people used to think spirits clothed themselves in the smoke of the dead. We take him in, to make his spirit one with ours, so he can continue on in our deeds and adventures. I know it's not your way. But he would be honored."

Alaji stepped into the smoke and breathed in. Her lungs burned, but that was right. That was as it should be. The spirit of a warrior should burn.

She stepped away to keep from spoiling the moment by coughing out loud. They sat together until the fire burned out, then rested as well as they could on the soggy ground.

No one had asked Yemerik to partake in the ritual, nor had he tried to join in.

3

They traveled southwest through the bog, trudging through shallow streams and muddy banks. Alaji managed to catch a few fish the first night, which they roasted into a stew with some root vegetables Brithol gathered. The meal wasn't much, but it was better than nothing.

As it grew dark, she sat with Phaesha and compared the basics of their fire-making spells. They began with hand formations, which were key to the invocation. There were more similarities than differences in their techniques. They were, essentially, different variations of the same spell. The motions to protect the flesh from being burned were built from the same concepts Alaji had always used to set branches and reeds on fire: it was simply a case of inverting some movements, slowing others, and adding in a few flourishes she'd never been taught.

Phaesha had terms for every movement, and she was versed in far more versions. But as soon as Alaji saw her cast up close, she realized Phaesha lacked the subtle control the women in Alaji's village possessed. Phaesha's fingers quivered if she held a form too long, and she had trouble with movements Alaji had mastered as a child. Alaji had been told her people had spent far longer mastering each task than most wizards. But she'd never really seen what that meant up close. Phaesha had a wider range of abilities, but she lacked Alaji's depth. Acquiring that would take years of work, and it was unlikely Phaesha would be willing to focus that intensely on a single spell.

Alaji showed her exercises she'd learned from her mother long ago. Phaesha wouldn't be able to cast the spell of the hearth as fluidly as Alaji any time soon, but they'd likely help her increase control and intensify the strength of her fire.

Before the end of the first night, Alaji was able to protect her fingertips from being scorched while casting. She could even hold a reed between her fingers, light it on fire, then continue holding it while it burned. The technique was so simple, she wasn't even bothered that she was learning magic beyond the realm of women. How could she be, when it was clearly a natural extension of the spell she'd been raised to cast?

Phaesha, satisfied that Alaji had learned the basics, conjured a handful of fire out of the air and hurled it into the stream they were camping by. The blast fizzled out, but not before splashing water against the far rocks and sending a cloud of steam into the night air. "Watch my hands," Phaesha said, repeating the motions. Once more, they formed patterns Alaji knew: first the protection spell she'd just learned, then the incantation to focus heat she'd been taught as a child. But Phaesha held no object to release the heat into. She channeled the energy into the air itself and shifted her hands to shape the fire. "Do you see?" she asked, and Alaji nodded. "Good," Phaesha said, before tossing the second ball of flame into the sand, where it flattened out to be quenched by the gentle waves of the stream. "Then do as I did."

Alaji nodded and closed her eyes to concentrate. She copied the motions she'd just seen, first the protection, then the invocation. But halfway through she felt her hands shaking. This was wrong, unnatural. The spells of the hearth existed to warm a home. Even when she repurposed them for war, they were still a woman's magic. This had no use but combat. It was theirs no longer: this magic belonged to something different.

"Stop," Phaesha said. "You have lost the spell."

"I'm sorry," Alaji said. "Could you show me one more time?"

Phaesha opened her palm and began the motions. Alaji watched, as if she'd forgotten, but really she simply wanted a moment to rest and think. Her gods were the stuff of children's stories, she told herself. But, here, in this time of oceans of ice, enchanted castles, and beasts as large as the Lord of Boars, they seemed more real than ever. She could convince herself they weren't real, but she couldn't ignore the feeling they were somehow watching her.

"Do you have it?" Phaesha asked. "Or should I demonstrate yet again?" There was less bite to her voice than Alaji would have expected. Still, the point was clear.

"No," Alaji said. "I think I have it."

"Then show me." When she taught, her demeanor changed. Alaji had already become accustomed to two versions of Phaesha. The first was the sneering, acerbic sorceress who followed Ulithaine around and occasionally threatened to kill one of their company. The second was the curious young woman who appeared when the two of them were alone. This new personality was poised and controlled like the first, but she lacked the cruelty. She was focused, patient, and direct. If Alaji had to guess, she'd have said she was learning what Phaesha's mother was like.

Alaji began the spell again. This time, she kept her eyes open. She traced the pattern of protection and began the spell of invocation. Again, she felt it. The uneasy sense her gods were watching her break their laws. But now she grew angry instead of scared. If Yemerik was wrong, if they did exist, it wouldn't matter whether she failed this spell, refused Phaesha's teaching, or mastered the magic: she'd already taken a spell that wasn't meant for her. That wasn't something the gods forgave. Learning another couldn't make a difference. Not unless it gave her the power to fight them off.

It was an absurd notion. But it brought a grin to her face and steadied her fingers as she finished the motions and whispered the spell. Why not? She'd helped slay a wizard in this time, a man who'd lived for centuries and controlled power that rivaled her people's legends. If he could be killed, perhaps there were better strategies than begging her gods' forgiveness.

As she finished the spell, fire exploded around her hand. It didn't burn her, but she felt the heat against her forearms. She swung the mass at the stream, but aside from a few flames that fell away, it stayed in place like a clump of mud. She shook it, and more broke off, falling to burn out in the wet sand.

"Easy," Phaesha said behind her. "Do not be afraid. Reform it."

"I'm not afraid," Alaji said. "I... I've seen this. I've seen something like it."

"It is a common mistake."

"No," she said, tilting her hand, so some more of the fire slipped out. "I saw it done intentionally. An old woman...," she trailed off. "I'm sorry. I want to learn this right." She stepped to the edge of the water and dipped her hand in. The remaining fire was quenched instantly.

"Do you need to see the spell again?" Phaesha asked.

"No," Alaji replied. "I remember how it's done. And I think I know what I did wrong."

—

The next day, Alaji practiced as she hiked, plucking plants out of the ground and reducing them to cinders between her fingers or tossing clumps of flame into the marshes. She'd wandered a bit away from the group to get closer to a bush that was larger than most of those around her.

"Hold up."

She almost jumped when she heard Ulithaine's voice. There was little that seemed quiet about the man, but when he tried, he moved with the grace of a fox. She turned, briefly worried she was going somewhere she shouldn't, but his face was relaxed.

"Sorry. Wanted to make sure I didn't find myself at the wrong end of your sorcery. We still have days before I'll have a chance to change my clothes. The walk would feel longer if there was a hole burned through my tunic." He smiled, as he always smiled when there wasn't battle nearby.

Alaji found herself smiling, too. "Longer still with a scar branded to your chest," she said. "You move too softly."

"An old habit," he said. "What are you doing out here?"

In lieu of an answer, she snapped off several branches, shoving them in an empty pouch. The last, she held up. It smoldered in her hand then erupted into flame. The leaves withered and fell away as embers. "What about you?" she asked.

"I wanted to speak. About what's next. About the gate and beyond."

"You should talk to Yemerik. He's the one who understands that sort of thing. I don't even know where he's planning on going next."

Ulithaine chuckled. "Why does it matter where or when Yemerik wants to go? If you wanted to go to one place and he another, what could he do but follow? It's that or die, isn't it? He lives by your generosity." There was no insinuation or insult evident in his tone. He said this the way he might comment on the weather or a bird flying overhead. It was an observation, nothing more.

"He's from a different time," she replied.

"That is plain to see. With you, it's less clear. I don't think I'd like a time where Yemerik fit in."

"You'd like my time even less," Alaji said.

"Is that where you're going then?" he asked.

"Not at first. I can't get back yet. I need help from Yemerik's people. Then... I don't know. There are things I need to do. After that, I'm not sure. After everything I've seen, a simple life among fishermen and farmers seems unfulfilling."

Ulithaine began laughing. "I'm sorry," he said. "I was just trying to imagine you as a fisherman's wife. It is not easy to picture, even after seeing you fish. Don't be insulted. I mean no disrespect to the profession, but it seems a waste of your talents. Unless everyone in your village controls time as you do."

"No. It's not like that. I'm not even supposed to.... It doesn't matter. Once I do what I need to, I'll find something more."

"Why not come with us?" he asked. He'd stopped laughing or even smiling. He was sincere, at least as far as Alaji could tell. "Listen,

I don't understand your quest or Yemerik's, for that matter. But you'd be better off with allies. We can help you reach your home. Then, once that's done, we could leave for a new era. Explore world after world."

"I'd need to speak with Yemerik," Alaji said, cautiously.

"If you choose to," Ulithaine replied. "But it's clear he needs you more than you need him. He sees your power as plainly as the rest of us. He knows he can't go on without you, can't even survive. Whatever he says will spring from that. He'll manipulate you to his own ends."

"That's true with you, as well," Alaji said. "Isn't it?"

"Of course it is! If you were a weak girl, I wouldn't offer an alliance. But you and I have strength. If you join us, I'll use that strength. I could overcome foes I couldn't otherwise, accomplish more than I could without you. This is how Yemerik views you, too. But I'm honest about it."

"He's honest," Alaji said. "We have an agreement: I'll help him return home, and he'll do the same for me."

"Tell me something, then. If he understands all of this, then why can't he get you home first? Or does it not seem convenient that your goals depend on his being achieved?" Ulithaine crossed his arms, and Alaji turned to go. "No, wait," he said. "Wait. I'm sorry. I hadn't meant to discuss this. Not in that way. I just wanted to offer my help. To keep our company together a little longer, at least, and not part ways at the other end of the portal. There's so much you could do to help us, and so much we could do to help you. Both of you. Who knows what else is out there. More like the hound, perhaps, or even worse. You could use the help."

Alaji sighed. "I will talk to Yemerik. And we'll decide what makes sense."

"Thank you," Ulithaine replied.

—

She didn't get a chance to speak with Yemerik that day. His

mood was too foul on the hike, and by the time she was finished practicing with Phaesha, he was sound asleep. She considered waking him, but it seemed a bad way to start the conversation.

Instead, she waited until the next morning. She woke to find Brithol gathering wood and Phaesha arguing with Ulithaine about the direction they should be walking in. When Yemerik was up, she motioned for him to walk with her. She didn't want the others hearing.

"What is it?" Yemerik asked.

"I spoke with Ulithaine yesterday," Alaji said. "He wants us to stay together after we're through the gate."

"Scratch the Jar," Yemerik cursed under his breath. Then he added, "Of course he does."

"He offered to help us reach the Citadel and then—"

"You told him about the Citadel?" Yemerik cut in.

"No. I told him you were trying to reach your people. That's all."

"Oh. Sorry. I thought you meant…," he trailed off while Alaji just stared at him.

"We don't know what we're going to come across, especially if you're right about someone tracking us. If we come across the old woman who broke the talisman, we'll be glad to have the help."

"Ulithaine is not magnanimous," Yemerik replied. "He is a coldblooded killer. Not much different than Hollik."

Alaji shook her head. He was nothing like Hollik, but she didn't want to debate that point. "He's not pretending to do this out of kindness. He can use our skills while we travel with him."

"Your skills, you mean."

Alaji shrugged. "Does that matter?"

"He… listen. He's used to getting what he wants. If you agree to travel with him, he'll find excuse after excuse to sidetrack us on various adventures and expeditions. He'll pull you so far away from what you want, you'll forget all about what you set out to accomplish."

"I will never forget my brother," Alaji said angrily.

"You'll never reach him, either," Yemerik said. "If you do this, he won't allow it."

"He'll help us," Alaji said. "He has no reason not to."

"He has every reason not to! He'd lose a sorceress who can manipulate time. He'd do anything to keep that from happening. Starting with killing me."

"I'd leave if he did that," Alaji said. "He knows I'd leave."

"Even if it wasn't his fault? Even if it looked like dumb luck or my own stupid decision? What would you have done if I'd fallen instead of Thirove? Because I promise you, if we stay with that man, he will make sure something like that happens. He'll arrange it or simply play the odds and wait for me to die. Hell, if someone else kills me, he'll probably avenge me then stand downwind while smoke pours off my body. But it would just be a matter of time."

"I'll keep you alive," Alaji said.

"You'd try. And probably keep succeeding for a while. But eventually you'd be too far away or too busy or something would happen you couldn't work around. Just like Thirove."

"Stop talking about him!" Alaji screamed.

Yemerik jumped back, surprised by the sudden outburst. "I know it wasn't your fault," he said, defensively.

"You don't know anything. I cut the rope to keep you from going over! If I hadn't been keeping an eye on you on the cliffs…." She shook her head but didn't finish the thought. Instead, she said, "You have no idea how many times I've saved your life."

"Probably not," Yemerik admitted. "But it will all have been for nothing if I'm killed on one of Ulithaine's idiotic quests for glory or treasure or whatever else he's after."

"We both almost died when we reached this time. Krishind's hound would have torn us apart if it weren't for Ulithaine's men. We're safer with them than we are alone."

"That's ludicrous. He was there to save us precisely because he's the kind of man who chases after things like that monster. Keeping around him means more of the same."

"He kills them, because they need killing," Alaji replied, defiantly. "Isn't that the sort of thing the Citadel is supposed to do?"

"At a large scale. With a logical methodology. The Assembly eliminates these sorts of problems at the source, before they even appear. We don't rush monstrosities while swinging swords and axes."

"Well, I don't see your Assembly here. Swords work well enough."

"The people living in the ice city might disagree with that."

"Is it so different than the cities the Citadel wipes away?"

"When the Citadel formalizes action on that scale, we consider the ramifications. There are career ethical specialists who review the decisions before and after they're put into effect. We take into account the long term historic trends and analyze the outcomes. We don't cut off someone's head because they make us angry or as some sort of poetic justice. And we sure as hell don't do things to get songs written about our exploits!"

"You have no right to judge these people. They saved your life. Besides, since when do you care when people die? On the plains, you wanted me to kill for you. You were angry when I showed restraint."

"Damn it. This isn't even about…." He let out a frustrated grunt. "No, you're right. I'm getting off track here. This isn't about murder. It's about whether we can trust them. And they've lied to us, used us, and endangered us. Sure, I'm grateful they didn't leave us to the hound. But that doesn't mean they're trustworthy. They're interested in legends and gold, not in our wellbeing, not in making the world a better place, and certainly not in returning you to your time."

"Ulithaine promised to help me. He said he'd help you get back, then help me do what I need to do."

"Once I reach the Citadel, they'll be able to take care of the rest. You won't need Ulithaine's help after that."

"What then? Am I supposed to go back to the life I had?"

Yemerik considered this silently for a moment. Finally, he answered, "Yes. But it won't be the same. Hollik won't come as fast. He won't be as bold. There's a very good chance it will all happen differently, and your people—"

"This isn't about them! I'm talking about me. Once my brother's safe and Hollik's dead or driven off, what am I supposed to do?"

"I don't know. Live your life, I suppose."

"I don't want that life," Alaji said. "Not anymore. You said you'd talk to your people."

"Yes. And I will. I'll explain who you are and what you've learned to do. I'll tell them that you want to work with us."

"You also said they'd refuse. That they'd want to send me back."

"It's possible they'll view this as a special case. They bring in experts sometimes." He shifted to keep from sinking into the mud. Firm ground was hard to find.

"What kind of experts?" Alaji asked.

"I don't know. All kinds. People who developed new philosophies and ways of looking at the world. Experts in history. Sorcerers who create unique types of magic."

"What about people like Ulithaine?"

"No. Of course not. He's a barbarian."

"Then what am I?" Alaji asked.

Yemerik shut his eyes and took a deep breath. "I already told you. You're not like them. You're not like him, no matter how hard he tries to make you forget that."

"I'm more like them than I'm like you," Alaji said. Her voice had quieted. She was calmer now than she'd been, more focused. "Helping Ulithaine isn't the same as working for the Citadel, but it's better than fishing. It means more, anyway."

"Then why draw this out? Pull out your knife and kill me. If you really want to be like Ulithaine – if you don't care about your home or your people or giving your brother a chance – go ahead."

Alaji rolled her eyes. "Don't be stupid."

"I'm trying to be honest. If we stay with Ulithaine, this isn't going to end at the Citadel or your village. It ends with me dead and you taking them through time to have pointless adventures that supposedly bring you closer and closer to your brother, but you never quite get there. If we don't get away from them, I'm as good as dead, anyway. So no pretending. No dramatic twist where I slip off a cliff or get eaten by a giant octopus after some plan goes wrong. Just kill me and be done with it. I promise you, they won't be mad."

Without another word, Alaji stormed off.

4

The morning of the third day finally brought them to trees. Not towering forests or lush groves, but even limp pines barely taller than a man were a welcome sight. The game improved, as well. Alaji managed to kill a pair of hens and several squirrels, along with catching a half-dozen fish. Phaesha had watched her work and gasped when Alaji's arm would seem to appear in the water instantly. Her astonishment made it difficult for Alaji to feel embarrassed about the times she withdrew her hand empty after misjudging how the water bent the light.

It was all unnecessary, of course. The streams were full of fish, and they could have just as easily made a net. But no one suggested this, and Alaji was happy to show off her skill, in no small part because it grated on Yemerik, who clearly would have preferred she refrained from demonstrating her magic to Ulithaine or any of his people. But after their argument, Alaji found it difficult to care what he wanted.

She did not, however, commit to Ulithaine's proposed alliance. He asked again, soon after. "Did you speak with Yemerik?" He came up on her as before, unheard or seen, at a time when there was no one else nearby.

"You know I did," Alaji said.

"How do I know that?" His voice was playful.

"Because we're acting strangely. And avoiding each other. Or did you stop noticing things like that."

This clearly amused him. "Not entirely. I take it he didn't embrace the idea."

"He doesn't trust you," Alaji said.

"Of course not. I'm reckless. Timid people tend to have problems with that."

"I don't trust you, either," Alaji said. "Am I timid, too?"

"No," Ulithaine replied, "Just cautious. The real question is, do you trust him?"

"I trust him not to give up. And I trust him to get me home as he promised. That's enough for now." Her voice wasn't as firm as she'd meant it to be, and Ulithaine smiled.

"It still doesn't make sense to me. Why he can't get you home first."

"Then ask him to explain it."

"Why? He's already made up his mind. But then, if I cared what he thought, I'd have gone to him. Tried to talk him into an alliance instead of you. But there's no sense in that. You're no slave girl – you make your own path."

"What if I choose not to go with you?"

Ulithaine grinned. "You won't," he said. "But take your own time reaching that conclusion."

—

As they continued, the trees quickly grew in height, though even the healthy ones were thin and wiry. The landscape was still covered in rivulets and streams, and they never seemed to find solid ground for more than an hour before plunging into another bog thick with insects. There was a patchwork quality to the forests.

Many were drowning in streams or lay uprooted in the mud, while strips of silt marked redirected or dried up waterways.

On the lower slope of one hill, they found a barren patch that stretched for several hundred feet. Large patches of earth had been upended by a massive mudslide, likely the result of a heavy winter and warm spring. Further down, they came across a grove of pines which had caught hundreds of fallen trees like flies in a web. The area was so thick with rotting logs, they had to turn back and find a different path.

In other places, they found stretches of blackened trees growing through a bed of charcoal and ash, the remnants of fires feeding off of the debris left by the floods and shifting waterways.

Periodically, Alaji's gaze would drift back to the glaciers. If their runoff could wash away forests and reshape hills, what could the ice sheets themselves accomplish?

—

"You're distracted," Phaesha said, irritated. She'd shown Alaji the basic motions for creating fire at a distance three times, but her attempts to duplicate the effect did nothing more than create a light breeze on the hilltop where they'd stopped for the night.

"It's nothing," Alaji said, stretching her fingers. The joints popped as she did so. She focused in front of her and started the spell again. Her fingers began with the invocation for fire while she whispered the incantation to transfer the flame. It was counterintuitive: the spells needed to begin and end together, but they were of differing complexities. They had different rhythms.

And, of course, she found it nearly impossible to stop brooding over her arguments with Ulithaine and Yemerik.

The spell fizzled, and Phaesha struck her. Not hard, but with enough force to startle Alaji. "The Leaping Flame is not magic for children. It is not for the undisciplined. Do it right or not at all." Her voice was stern, but there didn't seem to be any real anger. If anything, she seemed to enjoy teaching.

"I'm sorry," Alaji said. She took a breath and shut her eyes. She thought about the sound of the spell and its flow. She ran it through her head a few times, working out the pace. Then she exhaled, opened her eyes, and began, focusing on the Leaping Flame and trusting her hands to conjure the fire on muscle memory alone.

The spells finished together, and a spark of flame appeared several feet away. The will of her gods had been thwarted again, and she'd brought shame to her people's customs. Alaji smiled.

"Good," Phaesha said. "You have learned a trick to impress infants and startle rats. You might even light a candle, if it is nearby. If you wish to do more, you will need practice."

Alaji ran through the spell again and again. On a few tries, she mistimed the spells, and the flames failed to materialize. On others, the spell provided a brief flash or handful of sparks. But on her tenth try, there was an explosion of fire that burned through several leaves on a nearby bush.

"That is better," Phaesha said. "That is much better. Most take days to progress this far. Though most learn these spells when they are younger."

"Thank you," Alaji said, glancing past her to the men by the campfire.

"But you are still distracted."

"It's Yemerik. We're trying to figure out what to do once we leave this time."

Phaesha nodded. "Ulithaine instructed me to pressure you into staying with us. I told him I did not want the competition." The right corner of her mouth curled the slightest bit towards a smile. "But if we were to keep traveling together, I would continue to teach you. And learn from you. You know little, but what you do know, you know well. I am already better for our acquaintance." She plucked off a small, brittle branch and reduced it to ash in seconds.

"So am I," Alaji said.

"Of course. I know much more than you do," Phaesha said, smiling wryly.

PART 8: PHAESHA AND ULITHAINE

1

As they emerged into a clearing, Ulithaine raised his arms in front of him to gesture at the camp. He laughed and proclaimed, "My friends!"

Yemerik stumbled out of the woods, and his eyes widened. Dozens of men, women, and horses were moving around a large encampment. He turned to give Alaji a look of alarm, but she didn't return it. "You should have mentioned them," he said to Ulithaine, who gave him a look both confused and amused.

With one eye opened wider than the other, a half smile, and crooked head, Ulithaine replied, "I told you I had companions."

"But not an army," Yemerik said.

"An army? You flatter us! Do you hear that, Brithol? He takes our tattered band of rogues for an army!" He clasped Yemerik's shoulder. "You're not concerned we'll be unable to fit through the gate, are you?" The long days in the marshes had worn away his patience, so his laughter came out more mocking than good-natured.

"That's not what concerns me," Yemerik said pointedly.

"Don't worry. You'll find them a merry lot. Not unlike myself." He flashed a smile to put the smaller man at ease. Either that or to threaten him: Yemerik wasn't entirely sure. Ulithaine's attention snapped back towards the camp as three men charged across the field. One was quicker than the others.

"Ulithaine! Defend yourself," he bellowed.

"Stand away!" Phaesha said, pushing Alaji further back, as the two men collided. Alaji pulled a knife, but Phaesha shook her head. The other two caught up, and Alaji realized she knew one of them. Yemerik had already reached the same conclusion and had drawn back. It was Wray'tol, the massive warrior who'd tossed him across the front of his horse.

"Geffe!" Ulithaine hollered. "Calm yourself!"

"I'll kill you!" Geffe cried, wrapping his arms around the warrior. He lifted Ulithaine into the air, half crushing him. "You march to your death and leave me behind! And then you've the audacity to return to the lands of the living! I'll kill you!" He was laughing, crying, and shouting all at once.

"Put him down," Brithol said. "He's been through a great deal, and needs to breathe."

Geffe relaxed his grip, and Ulithaine slid to the ground, gasping. "I'm sorry," Geffe said. "Sometimes I forget—"

Before he could finish, Ulithaine wrapped his arms around Geffe, squeezed him as he'd been squeezed, and hoisted him into the air with a laugh. "I missed you, old man!" Ulithaine set him down and the two collapsed onto the ground, where they sat, trying to catch their breath. "The deeds we did, old man, this brave company and I."

"Yemerik," Wray'tol said, seeing the small man loitering away from the action. "I bet that you'd die out there. I lost a Fiejoran crown. And I'm glad for it!" He laughed.

"He's a slippery one," Ulithaine said. "Clever, shrewd. A good man to have at your side. It's a rare one who doesn't lose his head, and the gods delivered us two of that breed." He glanced at Alaji. "We thought it fitting to repay the gods' kindness, so we sent them a wizard to play jester."

"Then it's true. Oriv the Oppressor is dead?"

"At long last." Ulithaine unsheathed his sword and held it

overhead. "With this blade, I untethered his head and unburdened the weight from his shoulders." It hadn't been that sword, of course – the sword he'd used had been taken from the guards and likely lay buried in a crater of ice. But no one challenged his account.

"When we heard the city of crystalline ice had crumbled, we hoped. But we feared you'd been lost. How did you escape?"

"By wit and fist and sword and spell," he said. "And we've returned with the wizard's treasure and greater prospects." Ulithaine looked to the south. Part of the archway was visible, though the far section was hidden by a cloud. "Much greater."

—

"Is there anything to eat?" Alaji asked Phaesha. She was anxious to get away from Ulithaine before the rest of the camp ran over to greet him and express their relief at his miraculous escape from certain death. Besides, she'd caught the scent of cooking meat on the wind, and the thought of something more substantial than squirrels, nuts, and roots was appealing.

With a jerk of her head, Phaesha gestured for Alaji to follow her. Yemerik trailed behind, as well, not wanting to be left alone with Ulithaine and his men.

As Phaesha approached the camp, her sneer reappeared. Occasionally, if anyone looked at her, she snorted at them. Before they even stepped foot past the first tent, they were approached.

"Little Phaesha." The man was tall, but not as tall as most of the warriors moving about. "I see Ulithaine pulled you through another fight."

"Clesteive. I have no patience for boot-cleaners. Where is Phrathaile? We have done great deeds and would have food in our bellies!"

"You mean Ulithaine performed great deeds. And Thirove and Brithol, perhaps. While you made tricks to amuse them." He flicked his beard.

Phaesha returned his gesture as well as she could, given her lack of beard. "Is that why Ulithaine leaves you behind? You don't amuse him?"

"He leaves me behind, because I'm not worthy of more. Some of us aren't so lucky in our parentage."

"If you seek to raise my temper, you should send me to Phrathaile first. On an empty stomach, I might forget myself and do something… regrettable."

He laughed, and it echoed of imitation. He was trying to speak like Ulithaine and wasn't even subtle about it. "And who is this? Does she have value?" He looked at Alaji. "She hardly seems worth the effort."

Phaesha stepped between them. "If you try to touch her…." She smiled cruelly. "If you upset her, I won't save your life, Clesteive. That one brought down more of the wizard's men than any of us, save Ulithaine, himself."

"How?" He demanded. "She is too small to fight and too young to be much of a sorceress."

"Try her and see," Phaesha said, already stepping away. "But ask yourself why else Ulithaine brought them here. Ask why he took them to the wizard's tower."

Alaji and Yemerik hurried after her, while Clesteive stayed where they left him, posturing and trying to think of a response. "Thank you," Alaji said.

Phaesha shrugged. "It is the way here. When I first joined them, they looked down on me, like I was a child. It was the same with Ishta, when she joined to repay her family's debt. The weak fare poorly, even if they're protected. The strong do better. But we must remind them we are strong."

"It's barbaric," Yemerik said, as much to Alaji as Phaesha.

"It is as it should be," Phaesha snapped back. "Better those who don't belong slink away like scolded dogs than face the horrors of the world head-on."

"Slinking away suits me," Yemerik replied. He flinched as Alaji elbowed him.

"Don't say such things," she whispered. "They'll think you're serious."

"I am serious," Yemerik said. "We don't belong here."

Alaji looked him in the eye. She didn't say, "I do," aloud. But she didn't have to.

"Clesteive isn't so bad," Phaesha said, interrupting them. "He is short and stupid, but he would fight until the last drop of blood spilled from his corpse. I saw him wrestle a bear once. The scar on the right side his neck came of it."

"I suppose he killed the bear with his hands. Or did he tear its throat out with his teeth?" Yemerik asked.

"Do not be foolish," Phaesha said, turning a corner. "Treinile shot it with his bow. Ah. Here is Phrathaile. He is what passes for a cook here."

At first glance, Phrathaile looked elderly, but as they approached, it became clear he was less old than used up. His face and arms were covered in old scars and burns from dozens of battles. His left eye was discolored and unfocused. "I am no cook. My talents are wasted around a fire."

"You have no talents," Phaesha said back. "The food is all that's wasted."

"Cooking is women's work," he said. "They should make a woman do it."

"I said the same thing to Ulithaine," Phaesha replied. "He told me he has no women to spare. So he gave the job to the closest thing around."

Phrathaile chuckled. "That sounds like him, I'll grant you. I take it you all returned from the north."

"Almost all of us," she said. "Thirove stayed behind."

The veteran took a deep breath. "I am sorry for that. He had heart, that one."

"He brought down his foes until the end. He died clean, but he left three of those who slew him to linger with their guts hanging out. We were going to silence their moaning, but Ulithaine thought

Thirove's spirit would enjoy their song. We carried his body onto the glacier and performed the rites while the wizard's city broke apart behind us."

Alaji stood tall during this account, while Yemerik sighed and looked away. Phrathaile nodded. "That is a good day's work, then. We will remember his valor."

"All will remember," Phaesha said. "They will write songs and tell stories."

Phrathaile nodded. "You are hungry, I'd imagine."

"Hungry enough to come here," Phaesha replied. "Give us stew and beer strong enough to dull the taste!"

2

"This isn't a good place for us." Yemerik had followed Alaji around since they'd arrived. It was getting dark now, and the celebration showed no signs of dying down. She wasn't really listening to him, though. She was more interested in what was going on at the other end of camp, though she was content to watch and listen from a distance.

Ulithaine stood on a table beneath the stars and hollered the names of their dead. They had no trouble understanding him, even over the cheering: "Thirove! Wuerra! Treinile! Urjim!" The list went on, until he shouted, "Ivistim!"

"But Ulithaine! I am here!" a voice cried out.

"What fortune is this? Look! Ivistim's been returned to us!"

"He was never dead, Ulithaine! I think you were just being hopeful!" another voice called out. And then there was laughter and insults and fighting and more laughter. And then came the stories of the dead and their valiant ends. In the past hour, they'd heard three completely different accounts of Thirove's last stand. How he leapt in front of an arrow to save a companion. How Oriv had skewered him with a spike of ice, only for Thirove to pull it out of his stomach and bludgeon the wizard's guards to death with it. How he'd been stabbed through the neck and still managed to crush the skull of his killer with his bare hands. If any of Ulithaine's men were sober enough to notice the inconsistencies, they kept their thoughts to themselves.

"Did you hear me?" Yemerik asked. "It's not safe here."

"They won't hurt us," Alaji replied.

"Of course not. Four dozen drunken barbarians riling themselves up with tales of bravery. I'm sure we're in no danger."

"Don't mock them. They are mourning their dead."

"Is that what you call it?" Yemerik rolled his eyes. "I've seen this kind of behavior before. This is a bad place to be."

"What do you suggest?" Alaji asked. "Run away in the night? They'd ride us down in the morning. Besides, they know where we're going. It doesn't matter, anyway. We have an arrangement."

"Yeah, you and I have one, as well. I'm very little use to you dead. Which is how I'm likely to end up if we stay here long."

"Don't be stupid. Ulithaine wouldn't keep anyone who couldn't hold their wine. They are proud and strong, and they make too much noise, but he wouldn't have risked Phaesha's safety."

"Phaesha can take care of herself."

"Not when she first arrived. She wasn't thirteen when her father died. One of Ulithaine's company struck her once across the face and Ulithaine broke his arm and sent him away. He is less reckless than you think."

"Broke his arm. Well that's reassuring," Yemerik said.

"He is not always gentle, but he is fair," Alaji snapped back. "And he speaks better of you than you do of him."

"He's dangerous. And I've lost track of the number of times he's lied to us. Why should we trust him to do what he promised?"

"Yes, he lies. You lie, too. Everywhere we go, you tell people what suits you. How do I know you'll keep your promise to get me home?"

"You don't have to trust me to honor my word. Just trust I'll be smart. And that's in both our interests. But not in his. Look at him." He motioned to Ulithaine, who was dancing around the table, pointing to his men. "He doesn't want a world that makes sense. He can't even conceive of a world like that." Yemerik stopped talking when Alaji stood up and started walking towards the celebration. "Where are you going?"

"To have a drink and listen to stories. Maybe tell a few."

"That's stupid. Those men could kill you."

"And I could kill them. But I'd rather drink with them." She hurried away before Yemerik could think of a response.

—

Despite her bravado, she felt uneasy the moment she arrived in the midst of the warriors. The men were raucous and energized, and there were a number of women she didn't know mingling with them. These weren't warriors or sorceresses like Ishta and Phaesha, neither of whom were standing around the table.

Alaji navigated the shifting crowd, looking for a place to stand where she wouldn't be trampled. To one side, she noticed Phrathaile dispensing mugs of mead and beer. Alaji approached, and he handed her a cup. She was about to turn away when he stopped her.

"Phaesha's by the fire, brooding and practicing her ways. Might be a good thing to join her," he added, glancing around at a few of the men nearby. He took two more mugs and handed them over without explanation. Alaji managed to grasp both handles in her free hand, allowing her to carry all three at once. She thanked him and hurried towards the bonfire.

It wasn't far from the table and crowd, though it was isolated enough to grant some solitude. The noise from the celebration still carried, of course. Alaji found Phaesha sitting on a downed tree trunk, breaking small branches off of logs stacked in front of her. She set these on fire with a spell, then tossed them into the pit to burn. "It is a good method of practice," she said without looking up. "Your version of the spell, it forces the caster to learn control and patience. There is little distraction."

"Thank you," Alaji said.

Phaesha tilted her head. "It is truth, not compliment. It is also true that your people were cowards. It is easy to create fire in the air and to channel it forth." With a flick of her wrist and a few whispered words, she sent a ball of flame into the fire. A few of the logs shifted and a plume of sparks billowed upward as she did this. She paused to recover a cup of beer from the ground beside her. With a gulp, she finished it.

"Here. I brought extra," Alaji said. She handed over one of her mugs, then set another down, twisting it back and forth a few times to compress the dirt into a flat surface. Then she sat on the tree trunk and drank from the last mug. "I suppose we were scared," she admitted. "It's all we knew."

"They were scared," Phaesha said, looking up. "Not you. You learned magic they did not. Magic I don't understand."

"I was scared, too," Alaji said. "I hid my count. That's what I call the time spell. I never used it until I thought I had to. I was sure they were going to kill me for it. If I ever give them the chance, they probably will."

"You are many things, Alaji. Not all are good. But you are no coward." She picked at one of the logs and peeled off a section of bark. Then she moved her fingers and traced the fire into the scrap. When she finished, she tossed it in with the rest. "Why return, then? If they want to do you harm, why not leave them?"

"My brother," Alaji said. "I need to go back and save him."

Phaesha was picking at another clump of bark. "He's dear to you?"

"Of course," Alaji said. "He was my brother. Is my brother. It's complicated with time travel."

Phaesha nodded in understanding. "My brother was not so kind. I was sad when my father offered him as penance in the desert, but I was relieved, as well. I was so sure it was going to be me. But it was more than that. He was violent when he drank. Dangerous. My mother once told me I should go to her if he ever hurt me. She said she would kill him rather than see me injured. I did not want to carry the guilt, so I stayed silent. But when the god took him... it was like I was free of something. It is a horrible thing to say, I know. But I am a horrible person."

"I don't think so," Alaji said.

Phaesha snickered. "You mean well, but I would rather be worse than better. Good people do not survive long. Maybe it is different where you are from, but it is better here to be cruel, to be horrible. My mother is monstrous to her enemies. She uses magic she has never shared with me to drive her foes to agony and death. She still lives. My father was a generous and loyal man, and that is why he is dead."

"I'm sorry," Alaji said. "I'm not sure what happened to my father. He was in a battle when I was taken from my time. He probably died there. And my mother... I don't know what became of her, either. I spent most of my life thinking she hated me, but now I think she was trying to teach me something."

"That is how it is with parents. The worthy ones at least. They give birth to babes and choose whether to mold them into something with the will to survive. Parents who don't do this, they raise their children like the wizard's servants. Those people dressed as men, but they were still babes. They wore armor but were naked underneath. They were raised to love and live in peaceful times. When war comes for people like that, they die. It is neither good nor evil. It is just the way of things."

Alaji stared into the fire. "I suppose that's how my mother saw it."

"Then you should be grateful. Look at you now. You are strong, quick. You kill when angered and take what you want from the land.

You stand before monsters and wizards, and survive their wrath." She paused, then said, "You belong here. You have a man's heart. A warrior's soul."

"What about Yemerik?" Alaji asked, softly.

"What of him? He has no such strength. He is like the others, raised by timid parents in timid places. Sheltered from the ice and beasts, no doubt. If you enjoy his company, keep him like you would a pet. No one will challenge you, not after they see what you can do."

"I don't know. Yemerik thinks if we stay, we'll wind up with you until we die."

"There are worse lives," Phaesha said.

"But there are things we need to accomplish. He needs to reach his Citad- his home. I've sworn to go back for my brother. I'm not sure those goals interest Ulithaine, even if he says otherwise." A ways from the fire, Ulithaine was still standing on top of his table, though he was no longer alone. He'd taken the hand of a woman wearing a red dress embellished with fur and pulled her up beside him.

Phaesha sat silently for a moment. "I do not know about any of that. I want you to stay, because there is much you can teach me. And I want you to leave, because while you're here, I am not so special." She cleared her throat and added, "You have value to him. More than you realize." She nodded in Ulithaine's direction. He was kissing the woman passionately while the men below him cheered. "You could take her place, you know? Not because he desires you, but simply so you'd stay."

Alaji stared, confused. "I don't want him that way. He is too tall."

Phaesha seemed startled. "How can a man be too tall?"

"I don't know, but he is. I find him intimidating, not attractive. Some of the others, maybe," she admitted, looking around at his men. "But not him. Why would...." She shook her head, then looked back to see Phaesha staring at the couple. "You love him," Alaji murmured.

"I thought all women did."

"I don't," Alaji replied. "Who is she? The girl."

"I do not know their names. They are seldom worth learning. Sometimes, they are like Wuerra, archers or mercenaries. Or sorceresses," she added, solemnly. "But most of them are women who follow because they feel they owe him something. The daughters of farmers plagued by some monster he slew. Or he freed them from slavers, and they are too stupid to run home. They are worse than whores," she added, spitting. "At least whores demand money. These feel obligated. And they do not know he hates them for that. Ulithaine would never love a woman unless her will brought her to his bed. But he'll lay with them if they are pretty."

"Does he know how you feel?"

"He knows enough. I have offered myself to him, and he laughs, as if I am joking. Sometimes he tells me things. That I am too young, or that he has known me too long. Or that he cannot betray my father. But those are lies. That woman is no older than I am." She drank rather than go on.

"At least he cares for you," Alaji said.

"Who knows what he cares for or what he feels? I have enough of my mother's magic to be useful, and he does feel obligated to my father. But if he loves me, it is not as I'd like."

"Maybe it will change. My mother once told me that men change how they look at us. She said my father didn't love her at first, but that changed after they were married."

"Bah. I would not be bound to Ulithaine. I want him for a time. Perhaps forever, but not like that. You cannot control men like Ulithaine, and I would not be bound to a man I could not control."

"Then... what do you want?"

She shrugged. "I don't know. Sex, I suppose, but that is not enough. I had him once. For a single night, even though he'd sworn otherwise. He drank so much, he did not know me. Or did not care. Who can say? It was not as pleasant as I'd hoped. Other men I've been with have given me more pleasure. But perhaps it would be better if he hadn't drunk so much."

Alaji sat quietly, not knowing what to say.

"He never speaks of it. He regrets it, I'm sure. And he does not desire me. That is my problem. I do not look like them." She motioned again in the direction of the woman standing beside Ulithaine. A moment later he hopped down off the table, reached up to grab her with both hands, then lifted her into his arms. His men cheered as he carried her towards his tent.

3

Alaji woke early the next morning. Two of Ulithaine's men were arguing outside of the tent she'd shared with Phaesha and Ishta, the only other women in the camp who'd gone to bed alone. She didn't recognize the voices, but doubted she'd be able to get back to sleep. Besides, she'd had a great deal to drink and needed to relieve herself. She stood as quietly as she could and moved to the flap. If the situation had been different, she'd have taken the opportunity to examine the construction of the tent more thoroughly. The fabric and design were new to her and intriguing, but then what wasn't?

She considered waiting for the men to leave first, but she didn't feel especially patient. So she opened the doorway and stepped out, still making as little noise as possible. Phaesha had drunk far more than she had, and Alaji didn't want to wake her.

The two men outside were disheveled. Their eyes were bloodshot, and they were smeared with mud. Neither smelled good, either. The smaller of the two was also the older. He was more muscular and bald, though he had a long mustache and a pointed beard. The taller man was slender and young. He wore no shirt and seemed to be picking a fight with the other man.

Both turned to stare at Alaji when she emerged. They blocked the path in front of her, though they didn't seem to be doing so intentionally. She could have simply turned around and gone the other way. It would only have meant going around a few extra tents, but it would have felt like a retreat.

"Move," she said, quietly but with force.

The men snickered at this. The shorter man still towered over her. It was the taller who spoke, though. "Who are you supposed to be?" He asked. He stepped forward in an intimidating manner, chest puffed out and head held high.

"I'll show you," Alaji said. She paused a moment, then, in her head, she counted one. She reached down and pulled out her knife, drawing it slowly so as not to seem threatening. Two and three. The taller man chuckled as she moved it towards him. He didn't really know how to react to this. She wasn't attacking, but he shifted backward to keep some distance. Four. He laughed as she held it out. Five. He started to reach for it, thinking perhaps she meant to give it to him.

She stepped back to one, and the blade was almost touching his throat. "That's who I am," she hissed, pressing the blade against his neck.

With a sharp, surprised yelp, he fell back, dropping to the ground. He rubbed at his throat and looked at his palm, as if expecting to see blood. He kicked himself backwards, away from Alaji. The other man spread his hands and stepped back.

Alaji returned her knife to its sheath. "Stay out of my way," she said, trying to sound as much like Phaesha as she could. "I have no use for your foolishness." She walked by them, not bothering to stand clear. In theory, they could probably have tackled her or struck her if they wanted to. But they were scared. Terrified, even. She had nothing to worry about from them, and she knew it.

Once she'd finished her business behind a bush, she found a stream. She washed herself and drank some of the cool water. It helped clear her head, so she stood up and stretched. It was cold, and she was underdressed, but the air felt good.

She knew she should look for Yemerik, but she was still angry after their argument the previous night. So instead, she went further into the woods. She used her count to move away from the camp quickly. Then she went on the hunt. There wasn't a great deal of game that far north, but there was more than she'd found in the swamps. Besides, it was still early in the day.

When she finally returned to camp, most of the men were up. She walked in slowly, carrying the weight of a doe across her shoulders. Its blood ran down her arms and had made a mess of her clothes, but she didn't care.

The men took notice and pointed at her. Some laughed, some gave puzzled expressions, and others simply nodded in surprise. The man she'd given a scare earlier simply hung his head and wandered away.

Alaji brought the deer to the table Ulithaine had been standing on the night before. A number of the women were gathered together at one end, including the one Alaji had seen with Ulithaine. They gave a look of shock when Alaji approached them. She rolled the deer's body off her shoulders and let it fall onto the top of the table. Several plates and cups fell off as she did this.

A half-dozen men had gathered around, but they were dumbfounded by the display. The women, all of whom were taller and older than Alaji, likewise had no idea how to react. Alaji smiled and stood as tall as she could. Then, in a booming voice, asked the women, "Which of you is going to clean this for me?"

The men nearby burst out laughing. Alaji stifled a smile. She was one of them now. One of the men.

—

Yemerik wandered into camp a few hours later. He'd slept in the woods to avoid Ulithaine's men. He dragged his feet and probably looked like he was hungover. In that respect, he fit in well with almost everyone around him.

He found Alaji sitting by the fire sipping a mug of spiced wine. Her shirt was bloody, though she didn't seem hurt. Four warriors sat nearby, listening to her tell the story of how she'd eluded Krishind's hound. "I could smell its foul breath in the air, it was so close. And if I could smell it, it could smell me. Any hope I had of outrunning it was gone the moment I came on the clearing. So I did the only thing I could think of." She reached down and picked up a small chunk of wood which had tumbled out of the fire and gone out. "I lit the grass and choked it with the smoke." She demonstrated her spell, and flame bit into the wood. She tossed it on the ground and stomped it out. "I hid in the grass while it pawed through the weeds, unable to breathe but unwilling to give me up. I snuck away and was almost across the plain before it saw me."

Yemerik approached as casually as he could then cleared his throat and motioned to her.

"Is it important?" Alaji asked, loudly. The men hanging off her words turned towards Yemerik.

"I was just hoping to go over our plans."

"Get some food," Alaji said. "I want to finish my story. We can talk later." The men snickered.

"Of course," Yemerik said, forcing a smile. "Later, then." He turned to leave, but one of the men shouted after him.

"Hey! Is it true you ran off and left her to lead the hound away?"

"Are you calling me a liar?" Alaji demanded. The other men laughed at her fervor, while the first began stammering a response.

"It's true," Yemerik shouted back. "Though I worried for the wellbeing of the hound." This elicited a roar of laughter. He hurried away before he had to contend with any more questions or innuendoes, somewhat pleased with himself for stealing a bit of Alaji's thunder. He found a relatively quiet spot beside a solitary tree and sat with his back to the trunk. He rested his head against the bark and shut his eyes. Every now and then, he heard Alaji's voice carry to him, usually punctuated by laughter.

"A good morning to you, Yemerik." The voice came out of nowhere a few minutes after he'd sat down. "You look thirsty."

"Good morning, Ulithaine," Yemerik said, before opening his eyes. "I was just about to go looking for something to eat."

Ulithaine stood over him, holding a cup, which he offered. Yemerik accepted it and sipped the contents. Just water, fortunately. While he drank, Ulithaine spoke. "I hope your night was well spent. I'm afraid I didn't have an opportunity to introduce you to our companions. I fear sometimes I am not so great a host."

"They seem merry enough," Yemerik replied, not bothering to fake sincerity. "Besides, it looks like Alaji is making friends."

"Indeed. She fits in well, I think. I suspect you will find a place, given time."

"I have my doubts," Yemerik said. "Your compatriots do not strike me as the sort who appreciate learning or art."

"Nonsense. A third of them are poets and songwriters. And Gritle is something of a painter, when the mood and opportunity align. I'm sorry you did not have a chance to know Portmire. When he lived, he'd a love of old maps and stories."

Ulithaine's tone was hard to read. Was he joking, mocking, or did he actually think Yemerik was stupid enough to believe Ulithaine was trying to win him over? Yemerik couldn't decide. Against his better judgment, he pressed the issue. "Then I must apologize for misjudging your people. Clearly they are scholars. It is a shame we won't have a better chance to know each other." His tone wasn't so ambiguous. He spoke sarcastically and stared Ulithaine in the eyes.

Of course, the warrior smiled. "Indeed. If you must part ways as soon as we're through the gate—"

"We must," Yemerik cut him off. "Our paths lie in different directions, wizard-slayer."

"It is unfortunate," Ulithaine said, sighing. "I'd hoped we might find some common ground. We're not so different, you know."

"I think we're very different," Yemerik said.

"I didn't mean you and I. No, I meant Alaji and myself. We see eye-to-eye. And we complement each other well in a fight. She aided me against both the hound and the conjuror. Those are deeds that will not be quickly forgotten."

"They will once you're gone," Yemerik replied. "Once you leave this time, there'll be no one here to tell the tales. And wherever you end up, they'll lack any context for the wizard's power or the size of the hound. Depending on where you are, they could just as easily dismiss your stories as fables. Or they could wonder why it's such a big deal. There have been eras where law-abiding mages are conscripted to deal with wizards more powerful than Oriv. Where people like him are nothing more than common criminals. Your fame and legend may not mean as much where you end up as they do here."

"Then it's good I value other things," Ulithaine said. "Besides, I do not think I will go to such times."

"No, probably not. I think you'd be better suited to the past."

"Why do I feel like you're trying to insult me?"

Yemerik shook his head. "I am tired of a great many things, but first among them is pretense. If you thought you could leave my body in a ditch without driving Alaji away, you'd do it without thinking twice."

"You really don't think much of me," Ulithaine said. "No, I wouldn't leave you dead anywhere. I only kill when threatened or when it's justified. You don't threaten me, and you haven't committed any great crimes. At least none I'm aware of."

"Fine then. You'd leave me alive in some untamed land, knowing the chances of my surviving were slim."

"Now that sounds more like something I'd consider," Ulithaine said. As usual, he sounded amused. "I am not in your debt, after all."

"And you don't particularly like me," Yemerik added.

Ulithaine shrugged noncommittally. "If it means much, there's nothing I hate about you. A few habits I find grating, if we're being honest. Mostly, though, I find your behavior ill-suited for this world.

It makes it difficult to interact with you. I suppose that's why you're so anxious to leave it behind."

"That's right," Yemerik said. "What about you? Why are you eager to abandon everyone you've ever known, beyond this handful in your service?"

"Service," Ulithaine repeated the word as if it were foreign. "No. These are brothers-in-arms. Comrades. They are my family; the only family worth having! As for the rest, it is not that I want to cast it off. But I would embrace the chance to see a new world. To go to a different time and have different adventures."

"Different times, you mean. That's why you want Alaji with you. Our agreement only opens the door once."

"Once is more than I'd have without you," Ulithaine responded.

"How do we know you'll let us go after?" Yemerik asked.

"Oh, I have every intention of convincing you...." His grin widened. "I'm sorry. You asked for honesty. Of convincing Alaji to travel with us longer."

"And if she refuses? Will you try to force her?"

"It won't come to that," Ulithaine assured him. "She enjoys our company."

"But she needs mine," Yemerik replied. "I'm the only one who really understands how this works."

"Perhaps. But I suspect others could figure it out. That's not a threat, in case you're wondering. As I said, I have no intention of harming you, particularly while Alaji values you so highly. But it is something to think about."

"So is what she'd do if I was killed. Or even if I disappeared. Or there was some kind of accident. She's not stupid, and I've already shared my concerns with her. If anything happened to me, she'd vanish. Without me to slow her down, she'd be at the archway faster than you could follow. And then she'd be gone, and you'd never see her again."

"A loss, to be sure. And yet, I'd be alive and you'd be dead. But truly this talk has turned in a macabre direction. I've told you already, I won't hurt you without reason. Though, while we're airing concerns, I might add that something has been gnawing on me for a time. I can't escape the thought you might not welcome us going through the portal with you. That you might prefer we stay behind. And, as you say, you've a better understanding of this than we do."

"Under different circumstances, I might consider it," Yemerik admitted. "But I don't have many options for stopping you."

"That's good to hear," Ulithaine said. "We really haven't spoken much about the details. I'm curious what would stop you from taking us to a time worse than this one and leaving us to rot there. What ensures you'll bring us somewhere that suits our skills and fancy?"

"I don't know what's out there. We didn't come here expecting giant monsters and power-hungry sorcerers. Jumping through time has more than a little risk associated with it. I'd expect that would appeal to you."

"Perhaps. But I'm no fool. I'd like some guarantee you won't double cross us."

"How? The gate stretches from mountain to mountain. How exactly would I stop you from stepping through? After that, it's all chance."

"See? That's the sort of detail that's nice to have. Tell me, though, how does it operate?"

"Now you see, that's fascinating." Yemerik leaned forward. "It uses principles of aleatoric magic and temporal alignment that you couldn't possibly comprehend. The concepts involved are so far beyond you, I couldn't begin to explain the underlying theories if I had years." He leaned back. "Get us to the gate, and we'll do as we've sworn. Then we'll part ways in whatever era we come to."

"Assuming Alaji doesn't come around to my way of thinking, of course," Ulithaine added. "We'll rest here another day, then ride for the archway tomorrow." He walked away slowly, pausing to wave to a few of his companions returning with arms full of firewood.

Yemerik pretended to lose interest, but he kept an eye on Ulithaine and caught a glimpse of the warrior looking concerned. Yemerik smiled. It had taken a while, but he'd finally gotten under his skin. It was a small victory, but he savored it.

4

Alaji's deer was skinned, though not by any of the women. When no one else leapt at the task, Phrathaile set about getting at the meat. He left the skin hanging just outside of camp, though he did not get around to treating it. The meat didn't go to waste, though: he cut it into cubes and added it to the stew pot to cook slowly for dinner.

Before lunch, two of Ulithaine's warriors had pledged undying love and allegiance to Alaji. She could tell it was in jest, but it still filled her with pride. She had a place here, if she wanted it. She knew there were limits to how far she could trust them, but there was a certain nobility to these men.

She spoke with Yemerik, though the conversation was brief and unproductive. He'd little to say he hadn't already said. Finally, after rehashing the same argument for the third time, Alaji grew frustrated and exclaimed, "This is pointless! I'll make my mind up when we're through the portal!"

"This isn't just your decision," Yemerik reminded her. "I have a say in this, too."

"If we disagree, then what? There are only two of us."

"So we need to be agreement."

"And if we're not?"

Yemerik sighed in frustration. "You need to listen to me."

"This is like before, on the ship. I argued with the other you. The one who will not come to pass."

"How did you resolve it then?" Yemerik asked.

"I reminded him that he couldn't go on without me," Alaji said. "He realized I was right."

"You're not right this time."

"Maybe not about Ulithaine. But I'm right about the rest. You need me to go on. If I don't help you reach the Citadel, you will never find your way."

"And if I don't help you back to your time—"

"I can probably get there using the portal," Alaji shrugged. "Maybe it will take a while. And maybe I'd never succeed. But I would have a chance. Perhaps a better chance than if we continue forward."

"It's not that simple." Yemerik clenched his hands together, but they still trembled as he spoke. "If you arrive at the wrong time, a little early, you could change everything. Wipe your people out of existence. Assuming...." He shook his head. "Fine. Assuming we didn't already do that when we interfered with the distant past."

"You said—"

"I said the Citadel would fix any changes we made. And the damage might have negated itself. Time has ways of sometimes... never mind the details. There's a chance your people existed forty or fifty thousand years ago, and there's a chance they never existed at all. And the only safe way to find out—"

"Is your Citadel, right?" Alaji was almost screaming. "Your people will go back and set everything right, and I should take your word for it!"

"I am the only one with any real grasp of what's happening. I'm the only one who understands how time works and how it develops. So, yes, you should take my word for it. Because, I promise you, Ulithaine doesn't know a thing beyond slaughtering and telling lies."

"You don't understand everything," Alaji said.

"No. Of course not. No one—"

"You don't understand people. And you're no good with anything you haven't studied."

"This is Ulithaine talking. He talked you into—"

"No, you told me," she said. "You warned me, before I went back in Hathari. The older you said you'd understand things about time and history, but little else. You said I should trust my own judgment."

"That version of me obviously didn't expect us to fall in with a pack of madmen."

"You say you're the only one who can bring me home. I'm not sure whether to believe you or not. But I don't know better, so I have to assume it's so. That's why I went back for you in Hathari. It's why I came this far. But you say Ulithaine is too dangerous. I believe him to be a good man. A killer and a liar, yes, but one who will help us. We'll keep him with us, at least for a time. We'll bring him from era to era. He can have his adventures, and we'll have company and protection. This is my decision."

—

That evening was a far more muted affair than the party the night before. They ate and drank and laughed while stories were told, but nothing was done to excess. As the night wore on, they broke down the massive table and threw the pieces to the fire.

Phaesha and Alaji worked on their magic, while Yemerik skulked. Alaji was still nowhere near as adept as her teacher, but she picked up individual spells quickly. She could conjure handfuls of fire from the air and throw them in front of her. With a wave of her hand, she could create flame wherever she wanted, though it lost power the further it was from her. Phaesha moved on to other, similar enchantments, including one that summoned ice instead of flame. The movements were foreign to Alaji, though, and she'd yet to recreate the effect.

Meanwhile, Alaji showed Phaesha the weaving spell, which was completely new to her. "Why would a sorcerer waste their time with such a thing?" she asked.

"They used to teach it in my village before the healing spell. The movements are similar. The spells are similar. It's like weaving flesh instead of thread," Alaji explained. "If we tried to start with healing, you'd likely kill whoever you were casting it on."

Phaesha shrugged. "There are men here I could experiment on. They wouldn't all be missed," she said, before breaking into a rare smile. "I will practice your weaving spell," she promised.

—

Alaji woke the next morning when Phaesha shook her. She sat up quickly, immediately aware there was a great deal of commotion coming from outside.

"It is time," Phaesha said. "We are leaving."

Alaji dressed quickly and packed up her belongings. As soon as she was out of the tent, Ishta began dismantling it. There was almost no light yet, just a thin band in the east running from the mountains to the glacier. Alaji tried to stand out of the way, though it was difficult to find a place she could wait without someone approaching with a bundle of spears or a roll of blankets. The group was disciplined and moved quickly. Within the hour, there was nothing of value that wasn't strapped to the backs of one of the horses.

Ulithaine rode up to Alaji. "You'll be riding with Ishta," he said. "I've asked Yemerik to ride with Wray'tol." He motioned behind them to where the massive warrior was standing by the small man. "He'll be fine," Ulithaine added, though there was a hint of amusement in his voice.

"I'm sure Wray'tol can take care of himself," Alaji said, before realizing it was exactly the kind of joke Ulithaine would make.

Ulithaine cracked a smile but didn't laugh. "I hope to reach the gate by night. The paths aren't easy, but my people know them well."

Alaji nodded, and he hurried off. She started towards Yemerik, but Ishta found her first. "Give me your hand," Ishta said, reaching down. With her help, Alaji climbed onto the back of the warhorse.

Alaji craned her neck, so she could see Yemerik. She caught only glimpses of Wray'tol hoisting him up. At least this time he allowed Yemerik to ride correctly, instead of laying him horizontally across the horse's back.

"He'll be well," Ishta said. "Wray'tol is foolish and lacks manners, but he knows his place. He'll look after your friend."

The riders were gathering into two groups. Slowly, Alaji realized they wouldn't all be leaving together. About a third of the men had gathered near Geffe. All the women were there, as well, with the exception of Ishta, Alaji, and Phaesha. Riders from the two groups rode up to each other and clasped hands. A few of the women were crying. The one Alaji had seen with Ulithaine was sobbing. She called to him and reached out, but he simply rode away.

"They're not coming," Alaji said.

"Some have obligations or family," Ishta replied. There was a hollow sound to her voice. "Some choose to stay. Others were not offered a choice."

Alaji's gaze lingered on the woman calling for Ulithaine. She'd hated this woman a few days ago, though looking back, she couldn't figure out why. Now she pitied her, and that made as little sense. She'd be as safe as any of them; safer, probably. And it should have been obvious that Ulithaine's company was a fleeting thing. That was how it was with men who live on the field, wasn't it? That was how it had been with Hollik, at least if the jokes she'd overheard had any basis in truth.

She shook herself. It was still early, and she wasn't really awake yet. Ulithaine was not another era's version of the warlord who'd attacked her people, no matter what Yemerik claimed. Still, the scene playing out with the jilted woman troubled her.

"Are you alright?" Ishta asked.

"Fine," Alaji replied. "I'm fine."

"There is water in the saddlebag if you can reach it," Ishta said, motioning to the left side of the horse. "Wine, as well, if that's more to your liking."

Alaji held on with one hand while she searched behind her with the other. The concept of a saddle was a new one, let alone bags laid out beside them, but she figured out how to open the flap and reach inside. She pulled out the first skin she found and drank. It was the water, which was probably better, anyway.

The groups finished their farewells then rode in opposite directions. By then, the sun had started to rise, and the sky was red. Geffe went southeast, and the rest of them rode west.

They rested only briefly and never all at the same time. Half of the group would stop while the others went on for a few miles. They'd then stop and start again as soon as their companions caught up. "Why in shifts?" Alaji asked the third time they'd done so.

Ishta shook her head. "I don't know," she said. "This is what Ulithaine asked. I did not question him."

"Is this how you normally travel?"

"No. This is new."

Alaji looked around at those present. These weren't all the same warriors they'd stopped with the last time, but there was one constant. "This is to keep us apart, isn't it? He doesn't want me near Yemerik."

Ishta paused for a moment. "He did not tell me his reasons for traveling this way."

"But he said you were supposed to keep us apart? That was your instruction, wasn't it?" Alaji was more frustrated than angry, but the sign of distrust made her tense.

"It was," Ishta admitted.

"Because Ulithaine doesn't want us to speak together until we reach the gate," Alaji said.

"He did not tell me that," Ishta said. "But it is likely."

Alaji sighed and shifted backwards a bit. Ishta turned her head quickly with a look of concern.

"I'm not trying to get away," Alaji said. "And if I was, you wouldn't know until I was gone."

"He told me about your power. He said I was to be mindful. You have an arrangement, I understand. And, if I can, I am to see that arrangement fulfilled."

"Did he explain it to you?"

"Of course," Ishta replied. "You are taking us to a different time, long ago or in the distant future. Perhaps you will lead us from time to time."

"You don't sound happy about it," Alaji remarked.

"I am not. It is unlikely I will see my parents again. I am honor bound to serve Ulithaine. That does not mean I want to die a thousand years from anything I've ever known."

"I'm sorry," Alaji said. "I understand. I'm a long way from—"

"You do not understand," Ishta interrupted. "Let me be clear. What I want does not matter. If you plan to betray Ulithaine, you should kill me now. You would find me easier to murder than to best, no matter your magic."

"I'm not going to kill or betray anyone," Alaji said. "What's this all about? Did Yemerik say something foolish? Is Ulithaine angry?"

"He is cautious," Ishta replied. "That much was clear. And he told the rest of us to be cautious, too."

The forests thickened as they rode. They took old roads which had been worn down to little more than paths. Occasionally, they came across strips of overturned trees left by the beast. They couldn't cross these on horseback, since any horse slipping on the mesh of logs would have likely broken a leg, so they lost some time navigating in search of a way around.

They continued onward until they were nearly beneath the gate. The riders stopped, and Ulithaine rode up. Alaji looked around. "Where is Yemerik?" she asked, growing concerned.

"I won't leave him behind," Ulithaine promised. "He is close by. But I think it is better if he is among the last to pass through."

"What?" Alaji asked, suddenly confused.

"Go ahead," Ulithaine motioned in front of them. "Open the gate."

Alaji laughed anxiously and shook her head. "It can't be done from down here." She pointed towards the top of the mountain she'd descended weeks before. "There's a table at the top. It has to be done there."

Ulithaine stared at her for several seconds. "You did not mention this," he said.

Alaji shrugged. "I didn't think it was important," she replied. "It shouldn't be a problem. The gate opens across the entire plain. I can climb up and activate it, then all of you can ride through with Yemerik."

Ulithaine paused to study the arch far above them. He stared at the mountains and the paths spiraling up. He examined sight lines, points where the arch crossed over the pathway, and he looked concerned. "Not alone. I'll go, too." He turned to the nearest rider. "Preille, send for Phaesha and Wray'tol. Tell them to bring Yemerik. Friemaine! Brithol! Tuj! You, as well." He turned back to Alaji and studied her. "Can I trust you?" he asked.

"Yes," she said, though it sounded more like he was talking to himself than to her.

He shut his eyes for a moment and seemed lost in thought. Alaji became slowly aware that all his men were staring directly at her. They looked tense, too. Finally, he opened his eyes and said, "I hope you understand the situation I'm in. I don't mean to act paranoid, but your companion has been clear he'd rather leave us behind."

"I wouldn't," Alaji said, though she'd have considered it in that moment, if she'd had an opportunity.

"I appreciate that. And I believe you, mostly. But it is important I make sure." He climbed off his horse and motioned for Alaji to do the same. The three warriors he'd selected dismounted as well.

"I won't close the gate without Yemerik," Alaji said, as she reached the ground. "There's a part of me that wants to, but I won't."

She laughed softly to try and lighten the mood, but Ulithaine's expression remained stern.

"Since I don't understand this thing, I can't be sure you can't wave your hand and pull him through or lock others outside. I have only your word we can just walk through. Your word and his. And that's no longer enough." Behind him, a horse emerged from the forest carrying Wray'tol and Yemerik. Phaesha's appeared immediately after. "That's close enough!" Ulithaine shouted. "We are making for the mountaintop on foot. You are to stay forty paces behind us. Keep Yemerik with you. If Alaji approaches without me or if you see her vanish, kill Yemerik immediately."

5

It was dusk, but they weren't more than halfway up. Ulithaine went first with Alaji close behind. After her, Brithol came, along with the other two, Tuj and Friemaine. Both carried bows and never took their eyes off of Alaji. By then, it was too dark to see Yemerik and the others, though she heard them from time to time. She kept moving, periodically giving Ulithaine an angry glare.

"Don't be like that," he said, calmly. "This is not meant to injure your pride or to do either of you harm."

"If anything happens to Yemerik, I will kill you," Alaji said.

Ulithaine laughed. "That's better! There's the spirit I missed. If any ill befalls him, you are welcome to try."

"I trusted you."

"You still can," Ulithaine said. "I can imagine how this must feel, but it's not a betrayal. I'm only trying to protect what we agreed upon. A trip to a better time. Perhaps after that—"

"After that, Yemerik and I leave, as agreed," Alaji snapped.

Ulithaine nodded. "If that's what you want. As soon as we've verified the world is fitting, we will send you on your way. With food, wine, and treasure, even. You will find we are generous to our friends."

"What does that mean? About verifying?"

"It shouldn't take long. A few days at most to find a town and ask a few questions. If you take us to a time that meets our needs, that will be all. If not, we will need to try again. I don't think that's unreasonable."

Alaji didn't respond. She simply continued on while it grew dark. Soon, they brought out torches. Ulithaine held his up and smiled.

"I have flint, if need be, but it will only draw out our hike."

Alaji waved her hand, and the top of the torch exploded in flame. Ulithaine nodded in appreciation, even though the flames had come dangerously close to his skin. He used it to light the other torches, one of which he handed to Alaji. Looking back, she was relieved to count three lights far behind them. At least that meant Wray'tol hadn't tossed Yemerik over the edge. She was relatively sure Phaesha wouldn't have permitted that, but confirmation was still nice.

A bit later, Tuj tripped over a stone and struck his knee badly. He stood immediately but walked with a limp. It quickly became apparent they wouldn't be able to maintain their pace. Ulithaine whistled loudly then raised his torch in the air before lowering it to his right. He repeated the motion twice more until one of those following duplicated the signal.

Ulithaine turned to Alaji and said, "This will delay us. You could have prevented that."

"I could have," Alaji replied. "If you hadn't ordered Yemerik killed if I used my spell."

"Wray'tol wouldn't have seen, and I'd have heard you out," he said.

"I didn't want to take chances," Alaji replied.

Ulithaine shook his head. "I'm sorry things have grown so tense. But I've invested a great deal into this arrangement. We both know Yemerik doesn't trust me—"

"He was right not to trust you," Alaji answered.

Ulithaine smiled uneasily. "Regardless, he's all but said he'd betray me given the chance."

"Maybe. But I wouldn't have."

"I'd like to believe you. But the truth is you still do as he commands. I couldn't risk him manipulating the situation. He does things like that, if I'm not mistaken."

Alaji shook her head, annoyed. "I defended you. I told Yemerik you were harsh but not bad. I argued that we should stay with your company, at least for a while. Maybe even until he reached his people and helped me. All you had to do was trust me. Whatever world you end up in, I don't think it'll be enough for you. Not forever. When you finally grow tired of it, I hope you'll remember that it could have gone differently."

Ulithaine didn't respond to that, but he picked up his pace, gaining a little distance on the others. He didn't expand the lead too far, but he kept ahead of Alaji for the remainder of the hike.

When they finally reached the top, he turned to Alaji. "Lead on," he said. She navigated as best she could. She'd been up there enough times to have learned the layout pretty well, but it was still difficult to find her way. Eventually she found the indented pedestal that controlled the gate.

"I can open it a little ways in the past. A hundred years or so should be fine. Maybe even a thousand. I'd want to talk with Yemerik before I went any further. And definitely if you want to go forward. I don't completely understand the glaciers yet and wouldn't want to open to a time when they're right on top of us. I'm not sure what that would do."

"The past then," Ulithaine said. "A few hundred years is plenty."

The indentation was full of mud, weeds, and water. There was a small drainage canal, but this was clogged. She cleared it with her fingers, then brushed out the larger debris as best she could. Then she removed the pendant housing a small piece of the talisman and lowered it into the indent. The waves of time spilled against her, and she shivered. Then she turned the shard several times. The feel of the energy changed, and she was relatively sure she'd managed to arrange it correctly.

She looked to find Ulithaine was watching her every move. "It's done," she said.

Ulithaine turned around to look at the portal. "Why isn't it open?" he asked.

"It's readied from here, but we open it at the gate," Alaji said. "That's just how it works."

"Give me the pendant," Ulithaine replied.

Alaji balked. "This is mine," she said.

"I will return it once we're through," he said.

"No," Alaji said. "I am tired of this. I will open the door and take you through. But I won't be robbed by you."

Ulithaine reached out for the pendant, but Alaji leapt backward. He sighed, angrily. "I'm not trying to steal from you," he said, sounding exasperated. His men shifted around Alaji, so they'd be able to prevent her from running.

"I don't trust you. Tell your men to back off, and we all go through the gate. But this stays with me."

"Don't back away from her," Ulithaine said. "Never back away from her. It only gives her a target." His eyes never left Alaji, even as he spoke. "Alaji. I am not your enemy, but I take this matter seriously. Give me the pendant now. I know your tricks."

Alaji stared him in the eyes. "I don't want to hurt you," she said.

"I don't want to hurt you, either," Ulithaine said. "And I won't. Not badly. But if you force me to take the pendant, I will."

"Alaji! Stop!" Yemerik's voice called out.

To her left, Alaji saw Phaesha approach with a blade held to Yemerik's neck. Wray'tol stood beside her holding a torch. "Do as he says," Phaesha added.

"You'd crawl from a fight in this way?" Alaji asked Ulithaine.

The warrior chuckled and smiled. "Take him back down the path a ways," he told Phaesha. "Kill him if Alaji approaches, but don't hurt him otherwise."

Phaesha pulled Yemerik back the way she'd come. Wray'tol remained where he was, leaving Alaji surrounded by five men, each a dozen paces away. She might be able to slip by them, but she'd never outrun their voices, and that's all they'd need to kill Yemerik.

Ulithaine raised his hands slowly. "Stay still and don't interfere unless she comes at you," he told the others. Then, to Alaji: "Just give me the pendant."

Alaji's knife appeared in her hand. "I don't want to hurt you," she said again.

Ulithaine moved slowly, shifting forward towards her. She swung her blade at his arm, then stepped back in time just a moment. The tip of the knife cut into his forearm, drawing blood, but he didn't flinch. Instead he stayed ready. Alaji drew back her arm, and her count restarted at one.

Ulithaine held his ground. He inched forward again, while Alaji shifted backward. His eyes were determined, and they followed every twitch on her face. Two. Three. He was watching, waiting for something. Four. He lunged forward, and Alaji's instincts took over. She jumped away and stepped backward in time.

She appeared a few seconds earlier. He was a few feet further away, but still close. This time, he lunged the moment she appeared, and she took another step back. But now her count was at one, and he was quick.

He moved before she could react. He struck her with his palms, knocking her backward. Before she even reached the ground, he was hurling himself towards her. He struck and knocked the wind from her. At the same time, his left arm pinned her knife hand to the ground. His fingernails bit into her wrist, and she yelled.

With his right arm, he pressed against her neck. He leaned close. "Easy," he said. "I'm not going to hurt you, not badly. Just relax and—"

She swung at him with her free hand and swatted at his face. He ignored the strikes and pressed down. Alaji couldn't breathe. She couldn't even cough. Her fingers clawed at Ulithaine's hair and pulled. Again, he didn't flinch.

"It was a good try," he said. "But you're out of time."

She gasped, and things began to darken. Still, she didn't loosen her grip on his hair. She gasped again, while her fingers twitched. Then her hand opened and fell away. Her mouth opened, fighting for air.

"It's okay," Ulithaine said, still in a reassuring voice. "I promise you, you'll be—" He screamed without finishing his sentence. The heat met his cheek, the light met his eyes, and the smoke caught his lungs.

While she'd held his hair, Alaji had cast her spell of the hearth. None of the complex versions Phaesha had shown her: the simplest one, like she'd learned from her mother. The one her fingers knew on their own, deep in her muscles.

The hair on the side of Ulithaine's face was burning furiously as the flame climbed towards his scalp. He still pressed down on her as the fire burned, fighting against the pain and fear, as Alaji fought to remain conscious. She started shaking as she smelled his flesh blistering. After a moment, he rolled away, scrambling for dirt to rub against his head.

Alaji coughed and spat dizzily. Her vision was blurred, and it was almost impossible to sit up. She grabbed at her knife, ignored all else, and found the count in her mind. She didn't know whether she could remain conscious, let alone concentrate enough to invoke her magic, but she knew the burn wouldn't distract her opponent long. She leapt forward at him on one, and he turned to confront her. He lashed out to grab her leg, as his men, ignoring his orders to stand back, charged in. But they were all too slow.

Alaji stepped back just a second and appeared over Ulithaine. She kicked downward, catching him in the face. His men charged anew, but it no longer mattered. One: he rolled back from the kick, and she moved forward and brought her boot down again. On two, she stepped back to one, delivering a second kick right after the first.

Ulithaine's face was bloody and scarred, and he rolled over. His men froze when Alaji vanished and reappeared once more, now kneeling against Ulithaine's back with her knife pressed against him. Her left hand rested against the butt of the hilt, in case she'd need to drive it downward.

"Stop or he dies!" she screamed, as loudly as she could manage, and the men froze. Friemaine and Tuj began drawing their bowstrings back. "Brithol!" Alaji wheezed. "Tell them!" He paused for a moment. "Tell them that I can kill him before they shoot. Tell them I could kill all of you!"

"It's true," he said, standing completely still. "You saw how she moves."

"The weapons," Alaji said, nodding to one side. The archers stood still, and Alaji tightened her grip on her knife. "Now!"

"Do as she says!" Brithol cried out, and they tossed their bows on the ground. The others dropped whatever blades they carried.

"Now get back. Twenty paces."

"He said not to move away from her," Wray'tol pointed out.

"I'm looking to end this without blood," Alaji said. "But don't think I'm unwilling to shed it."

Wray'tol looked around to find the others were all doing as she commanded. He inhaled deeply, nodded, then stepped backwards with his palms raised. "Fine. Just don't hurt him."

Alaji nodded and stood slowly once the warriors were no longer a threat. Half-conscious, Ulithaine whimpered on the ground. "Tend to him when I'm gone," she said, and started away.

Wray'tol moved to one side to let her pass, though he didn't take his eyes from her. She walked slowly, but used her count. In seconds, she'd vanished into the darkness.

—

Phaesha had heard the shouts. She'd heard the sounds of bodies striking stone. She'd heard the man she loved scream in pain three times, and she'd heard Alaji's exchange with Brithol and distant thuds when weapons struck the ground. But she'd seen nothing.

Her right arm curled around Yemerik and held the tip of her dagger against his throat. He already had a half-dozen scrapes where it had dragged against his skin. Phaesha's left arm pressed against his back for leverage. Ending his life would have been as easy as cutting into an apple.

Yemerik's arms hung at his sides. He'd tried to weaken her hold earlier, as soon as they'd been left alone, but she'd simply tightened her grip. The longest scrape on his neck was the price for that act of defiance.

"We both need to relax," he said, as calmly as he could. "Whatever's happening up there doesn't mean—"

"Shut up!" Phaesha screamed. "I will open your throat if you open your mouth!" That silenced him. "If I see Alaji approach, I will kill you!" She shouted into the night. "Ulithaine! Brithol! What is happening?"

"Phaesha!" She heard Ulithaine cry out. "Wait there!" His voice was strained and slurred.

Behind her, in barely a whisper, she heard another voice. "Water."

She swung around, prodding Yemerik to do the same. Alaji was no more than five feet from her, standing beside Phaesha's pack. She knew all too well what Alaji could accomplish in five feet of space. "I will kill him!" Phaesha said. Her muscles tensed.

"Wait!" Yemerik barked.

"Do you have some water," Alaji asked, rubbing her own throat.

"What?" Phaesha demanded.

"Water. I just wrestled with Ulithaine. My waterskin broke when I fell, and I can barely… is there any water in your pack?" She knelt down and began sifting through it. She located the skin, opened it, and drank. Then she wiped her mouth with the back of her arm.

"Stay back," Phaesha said.

Alaji stood slowly in the moonlight, cringing as she did. She was bruised, cut, and covered in dirt. "Yemerik and I are going through the gate," she said simply.

"No. I could kill him now," Phaesha said. "You were a fool to show yourself!"

Alaji shook her head. "I could stop you. Even if you do it, I can still step back and stop you. You know this. Listen. Yemerik and I are leaving now. We have a head start, but we can't wait," Alaji said. "We need to go to the portal now, and I need to know if you're coming with us."

Phaesha's face contorted in confusion. "You think I'd betray him?"

Somewhere back up the trail, Ulithaine shouted. "Phaesha! Hamstring Yemerik! Quickly! Before she finds you!" Phaesha didn't move.

Alaji ignored this and said, "Ulithaine had his chance. I kept my word, but he betrayed me. He attacked me and lost, and he will spend his days in this era. You can't stop me, not at this distance, so you can't change that. Nothing you do will get Ulithaine through that portal. But you can go places he never will. Or you can stay here with him. Those are the only two choices I'm giving you, and you need to decide now."

"Would I ever see him again?" Phaesha asked.

"No," Alaji said. "I don't think we could get back here if we wanted to."

Phaesha released Yemerik. He stumbled forward, panting. "We should hurry then. Unless you were lying and mean to kill me. Perhaps he'd think more favorably of me if he found me murdered."

Alaji handed the water to Yemerik. "We need to go now," she said to him. He nodded in agreement. There was rustling not far behind them. Fortunately, they were close to where the archway passed over the path. They ran quietly and quickly, while Ulithaine and his men called for them. Phaesha said nothing but ran with Alaji.

Finally, they reached the archway. Phaesha paused to gaze up at the gate.

"I'll only leave it open for a moment," Alaji said. "Stay right behind me." She stepped through the gate and was met by a blast of wind, sleet, and light. A winter storm spilled out of the portal, and a bolt of lightning cut from the edge of the top of the archway to the far mountain. On the other side, it was early evening. The sky, while gray and dim, was far brighter. Immediately, the valley and mountain were lit up. Alaji motioned for the others to follow. They did, despite the cold.

Phaesha turned and looked back. Far below, she saw horsemen swarming like ants, starting to run for their mounts and prepare for a mad dash towards the portal. They'd never make it. Behind her, she saw Ulithaine staring in disbelief. He was several hundred feet away. He looked at her and raised a hand. She couldn't make out his expression. He opened his mouth to say something, to call out. She did the same, though she did not know what she meant to say.

Before either of them could speak, Alaji flickered and the gate vanished.

PROLOGUE

"When are we?" Yemerik yelled through chattering teeth over the howling winds.

"The past! A few hundred years, I think!" Alaji yelled back.

"We will die here if we don't find shelter!" Phaesha yelled.

"Forget shelter," Yemerik replied. "We need to open the gate again. We need to try again."

They struggled through the snow to the stone pedestal. It was buried completely in snow and ice. "I have this," Phaesha said. She chanted quickly, and fire pooled in her hands. She threw it into the snow, and it began melting. Alaji began doing the same. They continued until enough of the ice was gone.

Alaji lowered the pendant into the indent. There was still some ice at the bottom, but the waves of energy poured out anyway. "Several months?" Alaji asked.

Yemerik shook his head. "I want to be done with this era. Can you do a hundred thousand years forward? The ice sheets should have receded by then. Going further would be better than the alternative."

Alaji's eyes widened. She had enough experience with his numbers to grasp the words and how they were structured, but she still relied on translating such things to her fingers, to powers of five, and this number was far larger than she could wrap her mind around. She could understand the words, but that was all. "I don't... I'm not sure."

"It... it should all work in orders of magnitude," Yemerik said. "If you can figure out a thousand, then go from there. Just increase it by two magnitudes."

She didn't understand all the words he'd spoken, but she thought she understood the concept. "I don't know. I'll try." She tilted the pendant, and the waves of energy shifted. They became deeper and resonated differently. She tilted them further, and the change became more extreme. She turned the pendant several times.

"There. Maybe. I don't know."

"Let's try it," Yemerik said. They made their way back down the path towards the gate.

When they were nearly there, Yemerik stopped. "Alaji. Give me one of the shards." She did as he asked. "Stay back up the path out of the line of the gate. If we open it when the glacier is on top of us, I'll be crushed. Do you understand?"

"You want me to step back and stop you from opening it?" she asked.

"Exactly."

"Hurry," Phaesha said, shivering.

Yemerik walked down the path until he was nearly under the arch. He looked back to make sure Alaji was watching and not waving her hand for him to stop. He took a deep breath and stepped forward.

An autumn breeze spilled through and mixed with the snow and ice behind them. Yemerik laughed. "Come on!" he called. Alaji hurried behind with Phaesha, and soon they'd stepped into this new world. Alaji took the shard back and closed the gate. A storm cloud which had spilled through with them melted into mist and began drifting down the mountainside.

"The mountain," Phaesha gasped. "What happened to it?"

Alaji looked behind her. She was right: the rocky slope which had risen above them had been shorn away. They were now at the actual summit. Only the arch remained above them. She breathed in the crisp autumn air and caught faint hints of wood smoke, leaves, and other scents she couldn't place. "There's more," she said. "The glacier is gone." She pointed north, towards an open steppe.

"Probably not gone," Yemerik said. "It's far out of sight, though. Hundreds of miles. Maybe thousands."

"It's all different," Phaesha said. She turned around slowly, looking in every direction. The valley floor beneath them had been reshaped. The lake to their north was gone, save a river cutting to the east. To the southwest, a small, round lake butted up against the side of the mountain. And beyond that, a series of mountains and small hills had risen up. Fields, buildings, and roads lined that area. Far to the south, partially concealed by a thick, dark cloud, lay the edges of a massive city.

"How is any of this possible?" Phaesha asked.

"The ice did this," Yemerik explained. "It carved the land then melted away. It's happened before, and it will happen again."

"What is that?" Alaji asked, pointing and squinting towards a form drifting through the clouds.

"An air ship, I think," Yemerik answered. "Difficult to say for certain, but that's my best... no, wait. It's definitely an air ship of some sort. See? There are two more."

"It is another world," Phaesha gasped, stepping forward. "What else is down there?"

Yemerik shook his head. He didn't have the faintest idea. "As far as I know, no one has ever come here before. Not the way we came, anyway."

Alaji refastened the pendant holding a shard of the talisman around her neck. "Then let's be the first to see it."

A TIME WHEN THE DEAD ARE
INDENTURED TO THE LIVING
AND BANKS RULE CITIES OF
STEAM AND MAGIC.

A UNIQUE SICKNESS
OF SPIRIT

COMING AUTUMN 2016

www.ingramcontent.com/pod-product-compliance
Lightning Source LLC
Chambersburg PA
CBHW030922120626
46554CB00001B/243